Cicada Days

AND OTHER SHORT STORIES AND ESSAYS

Samuel A. Whiteleather

Cicada Days

Copyright © 2021 by Samuel A. Whiteleather

All rights reserved.

ISBN: 978-1-60414-926-5

Edited by Mary Sell

Published by

Fideli Publishing, Inc.
Martinsville, IN 46151
www.FideliPublishing.com

Table of Contents

Part 1

Fictional Stories

A Calm, Quiet Voice

Every muscle in Eli's body quivered as he clung to the face of the rock outcropping. The tip of his right hiking boot was wedged tightly in a small ledge and by flexing his toes he could move his body slightly upward. His other foot was in a much worse position. It too was on a small ledge but this ledge was far narrower. He was only able to hold his boot sideways against the outcropping and he knew if he pushed down too hard, he'd slip.

His hands were in a similar situation. His left hand was wedged firmly in a solid handhold. He could feel firm rock all the way back to his first row of knuckles. By bearing down hard he could raise his upper body a good foot up. His right hand was in bad shape. His fingertips were wedged in a small crevice but only up to his second row of knuckles. Eli had to squeeze his fingers tightly just to maintain his grip. This grip gave him no leverage for upward movement and the pain that was gathering in his knuckles felt like a small hammer was tapping them continuously.

Eli looked down and felt his stomach tighten again. He figured he was a good 15 feet in the air or maybe more. *Gotta stop doing that,* he thought. He knew thinking about falling wouldn't help his situation at all. But his mind kept returning to it like a hungry dog returning to a pile of garbage. *What would the other students think if I had to be rescued from a field trip!* His cheeks flushed red from the thought of it. *I can just imagine the girls talking about it …* "Can you believe Eli fell off that rock outcropping? What made him decide to climb up there anyway? Poor Eli, it's a wonder he didn't die from the fall."

1

And the boys, what would they say? "Did you hear about Eli? I'd never have fallen off like he did if it was me up there. I would've kept climbing to the top. What was he thinking anyway?"

And now, clinging to the side of a big rock, Eli had to wonder to himself, *What* was *I thinking?*

***

The field trip had started out pretty normal. "OK, everybody on the bus," Mrs. O'Connell said when the big yellow bus pulled up in front of the school. Eli climbed up the steep black steps and picked a seat in the middle of the bus. He felt lucky when he slid across the cold vinyl seat and leaned against the window. *Yes! Window seat,* Eli thought.

The bus was full of sound as Eli's classmates yelled to each other about who was sitting with whom. Eli didn't join in. He sat quietly looking out the window. But on the inside he wondered, *Who will want to sit with me?*

He turned when he felt someone slide into the seat next to him. It was Alex. "You wanna trade me seats?" he yelled to the kid in front of him.

"No, I'm good dude," the kid replied. Alex slumped back in his seat.

"Hey," Eli said to Alex.

"Hey," Alex replied coldly.

"Where the heck are we going anyway?" Alex asked the kid in front of them.

"Some stupid historical site. I think there was an Indian battle there or something," the kid replied.

"Sounds boring," Alex shot back.

Eli looked back out the window. He didn't think the trip would be boring. He actually liked history. He had read all about the site. A big battle was waged there back when Indian lands were slowly but surely becoming claimed for America. An Indian prophet had led a group of braves to attack an encampment of American troops. He told the braves that they would be invincible as long as he kept praying with uplifted hands for protection. The prophet had stood on a high point overlooking the battle field while his braves attacked. In the end, the braves were driven from the field by the Americans. There is a rock near the site some call "Prophet's Rock" where legend has it the great prophet stood.

Eli heard the air brakes release as the bus pulled away from the school. He wanted to say something to Alex to get a conversation going, but he was afraid he'd sound stupid so he looked out the window. As the bus picked up speed, Eli watched bare fields of corn stubble and white farmhouses zip by as they made their way towards Prophet's Rock.

It wasn't long before Eli saw a big brown sign that read "Historic Battle Ground next left" looming up on the roadside. The bus took the turn and wound down a country road that was flanked with tall trees on either side.

The bus driver steered into a parking lot and Mrs. O'Connell yelled, "OK wait your turn!" as the students jumped to their feet and jammed into the narrow aisle. Eli waited his turn and soon was among the swarming mass of kids standing outside the bus in the gravel parking lot.

"OK class, quiet down," Mrs. O'Connell said. Eli liked Mrs. O'Connell. She had brown eyes and long dark hair that fell on either side of her face. When she smiled, her eyes shone and the wrinkles on her face lined up as if they were made for smiling. She was patient but firm with Eli's class.

"Please give your full attention to Mr. Okos. Mr. Okos is a local historian who will take us on a tour of the battle grounds."

Eli looked at Mr. Okos. He had short dark brown hair and wore a goatee. He was dressed in blue jeans and boots and Eli thought he looked like a biker dude. *Pretty cool for a historian,* Eli thought.

Mr. Okos began telling the story of the Battle of Tippecanoe. He told of the night attack led against an American general's troops. The attack was led by an Indian prophet who believed he had special powers. The Indian braves attacked the unsuspecting troops who somehow rallied to keep the Indians at bay.

Eli imagined what it must have felt like to fight for your life in the dark. He could hear the sounds of men yelling and see the flashes of yellow and red as muskets erupted in the night air. He could smell the gunpowder hanging thick in the air and coating the insides of his nostrils.

Suddenly Eli felt something hit him in the back of the neck. It hurt a little and Eli felt a tingly feeling up his spine, the same feeling he got when his dad would jump out and scare him. Eli turned around. Behind him was Alex and a few other boys. They were all looking at Eli and smiling. Eli felt his cheeks flush and his face get hot. He looked to where Mrs. O'Connell was standing but she had her back to Eli and the other boys. He wanted to say something, but he didn't want everyone to turn around and look at him.

"OK kids, let's head toward Prophet's Rock," Mr. Okos said as he started walking toward a rock outcropping that clung to the side of a wooded hill. "That's the spot where legend has it the prophet stood and prayed while the battle waged below him," said Mr. Okos. Eli hung towards the back of the group where he could keep an eye on Alex.

At the rock outcropping, Mr. Okos explained that this probably wasn't the spot where the prophet had stood but that it was somewhere near the site. Eli listened as Mr. Okos told of how the prophet held his arms raised during the battle to protect his braves from American bullets. "His protection didn't go very far though," Mr. Okos said, "as many braves died during the battle."

Eli looked up at the rock outcropping. Its surface was dark with lots of small holes scattered over it. The outcropping rose about 30 feet above Eli before it leveled off and joined the side of the hill.

Eli jumped when another rock hit his back. Alex had slipped behind him somehow. Eli felt his cheeks flush red and his breath shorten. He wanted to lash out at Alex but didn't want to make a scene. He could hear Alex and the other boys snickering beneath their breath. Eli stayed quiet and looked away.

"All right," Mr. Okos said, "let's head to the next stop."

As the group began to move, Eli hung back. He ducked behind a large sycamore tree that grew near the outcropping. Soon the group was out of sight and Eli was alone. Eli looked up at the outcropping. He saw several easy handholds. Eli felt a tightness in his chest from being made fun of by Alex and his friends. He burned with anger and was frustrated with himself for not standing up to Alex. His feelings were boiling to the top like a pot of spaghetti sauce left on the stove too long. His face was tight and he felt moisture gathering in the corner of his eyes. Looking up at the rock, he began to climb. He climbed with abandon and fury until suddenly he realized he could climb no more.

Clinging to the side of the rock, Eli felt panic creeping in. *You're going to fall!* an inner voice kept shouting. *Alex will pick on you the rest of your life for this! You're going to hurt yourself. Mrs. O'Connell will have to call for an ambulance. Your world as you know it will end!* His grip was starting to loosen and the aching in his trembling hands caused every muscle in his to body to scream "let go!"

But just when it seemed all was lost, Eli heard another voice speak. This voice was quieter than the first but much steadier. "You can do this Eli, be strong," the voice said. The first voice started to spew worry and fear again, but Eli shut it out.

"Stop worrying about what might happen or about what other people might think. Move now and move with all your heart and strength. Move now."

With one mighty heave Eli pushed up with his right foot and lunged upwards with his left hand. At first his hand hit flat cold stone and Eli felt himself slipping. But working his fingertips against the stone he suddenly found a small crack. It was narrow but deep. Eli thrust the palm of his hand inside. Pulling hard, he swung his left leg up until he found a small crevice and pushed up again. He had risen three feet in a matter of seconds and he felt a warming confidence building in his heart. Looking up, Eli saw two good handholds a few feet away. He went for them. Up and up he climbed until at last he felt the top of the ledge. "I made it!" he said aloud.

With one final push he heaved his head and shoulders up and over the top of the outcropping. He breathed a heavy sigh of relief. But suddenly he felt a shower of dust and pebbles hit his face. Eli was momentarily blinded but managed to pull the rest of his body up to flat ground.

As he lay on his stomach breathing hard, he heard laughter. It was Alex! *Oh no*, Eli thought, *I climbed my way out of danger only to be bullied again by Alex.* But from deep inside his heart came a voice again. "Be strong, Eli. Stand up for yourself!"

Eli rose to his feet and brushed himself off. Before him stood Alex and two other boys. They were blocking the path down the outcropping. "Where you been Eli?" Alex said, sneereing.

Eli felt blood flush to his ears. He knew what he had to do and he didn't care what it cost him or what anybody would think. He drew close to Alex and with unblinking eyes and a calm but steady voice said, "Alex, I know you don't feel real confident about yourself, and for that I'm sorry. But I gotta tell ya, tearing other people down to build yourself up won't satisfy your need for self-worth."

Eli paused and looked deep into Alex's eyes. "I am loved by my Creator and that's enough for me, and it can be enough for you, too, if you'd recognize it and pursue it. Now get out of my way and don't pester me anymore."

Alex laughed in Eli's face and with one hard push shoved him back toward the cliff edge. Eli's shoulders stung from the blow but he drew back and stood up to Alex. "Get out of my way, Alex!" he said again.

This time when Alex pushed him Eli was ready. He caught Alex's arms and redirected his body downward. Both boys hit the ground with a thud and Eli managed to roll on top of Alex. Eli had a tight grip on Alex's jacket collar. The other two boys watched on in silence, waiting to see what would happen next.

"Stop pestering me," Eli said. "You can do better than this." Eli rose to his feet and calmly walked down the trail without looking back.

Here Comes Another One

"Come on, we've got to be quick if we're going to beat this thing!" Esther's dad yells.

Looking off the bow of the boat, Esther sees a patch of choppy water speeding towards them. "Here comes another gust, Dad!" she calls. Just as soon as the words came out of her mouth, they are swallowed by the noise of the wind ripping through the rigging and waves breaking against the boat.

Her dad continues working with his back to her. Esther knew he hadn't heard her. He was busy pulling on a line that was caught. She knew if he couldn't get the line free, they wouldn't be able to pull in the front sail. With the front sail up, they risked capsizing the boat in the strong wind.

Down below deck Esther watches her mom hurriedly closing doors and securing all the sunscreen bottles, food bags and water jugs that were getting tossed around the cabin. As the boat crests another wave, Esther's mom grabs a handrail to keep from falling down. She looks up at Esther. The creases in her face look tight and her mouth is held firmly shut. Esther mouths the words "I'm OK." Her mom nods and goes back to her work.

Looking back out over the endless expanse of water her family's boat bounces around in, Esther sees that the gray sky above them is turning black. The clouds are moving fast and she can feel moisture in the air.

And then she sees another patch of choppy water. This time the gust looks much larger on the water and moves with lightning speed. "Dad!"

she screams, "Here comes another one!" Esther's heart beats fast inside her chest. It feels like it is coming up her throat and her mouth goes dry.

Her dad turns and looks at the gust still moving rapidly towards the boat. "Oh, no," he says as all expression slips from his face.

Esther wraps both arms around a winch on the side of the boat. Its metal body feels cold against her skin. "Hang on down below," her dad calls to her mom. Down below, Esther sees her mom gripping to the bottom part of the mast that runs through the center of the cabin. She can see her little brother and sister clinging to her mom's legs.

And then the wind gust hits. The boat tilts to Esther's side so much that she can almost reach down and touch the water. Above the sound of the wind, Esther can hear the boat creaking and popping from all the pressure the mast stays are putting on the deck. The big sail and the front sail put so much force on the boat that Esther wonders how the mast stayed upright.

"We've got to get that front sail in," Esther's dad calls above the wind. Taking one hand off the steering tiller, he begins working on the line. Looking hard at a spot on deck in front of the mast, Esther's dad calls to her, "I need you to crawl up front and untangle that line." He points to a spot where the front sail line is caught. "Once this gust gets past us, you'll have to get it done before the next one hits."

Esther swallowed hard. With her mom down below and her dad giving everything he had just to keep the boat on course, she will have to fix the line. She knows the fate of her family's boat and their very lives depend on her.

With one big surge of courage Esther rises from the cockpit and begins to climb up top. As she climbs, she sees small splashes in the water all around the boat. "Here comes the rain," her dad yells as raindrops start landing on the top of her head.

When the boat crests a big wave, Esther has to hold on tight as it rocks down into the trough of the next wave. Finally she reaches the tangled line. As she turns to ask her dad for instructions, she sees the rippled water from another gust moving toward the boat.

"Dad, what do I do?" she calls out.

"Pull the blue line over the railing," he calls back.

Esther gives the line a tug. It doesn't budge. Looking out over the water she sees the gust is getting closer. Setting her feet firmly against the boat deck, she pulls with all her might. This time the line comes loose.

Her dad immediately begins pulling in the front sail. Now that it is free, the blue line begins whipping wildly in the wind. It whizzes past Esther's face before smacking her squarely on the back. The blow takes her breath away and stings so sharply it feels like tiny needles are sticking up and down her back.

For a moment she lost her sense of purpose and feels a sob welling up inside of her. Pausing, she takes a deep breath and starts carefully crawling towards the cockpit.

And then the third gust hits. It slams the boat just as it crests a big wave causing the boat to tip sharply to one side. Esther feels her lower body being pulled towards the water. "Help! Dad!" she screams. But the hollowing wind swallows her words like a hungry dog wolfing down a squealing mouse.

The gust has brought with it driving rain that pelts Esther's body. Now she is hanging by the guardrail, her body dangling over the side of the boat.

From the corner of her eye she can see her dad making his way toward her. Just as he is within arm's reach, the boat pitches up and Esther feels herself falling.

She hits the water with a crash. Her head goes under and her world is quiet and dark. Her body is shocked by the coldness of the water and for a moment she feels lifeless. In that quiet moment she thinks of her Creator and her family and the love they hold for her. The love overcomes her fear and something inside of her awakens. With all her strength she surges toward the surface.

Her head breaks and she's back in the world of driving rain and wind. She struggles to tread water as a wave lifts her towards its crest. At the highest point she sees her boat. She could tell her dad had the front sail down and that both of her parents are busy bringing the boat around.

Before she goes down into the trough of the next wave, she can see the boat is pointed in her direction. As she treads water, she tries to keep her spirits up. All she can see are dark waters and above her are dark rain-filled skies. *What if they don't see me?* she thinks. *Or what if they miss me and can't come back around in time to save me?* These thoughts fluster back and forth in her mind as she rides another wave.

As she crests the wave, she sees the boat again. It's bearing down on her hard. *The boat is coming too close,* she realizes, *it's about to hit me.* The front of the boat looks like a huge knife slicing through the water. Summoning all her remaining strength she swims to the side just as the front glides past her. She reaches out and pushes off the side and screams as loud as she can.

Suddenly a head appears and her mom looks down at her. "Hold on, Esther!" she calls. In an instant the boat is past her and she struggles to tread water in the wake it leaves behind. On the back of the boat she sees her dad getting ready to throw a life ring. He takes one big swing and tosses the ring high into the air, a yellow safety line trailing after it. The ring lands with a splash a few feet from Esther. Swimming with all her might she grabs the ring just as the safety line goes tight. Her body starts moving through the water pulled by the ring.

"Hang on" her dad calls as he slowly begins pulling her toward the boat. When she gets close enough, her dad reaches down and pulls her on board. She immediately starts shivering as water drips from her clothes and hair.

"Let's get you down below," her mom says. She sees a bright light burning in the cabin and several warm blankets waiting for her.

"You did it, Girl" her dad says. Esther can see that his face is tight and tears are welling in his eyes, "You saved us."

She smiles at him as her mom slowly lowers her into the warmth and safety of the cabin.

Petey

"**C**ome on, Pete," I call to the big dog that follows a couple of feet behind me. His head is down and his big ears hang loosely on either side of his black eyes. "Why did you do that, boy?" I ask him through clenched teeth. Pete just looks up at me, his tail wagging slowly.

I want to take Pete and run away. I figure if I swing back up to the house and ease into the kitchen, I could stuff my pockets with cheese puffs, granola bars and Mom's homemade beef-jerky. We could live in the woods for at least three or four days.

I know it won't work though. My dad knows the woods behind our house pretty good. He'd probably come looking for us after a day or so. There's only one thing I can do about our situation, and that's face it.

"But we can go on one last run together, boy," I say to Pete. His ears perk up and his tail swings happily. "Come on!" I say as I break into a run down the hill behind the house. Pete runs around me and starts high-tailing it for the big woods. I run so fast that my legs feel like a pinwheel beneath me spinning out of control. The trees on the edge of the trail are a blur as I pass, and the horses in the pasture next to the trail jerk their heads up to watch us.

We run past the pasture and into the woods. The woods are two shades darker than the pasture and a couple of degrees cooler. It feels good to be protected from the afternoon summer sun. My heart is racing from the running and my breath comes in short gasps but Pete runs on. We pass the hut I built out of logs and an old wooden door I drug down from the barn. In the winter months Pete and I would hunker down in it, warding off the cold by building a campfire. *No more winters with Pete,* I think to myself.

We duck through the hole I cut in the barbed-wire fence that separates our woods from our neighbor's woods. Our neighbor's woods are big. There's a creek that runs through them and in the summer months I catch creek chubs and darters in it. The darters are my favorite. They are bright blue and orange and remind me of the fish you see in the tanks at Walmart. In the winter, the creek freezes and sometimes you can bust off chunks of ice that are big enough to float on. There's also a swimming hole with water over my head. It's the best feeling in the world to plunge into its cool waters after a hot day of bailing hay with Dad. It washes away all that scratchy chaff that clings to the sweat on your arms and legs. It's like taking a cool shower without the soap.

The woods are pretty big, too. There are some giant trees that reach way up into the sky. Some of them have large grapevines that are good for swinging. The woods are full of critters and neat plants to look at. Pete and I see deer, groundhogs, woodcock (it's a bird, just look it up), salamanders, frogs and turtles. In the spring, wildflowers bloom everywhere and spring-peepers (a small frog, you can look that up too) call so loudly from a swamp in the woods you can barely hear yourself think.

But probably the best part about the woods is that no one lives in them. Pete and I can pretty much do as we please. We are free to swim, hike, jump down a ravine or dig up a groundhog burrow. No rules, no parents, just big wild woods.

"Come on, Pete. Let's keep going," I say getting Pete back onto the trail, away from the groundhog den he stopped to investigate. I want to take Pete to one of our favorite spots. "Just a little bit further, boy," I say as we pick up the pace. As I run, I hear my dad's words in my mind: *We won't be able to keep him now, I'll have to take him in to the vet.*

***

I remember when we first brought Pete home. His long ears hung down on either side of his small face and his body looked like someone stuck a set of deer legs on the body of a chihuahua. His coat was tan with black spots. It was the color of my family's favorite college sports team, the Purdue Boilermakers. So we called him Boilermaker Pete, or Pete for short. He didn't stay little long. In a few months he was prancing around the house, his back nearly as tall as my dad's waist. One time my little sister was standing in the doorway to the kitchen when Pete came running in from the living room. He tried to run between her legs but didn't get low enough and she ended up on his back. She rode him about halfway across the kitchen before she fell off. That's the type of stuff that makes having a dog fun!

Owning a Great Dane has been fun. I liked to walk him through the campgrounds where my family camps with our horses. People would always say "I like your dog" or "Is that a Great Dane?" I would just nod my head and keep walking, beaming with pride on the inside.

Why did Pete have to bite someone! I don't know what made him do it. Maybe he was scared when that kid came up to him. It's not like he attacked the kid, but he did bite someone. Dad loves Pete, too, so putting him down must be the right thing to do.

***

"Pete, wait up," I call out. Pete stops and comes up to me. We've reached the spot. It's a high point at the back of the upper pasture. In one direction the whole pasture stretches out before you. In the summer it's full of green alfalfa that Dad cuts for hay. My favorite part of summer is the cool evenings after a first cut of hay. I love the smell. It's green and earthy and makes me feel like everything is going to be OK.

The whole pasture is surrounded by tall oak and hickory trees that grow on the edges of the ravines which fall away on every side. In the other direction, you can look down on the creek that runs below. It's a steep drop-off and Pete and I like to jump down it. Sometimes my little sister comes with us and she jumps too. You can slide all the way down to the creek if you want and splash into its cool waters at the bottom.

I look out over the creek as Pete stands beside me leaning his long body against my legs. I feel something inside of me welling up. It feels like someone is squeezing my heart forcing my feelings out and up to the surface. My face feels tight and I feel pressure around my eyes.

"Why did you do it, Pete!" I scream and before I know what I'm doing, I'm punching Pete in the side of his big chest. Tears start rolling and I'm nothing more than a blurry-eyed boy punching his dog 'cause he doesn't know what else to do. Pete just stands there, his big body easily absorbing the blows from my small fists.

I take a long, ragged breath and stop. Pete looks up at me and I know he has no idea what's about to happen to him. For him this is just another outing in the woods.

"Come on Pete, it's time to go back." We turn towards home. I walk in front this time, Pete following slowly behind. We walk in silence. I plod on hoping that somehow something might come along to change things. But in my heart I know it must be done.

When we get back to the house, Dad already has the car ready to go to the vet. I walk Pete over to the car and Dad loads him into the back. Pete sticks his big head out the back window and I put my hand on his muzzle one last time. "Good bye, Petey," I say. Dad puts the car in gear and pulls onto the road.

"Where you going?" my mom calls from the house as I start walking down the hill.

"I'm going to the woods, Mom." I walk on down the trail again, this time alone.

Belle

Eva woke to the feeling of someone shaking her gently. Her room was dark and it was warm under her covers. "Eva it's time," her dad whispered in the darkness. She climbed out of bed and sleepily pulled on a pair of jeans and a hooded sweatshirt. The sweatshirt caught around her thick blond hair but with a jerk she popped it over her head. Carefully putting her glasses on, she yawned and followed her dad down the steps.

Downstairs in the kitchen, one small light was burning. It was the light above the sink, the one her mom used while doing the dishes. The counter tops were all wiped clean and except for the movements of Eva and her dad putting on their rubber boots, the house was quiet and still.

Swinging the front door open, her dad hopped down the front steps with Eva at his heels. As they walked towards the barn, Eva could see thousands of stars twinkling through the branches of the tall pines that grew in her front yard. *What will I find when we get to the barn?* she wondered to herself. The night air felt cold against Eva's face, but much softer than the air of the past winter months. "Are you excited?" her dad asked. "Yeah," she replied, her breath steaming lightly as it escaped into the night.

Eva thought the barn looked like a giant black cat's head tonight. And as they drew closer, she imagined the big open doors were its mouth ready to swallow them. But her heart was cheered when she saw the light from the basement of the barn creeping up through the floorboards.

The basement was her favorite part of the big barn. Three sides of the basement were made of cobblestone walls that sweated coolness in the summer and kept the coldest of winds at bay in the winter. The front side of the basement opened into the lower pasture. In the summer her dad kept all of the doors open. Warm breezes brought in the smell of wildflowers and green pastures while barn swallows flew in and out as they tended their nests. In the winter, the doors were kept tightly closed at night protecting the animals from cold and trapping the smell of a freshly opened bale of hay in the depths of the barn.

As they descended the old wooden steps, Eva smelled fresh hay mixed with a hint of manure. Eva didn't mind the manure smell though, it was the smell of animal life, and for all of her nine years Eva had always loved animals. And there was one animal that she loved more than any other, that was the horse.

Eva had never had a horse of her own. But she had spent most of her young life riding and caring for her mom and dad's horses. She loved the feeling of riding a horse with her blond hair blowing in the wind, knowing she could steer the horse whichever way she chose. She loved taking care of horses too, filling their buckets with water in the morning and watching them slowly drink it down, or simply brushing their wet flanks after a long ride.

"Easy there, April," her dad softly spoke to the big black mare in her stall. Eva could see through gaps in the stall wall where April was standing. Her flanks were rising and falling rapidly from heavy breathing. "OK, come in here, Girl," Eva's dad said beckoning her to come into the stall.

Eva entered and asked, "What do you want me to do, Dad?"

"Just hold this lead gently," he said handing her the end of the lead.

Eva took the lead and pulled April's head down. She looked into April's big eyes. They looked like giant black marbles and seemed to read what Eva was thinking. "Easy girl," Eva calmly whispered. Even though she sounded calm on the outside, inside her heart was gripped with worry. *What if something goes wrong and April doesn't make it? I really want my own horse, but that's not as important as April being OK.*

April's breath was picking up and every once in a while she would paw the ground. The hair around her flanks was getting damp and Eva could smell the rich scent of horse sweat. April shook her head hard, causing the lead to fling from Eva's hand. "Whoa, April," Eva said, her hand slowly reaching for the lead. April pawed the ground and took a couple of steps backwards.

"Get a hold of her lead," Eva's dad said. Eva kept calm and slowly picked the lead back up.

"Got her, Dad."

April pawed the ground again before slowly dropping on her front knees. "Just let her go down," Eva's dad said.

Slowly, April lowered herself down until she was lying on her belly. Eva knelt down beside her on the stall floor and stroked her head. April snorted a few more times and then lay down on her side. Eva's dad moved behind April.

"Here it comes, Girl," her dad said. Eva looked and saw a dark object that was slowly getting bigger. "Come on April. Almost there," her dad whispered.

Eva's heart beat rapidly and she noticed her hands were moist with sweat. Her dad looked up at her. "OK, come here, Eva."

April was laying her head on the stall floor and her breathing was starting to return to normal.

Eva walked to her dad and saw the foal for the first time. It was laying on its side and its flanks rose and fell slightly with each breath it took. Its coat was just as black as April's and Eva could see a white patch on its head directly between its black eyes.

All around the foal was a layer of white sticky-looking stuff that steamed lightly on the stall floor. "What is that stuff, Dad?" Eva asked.

"It's the placenta, that's what kept the foal safe inside April's belly."

Eva touched the placenta. It was warm and felt like a wet balloon. She looked back at the foal, its black eyes looked alert and shiny. Its breathing was picking up and all of a sudden it raised its head and looked at Eva. All of the worry that had built up in Eva's heart slipped away like a silk sheet falling from a kitchen table.

Eva smiled at her dad and he smiled back. "What should we call her, Girl?" he asked.

After thinking for a few seconds Eva replied, "Belle."

Onion Patch

"Why don't you go up to the casket?" Max's dad asked. Max looked at the floor. His feet felt tight in his church shoes and his shirt collar was scratchy against his neck.

All around him a crowd of friends and family talked in hushed tones. "They think the guy that hit them was drunk," he heard a family friend say.

"I talked to a guy from the Sheriff's department and he said she was thrown from the car and pinned. By the time they got her to the hospital, she was already gone," his neighbor from two doors down said. Max tried to shut the conversations out but bits and pieces kept getting in, like pebbles thrown at his heart.

The accident was a blur in Max's mind. There was the sound of screeching tires and breaking glass. There was the hard slam when the car flipped over on its side. And there was the voice of his father helplessly calling to his mom as he tried to free her.

Max labored to block it from his mind, but the sudden loss of his mother left him reeling. *What would happen to my family now? Who will fix supper or mend our clothes? Who will cheer me up with sweet words when I've had a bad day?* Max didn't know the answer to any of these questions. All he knew is that they'd have to go on without her.

The room was bright with sunshine and as Max walked towards the casket, he passed his grandfather. He looked strange in his clean white shirt and black pants. Max was used to seeing him in his bib-overalls.

But his eyes still had a warm glow like always. His grandfather put a hand on Max's shoulder and squeezed as Max walked past.

All around the brown coffin were large white flowers. They smelled sweet but damp to Max. Max looked at his mother lying there. Her face was surrounded by thick brown hair neatly combed, and she was wearing the floral print dress she liked to wear to church. The lips that had kissed him so many times wore a shade of lipstick that looked strange on them.

Max felt like he was in a very bad dream. The person who had cared for him the most, who had spent the most time with him, who had held him in her arms so close he could feel her heart beat, was no more. Max's chest felt tight and the muscles in his face were tense. He wanted to cry, but he didn't.

After the funeral, Max's dad drove him to his grandparents' farm. "You'll be staying here for a while, Max, until I can sort things out," his dad said.

Max got out and grabbed a bag of clothes from the trunk, then waved to his dad as he drove away. Max looked at his grandparents' farm. The two-story house was white with a small porch on the front. The yard around the house was bare but for a few short trees. A large chicken coop stood next to the house and a flock of brown hens picked in the short grass next to it. Beyond the house was his grandpa's barn. It wasn't the biggest barn in the county, but Max's grandpa kept it looking good with a fresh coat of white-wash paint every few years.

Max had spent plenty of time at his grandparents' farm when he was younger. He would wander out to the barn while his grandma and his mom talked on the front porch or baked pies together. The barn was always cool and shady even on the hottest of summer days. Max liked the smell of fresh hay in the barn. He liked to look at his grandpa's mules in their stalls. They were tall and white. When Max talked to them, they'd prick their ears forward and raise their noses towards him hoping Max had brought them an apple core or a couple of carrots, which he did whenever he could.

Sometimes Max would sit and watch the barn swallows flying in and out of the barn doors as they brought bugs back to their hungry chicks. He'd climb up to the rafters and look into their nests to see the chicks stretch their feeble necks high, beaks open wide.

But now that he was thirteen, Max didn't come to the farm as often. When he did, it was to work. In hot summer months, Max helped his grandpa load hay into the barn. During the colder months, the mules' stalls always needed cleaning, and there was always firewood to split. Max didn't mind the work, though. He knew it needed to be done and liked knowing he was helping his grandparents.

***

Max saw the front door open and his grandma come out of the house. "Max, come here," she said to him. Max walked up the steps of the porch and dropped his bag. "How you doing, Kid?" she asked, pulling him in for a hug. She held him tight and rubbed his back lightly. "You're gonna be OK," she told him.

Max felt embarrassed to be hugged by his grandma, but being held again made him feel warm inside. Tears welled up in his eyes. He wanted to let them flow and cry in the shelter of his grandmother's arms, but he didn't.

"Come inside and you can change your clothes," his grandma said, leading him through the kitchen and into a back bedroom.

Max threw his bag down and changed into his bibs. It was a relief to be back in his normal clothes after being cooped up in church clothes all morning.

Max walked into the kitchen. His grandma was rolling out dough, her hands white with flour. "Your grandpa's out in the onion patch. Why don't you go help him?" she said without looking up from her work.

"OK, Grandma," Max said as he walked through the kitchen and out the back door.

In the far corner of the onion patch, Max could see his grandpa bent over picking onions. As Max got closer, he stood up and looked Max in the eye. Max held his gaze and knew his grandpa could read the hurt he felt inside. "How you holdin' up, Max?" he asked.

"OK," Max replied.

His grandpa nodded slowly. "Well, time will tell about that. Max, I'm gonna take a break from this. Why don't you finish pickin' the patch"?

"Yeah, I can do it," Max replied as he took a burlap sack half full of onions from his grandpa. He patted Max on the back and made his way back to the house.

Max looked down at the black dirt the onions grew in. Max's dad told him that the onion patch had once been part of a marsh. The marsh was drained years ago for farming, but after a hard rain it was easy to picture ducks and muskrats living there once again. Max liked the way the dirt smelled, rich and full of life.

Max dropped to his knees and started picking. This was the first time he had been alone since his mother's death. His mind drifted to her again. He thought of the way she held him gently in her arms on Sunday mornings before church, dressed in her floral print dress, the smell of her perfume filling his senses.

He thought of the way she fixed his sandwiches just the way he liked them, and how he felt loved when he opened his lunch bucket and saw them in the middle of a hectic day at school. He thought of the time she came to him after his dad had been rough with him for doing bad in school.

"Come here, Max. You'll do better next time," her voice as soft as lamb's wool. Max felt the urge to cry again. *Must be these onions.* All alone in the middle of his grandpa's onion patch, Max wondered if it would hurt to cry. *Maybe now is the time, here where no one can see.*

Max felt the first tear roll down his cheek and drop into the black dirt. It was followed by another and another, and soon Max's eyes were blurry with tears. *I'll get them all out here in the onion patch. I'll let this black earth take them all, so I won't have to cry them again.* "Take them, take them all," he said through clenched teeth.

When the tears finally stopped, Max dried his eyes with the back of his hands. He knew he wouldn't cry again. He knew that the only thing left to do was to keep on going without his mom. And so he did.

Authors Note: "Onion Patch" is based on the real-life experiences of my Grandpa, Max Whiteleather, who lost his mom at an early age.

Bareback

"OK girl, let's go," Eva called to the big mare named Belle. The horse perked her ears up and gracefully rolled into a canter. Eva gripped Belle's flanks gently, easily staying in the saddle. Strands of her blond hair trailed behind her as green alfalfa flew by beneath her. Eva kept Belle's canter in check by holding downward lightly on the reins.

She was riding in the high pasture. It was a sea of green alfalfa grass that waved gently in the summer breeze. The pasture was surrounded by thick woods on all sides except for the gap where the tractor trail came into it. The woods were shady and cool even on the hottest days of summer. Beyond the edges of the pasture, the terrain dropped steeply. Down along the bottom of the drop was a small creek that ran cool and clear. Sometimes Eva and her sister Ruth would play in the creek after helping their dad bail hay or after a long horse ride.

Eva loved the high pasture. Here in the early morning, you could see a deer, head down, grazing on the alfalfa. Or you might see a turkey walking the edge, head outstretched looking for bugs. Eva loved walking up to the high pasture on a summer evening after her dad had just cut hay. The air was alive with the sweet smell of drying alfalfa and clover. Eva wished she could bottle the smell up and keep it in her room to be opened on a cold winter day. She'd linger in the pasture until dusk so she could watch the lightning bugs flicker on and off in the fading light.

Suddenly Eva felt Belle's gait change. Her pace was beginning to quicken and her head was dropping. It felt like Belle was taking a giant leap with each stride. "Easy girl, slow down," Eva called out as her heart began to pound and her face grew tight with worry.

***

Earlier that day, Eva had asked her dad if she and her little sister Ruth could go riding on their own. Eva wasn't sure if her dad would say yes since she had only just turned 12. But she was very confident around horses from years of riding with her family. "That's fine," her dad said. "Just make sure to cinch the saddles tight and go easy on the horses' mouths."

"OK, Dad," Eva said as they left the house and walked down towards the barn.

In the barn, Eva got Belle out of her stall and tied her to a lead rope. Belle was a tall horse, with a brown coat and a white star on her head right between the eyes. Eva loved Belle. She had been there when Belle was born one cool spring night three years ago. She had helped her dad break Belle, and had been the first in her family to ride her in the high pasture.

Ruth got her horse, Thunder, out of his stall and tied him next to Belle. Thunder was smaller than Belle and had an all-black coat. "Which saddle do you want to use?" Ruth asked.

"I don't want one," Eva replied.

"But Dad said—"

"I don't care," Eva interrupted Ruth. "I want to ride bareback so I can feel closer to Belle. It's all right, Ruth, I can handle it."

"OK," Ruth said, shrugging her shoulders. "I guess I'll take the Australian saddle."

Eva loved riding bareback. She felt free and in more control of the horse without the restrictions of a saddle. She loved the way Belle felt beneath her when she was seated high on her back, legs gripping firmly to her flanks. She felt a kind of freedom rarely felt by someone her age. And besides, it was a beautiful summer day, blue sky above and a gentle breeze moving the light summer air.

Eva and Ruth worked together until Thunder was saddled and both horses were bridled. They led the horses out of the barn and Eva held Thunder while Ruth got on. "Whoa, Belle," Eva said as she prepared to jump on Belle's back. Holding the reins in one hand, Eva leaped onto Belle's back, belly first. Once she was positioned, she swung a leg over and sat up. Belle took a couple of steps sideways but once Eva was upright, she quickly gained control.

"Where should we go?" Ruth asked.

"Let's ride up to the high pasture," Eva replied. They walked the horses out of the barnyard and onto the tractor trail that led up to the high pasture.

***

"Whoa, easy girl!" Eva called to Belle who was now running full out. Belle made no effort to slow down but instead ran all the faster. Belle had gone from a controlled canter to an all-out run in no time. *What did I do wrong?* Eva wondered. She had dropped the reins and clung desperately to Belle's mane. Eva felt her body start to slip to one side. Her heart was beating hard inside her chest and even though they were going fast, Eva felt like everything was happening in slow motion. She knew her only chance of stopping Belle was to turn her head. But without the reins and no saddle to push herself back up this wouldn't be possible. The alfalfa was a green blur as it whizzed by below her. The ground seemed a long way down.

What will happen if I fall? she wondered. *Will it hurt, what will Belle do? Will she keep running and maybe plunge down the steep hills surrounding the pasture? And....what will Dad say about this?*

And then it happened. Belle took one extra hard lunge forward and Eva felt her body sliding towards the ground. As soon as she hit, she began to tumble and spin. She felt like she was inside of a washing machine. When she finally stopped tumbling, she lay still for a minute, the wind knocked out of her lungs. She lay staring up at the blue sky, relieved to be off the out-of-control horse.

Ruth rode up on Thunder just as Eva stood up and dusted herself off. "You all right?" Ruth asked excitedly. Thunder's nostrils were flared from the cantering, but Ruth had him in control.

"Yeah I'm fine. Where did Belle go?"

"She went out of the pasture and down the tractor trail, probably headed for the barn," Ruth replied.

Eva nodded and looked towards the tractor trail.

"Want a ride back?" Ruth asked.

"No, I'll walk."

On the walk back to the barn, Eva thought how her dad had been right. She hated that. But she knew the best thing to do would be to tell him the truth. She'd have to tell him she decided to ride bareback, even though she knew she wasn't supposed to. She'd have to tell him about losing control and hitting the dirt as Belle ran on without a rider. She knew now that although she was old enough to ride on her own, she wasn't old enough to make certain riding decisions. She knew it took experience to be able to do that, and she'd gained some the hard way today.

When she got back to the barn, her dad had Belle in a halter tied to her stall. He was brushing her flanks which were wet with sweat. She was breathing lightly and standing without stomping.

"Dad..." Eva started to say.

"I know, Girl," he interrupted. "What did you learn?"

"I'm probably not old enough to ride bareback yet."

"Yes, Girl, I knew that. I'm glad you learned that lesson without you or Belle getting hurt."

Her dad put the brush down and wrapped Eva in his arms. "Be more careful next time, Girl."

"I will, Dad," she replied.

Eva turned toward Belle and reached toward her. "Sorry, girl," she said as Belle brought her nose up and blew gently against Eva's outstretched hand.

Two Peoples, One Heart

Chapter 1

O utside her family's cabin, Loretta sees blue skies fading away to burnt orange. The cicadas of deep summer are beginning their chorus, which rises and falls in a rhythmic echo. The cicadas drown out the constant background noise of the cars and trucks that drive the state highway behind her cabin. In the kitchen her mother is tidying up after a supper of chicken and rice. Her father is reading in the back bedroom of her home. She walks across the wood floor to where her brother and sister are playing cars on a play rug.

"Can I play?" she asks.

"Yes, you can be the yellow car," her brother Isaac says.

"I don't want to be the yellow car. I want to be the blue car," she replies.

"NO!" her little sister Olivia cries out as Loretta attempts to disarm her of the blue car. "That's my car."

"Loretta, just pick another car," Mom calls out from the kitchen.

But Loretta won't settle for anything less than the blue car, so she walks down the hall with her head down, her blond hair falling on either side of her face. When she gets to her parents' room, her dad looks up from his book. He notices Loretta's blue eyes under her knit brows and sees that the corners of her small mouth are down-turned.

"What's the matter, Girl?" he asks.

"Olivia and Isaac won't let me play with them."

"Is there something you could do on your own?"

"Like what?"

"Sit and read with me?"

"I already read a book this morning."

"What if you play cars by yourself?"

"I don't want to."

"It's nice outside. Why don't you go for a walk?"

Loretta stands thinking as her knit brow slowly melts away and her face becomes more serious.

"Where would I walk?" she asks.

"Walk down to the riverbank and back up to the cabin," her dad replies.

She stands quietly for a moment looking at her dad with his close-cropped hair and the bristly beginnings of a beard on his face. "I guess I'll go for a walk," she says quietly.

Without another word she walks out the door, letting it slam behind her. As she walks down the steps that lead to the river, her dad rises up from the bed. He walks to the back porch and stands leaning against the railing, watching Loretta descend the stairs. When she is about halfway down, she turns and looks up at him. The evening sun makes her blond hair glow and small, shining spots gleam in the tops of her blue eyes.

"Have fun on your walk, Girl," he calls.

Loretta says nothing in reply as she continues down the steps. Her dad watches her until the pink colors of her shirt are swallowed by the dense growth of the riverbank.

Chapter 2

The riverbank is covered in green plants growing in dense clusters. Some are starting to show signs of yellow flowers at the tips of their long narrow stems. From the tops of tall trees, small songbirds add their clear and bright voices to the background buzz of cicadas.

As Loretta walks the well-worn trail that winds along the riverbank, plants swipe against the sides of her bare legs. Taller ones threaten her face and she reaches up to push them away as if she's moving through a beaded doorway. She's careful as she walks to avoid the stinging nettles her dad warned her about. She has been stung by them before and knows well the burning and itching sensation they cause. If she gets stung by nettles, she knows to look for touch-me-not plants. By taking the juicy stems of the plants and smashing them, she can make a liquid that when rubbed on her skin will help take the sting away. Later in the summer she likes to look for the ripe seed pods of the touch-me-not plant which explode when touched, throwing their tiny seeds high into the air.

She knows other things too about the forest along the river. She knows the most common owl heard in the evening is the barred owl and that if you mimic its call, it will sometimes call back. She knows about the banded water snakes that entwine themselves in tree roots along the riverbank. If you're not careful, you'll think they're just another root. She knows about the deer that use the riverbank as a passageway in the late evenings and early morning hours. She knows the taste of deer meat well, as the steaks and roasts that her mom prepares are some of her favorite meals. And she knows about the fireflies that come out at dusk and twinkle on and off as they dance over the tops of touch-me-not plants.

By now the sun is sagging low over the horizon and the forest is starting to darken. Loretta heads for her favorite spot in the woods and approaches quietly. In front of her stands a large sycamore tree. The tree's trunk is so large that Loretta and her family can barely encircle the tree standing hand in hand with outstretched arms. The trunk of the massive tree is white and dotted with brown bark that clings to the tree like bran flakes clinging to honey. At the top of its trunk, several large white branches sprout out and away from the tree. On their ends are large leaves that are bigger than a man's hand. They glow a greenish yellow in the light cast by the setting sun. If one looks closely at the tree, they'll find several holes and cavities. Some of the holes are big enough to stick your head into while others are smaller. Around the edges of these holes are the claw and teeth marks of the many small animals that have found shelter in the tree over the course of its long life. On any given winter night, when snow is falling and cold winter winds rage over the river-bank, raccoons and squirrels can be found in the tree nestled as snug as Loretta in her bed inside her cabin. In the spring and summer months, birds by the dozens can be found using its branches for nest sites and feasting on the abundant insect life found there.

But Loretta's favorite part of the tree is its hollowed-out center. Here, through a small opening, one can enter the tree and find relief from the heat of a hot summer day or the chill of a cold winter wind.

Loretta stares at the tree for a minute before entering. There is something about the tree that is not quite the same tonight. She wonders if it's the evening light that makes the tree more looming. Or maybe it's because one of its large limbs has died and has begun dropping leaves. And then her eye falls on a large Virginia creeper vine growing up its side. "That's strange," she says aloud. "That vine wasn't there the last time I was down here."

The vine is large and thick, about as big around as her arm. It stretches high into the tree before it branches out into several large shoots with five-fingered leaves that arch down from their own weight. Even though it's still summer, the leaves have begun to change and are a dark red color. The leafy arch of the red vine stands out in the green forest like a red flag on a cloudy day. Loretta doesn't understand how the vine got there or why its leaves have turned red already, but since she knows her tree like an old friend, she puts her worries aside and enters through the crack.

Inside it's cool and smells of sawdust and wet moss. The light is dim but Loretta can still see the spot against the outside edge of the trunk where she likes to sit. She sits down and starts to replay the evening's events. She thinks of the chicken and rice that she had for supper and how her dad wouldn't let her get a second scoop of brown sugar. She thinks of Isaac and Olivia and how they wouldn't let her play with the blue car. And she thinks of her dad lying in his bed doing nothing but reading a book. *How can they all just sit there in the house when they can clearly see I'm bored?* she wonders. *It's like they don't even care how I feel!*

As she thinks, she feels something poking her in the back. She digs the object out of the dirt and examines it in her palm. It's small, about the size of a Matchbox car. It is brown and has a body with legs and a head. On the head is a small face and markings that look like women's hair. "That's strange," she says. "I've never found anything like this in here before."

Placing the figurine in her pocket, she lays back down again. She is relieved to be in the quiet of the tree with only her thoughts to keep her company. Ever so softly, sleepiness begins setting in. She tries to fight it because she knows it's too late to fall asleep in the woods. But she is soothed by the darkness of the tree. Outside she can still hear the cicadas. Their rhythmic throb puts an end to her drowsy fight and she is soon fast asleep.

Chapter 3

Loretta wakes with a start to the sound of a barred owl calling. The one note call rings through the woods in a sharp burst of sound. The inside of the tree is now completely dark and the cicadas are quiet. She crawls to the crack in the tree and looks out. The cool night air feels refreshing on her skin and helps ease the pain of waking up from a long nap. She looks at the sky and sees stars twinkling through the leafy tree branches. As she steps out of the tree and into the night, she stops to investigate the stars. By standing under a dead limb, Loretta sees so many bright stars that the twigs of the limb seem like black skeleton fingers reaching into milky whiteness. Of all the times she has been outside at night, Loretta can't ever remember a night so clear. Usually on nights when she is allowed to stay up late, only a few of the brightest stars are visible. The glowing lights of the nearby city keep most stars hidden in an orange haze. Now as she looks up at the sky, there is only blackness speckled with thousands of blurring white lights. Some cluster together to form splotches of murky light while others stand alone, the edges around them pointed and bright.

As Loretta stands looking up, she is also amazed at how quiet the night is. She hasn't once heard the sound of a passing car. She also hasn't heard the distant rumbling of jets coming to and from the nearby airport. The only noises of the night come from the small crickets that sing in hushed tones in the grass around her. The night is so quiet and still that Loretta is startled by the noise of her foot hitting the forest floor as she starts toward the stairs to the cabin.

Loretta walks along the riverbank for some time before coming to a stop. *Hmm. I must have passed the stairs without seeing them.* She turns and walks back the way she came. She walks slower this time, carefully looking for the stairs. But to her dismay she ends up back at the sycamore tree. *What's going on? I should have walked right past those stairs.* Thinking the unusual darkness of the night has confused her, she decides to climb straight up the steep bank. She starts walking, grabbing small trees to pull herself up. Just as she is about at the top, she feels the prickly sting of a nettle on her arms. The pain and irritation are intense, but she keeps going until she reaches the top. She walks towards where her cabin should be, looking for the soft yellow light of Daddy's reading lamp leaking out the bedroom window. But instead of light there is only darkness. And instead of the mown grass, she finds only more trees and nettles. "I can't believe this," she says aloud. "Not only can I not find the stairs, I can't find the cabin."

She walks a little bit further. *This has to be where the cabin is. It should be right here.* But it's not. Trees and more trees are all that she can see. Her mind struggles to figure things out and panic creeps into her heart. "Daddy!" she screams into the night air. "Where are you!"

Instead of the sound of her father's comforting voice calling from the back deck, the night is empty of sound. Even the crickets have stopped, disturbed by the outburst. Loretta sits down on the forest floor. The skin on her arms still throbs from the pain of the nettles. She feels alone in the woods with the vast black sky sprawling above her. She thinks of her home and her family and begins to cry.

Chapter 4

Early the next morning the sun slowly rises in the east. It rises over a dense forest of tall trees. Songbirds are calling as they hop from branch to branch looking for the bug life they'll eat for breakfast. The sun's first rays bring out the sparkling greenness of the river running at the bottom of the bluff. The river runs clean and free. Its bottom is spotted with dense mussel beds over which swarms of fish swim and feed. Along the riverbank, a belted kingfisher opens with a burst of cackling sound as it flies to its perch to begin hunting for the day.

The call of the kingfisher wakes Loretta from the light sleep she fell into the night before, when she grew tired from crying and worrying. She rises to her feet and for a moment she can't remember why she's not waking up in her bed inside the cabin. Then it all comes flooding back. She looks to the spot where the cabin should be and seeing only trees, she knows that it wasn't all a dream. She thinks of her family and realizes that if the cabin isn't there, they're not there either. She'd give anything right now to hear the call of her mother's voice from the kitchen telling her that breakfast is ready.

Slowly accepting her fate, she thinks of her dad and what he might do if he were here. She remembers the time Isaac cut his head while on a family outing. She watched her dad calmly clean the wound and dress it before loading her brother into the car to take him to the emergency room. She remembers the time when he took her family to a cave that required a watery crawl through a small hole in order to exit. Her brother and sister panicked when the icy water got to their knees and they began to cry. Her dad looked her in the eye and calmly asked her to help him get them out of the cave. Loretta, pushing aside her fears, listened quietly as he told her the plan. She worked with her dad to get everyone out of the cave and learned an important lesson about staying calm and thinking things through in an emergency situation.

Now she must put those lessons to the test and decide what to do next. Her first thought is food. She knows that although a little late in the year, there may be a few black raspberries around. She notices a small clearing where the sun's rays cast a bright light on the forest floor. Walking into the clearing, Loretta finds a small patch of raspberries. The morning dew stands on the large black berries making them taste cool as she begins popping them into her mouth. The berries are sweet with a hint of sourness and the thick juice feels good on her tongue. After satisfying her hunger, Loretta sits down on a log to think. "Well, just because the cabin is gone doesn't mean there aren't other houses still around," she says aloud. "Maybe I should start looking for someone who can help me."

Not wanting to lose sight of the river, she starts walking along the bluff moving upstream. She walks until the sun is high in the sky before deciding to take a rest. A strong thirst pulls her down to the river's edge. She cups her hands and takes a drink of the cool, clear water. The river looks the same on the surface but has a different feel to it. The water smells like fresh rain with a hint of fish, a much cleaner and fresher smell than what Loretta remembers. She can also see clearly the large rocks that dot its bed and the green moss and plant life that cling to them. She hasn't seen any Styrofoam cups or empty bait containers on the bank either. This is unusual for a river that runs through several large towns.

As she rests by the river, she reaches into her pocket to examine the figurine she found. It's tannish brown and looks like it's made of clay. Around the waist of the figurine is the impression of a belt like a woman would wear on top of a skirt. *This is really neat. It looks like one of the pieces I've seen at the State Museum with Dad.* She puts the figurine back in her pocket and starts walking again.

As the day wears on, Loretta begins to grow hungry again. She finds another forest opening and eagerly looks for more raspberries. Spotting the purple arching stems of a large clump, she walks toward the far end of the clearing. As she approaches, movement catches her eye. Stopping, she scans the raspberry patch. Her eye catches on a dark patch of black fur and she freezes. The fur is much thicker and denser than any raccoon she has ever seen and when the creature moves again, she can tell that it is much bigger too. As she watches, she sees a large ear emerge from the briar patch followed by a long snout with a black nose. Next a paw with five shiny black claws reaches out and pulls a clump of raspberries off the stem. The paw drops the berries into an open jaw of long white teeth. "Oh, no," she whispers. "It's a bear."

Chapter 5

As Loretta watches, frozen with fear, the bear turns to grab another handful of berries. As it turns, it sees her. It stands on its hind legs and Loretta can see the full scale of its massive body. The bear looks at her, studying the blond-haired creature standing before him. Loretta is overcome with fear and screams at the top of her lungs.

She runs out of the clearing, the raspberries tearing at the skin of her legs. The bear, equally scared by the scream, turns and runs the other way disappearing into the thick woods.

Loretta runs back to the banks of the river before stopping to catch her breath. She stands still and listens to make sure the bear isn't chasing her. The woods are quiet except for her heavy breathing. She walks into the water to ease the pain of the scrapes and scratches left behind by the briars. The water feels cool against her legs.

By now the sun is making its way towards the horizon and the familiar drone of cicadas fills the air. Loretta's stomach begins to growl again, but she isn't willing to risk disturbing another bear. She sits on the bank collecting her thoughts. All day she's walked and hasn't seen or heard the first sign of other people. She is discouraged by the day's events. Her walk to find people has failed. The gnawing hunger in her belly is building. She was almost eaten by a bear, and she misses her family with all her heart. As the woods along the riverbank begin to darken and Loretta thinks of another night spent alone, she remembers probably the most important lesson learned from her dad. She remembers praying with him at bedtime. She remembers the calming effects their prayers had on them both. She recalls saying a prayer at school when the stresses of being a kid overwhelmed her.

And now sitting on the riverbank, feeling all alone in the world, she prays to her Creator asking him to bring her peace and wisdom.

Chapter 6

The next morning, Loretta wakes to the sound of a Kingfisher calling as it flies from a tree branch. She stretches her arms and looks at the river. It's flowing just as green and clear as it was the night before. Over its waters hover small clouds of tiny bugs that dance and move in a rhythmic cycle.

After drinking from the river, Loretta begins hiking along its banks. She passes through more dense forest before coming to a clearing. As she scans the clearing, she notices vines that grow from small mounds of dirt. The vines are thick-stemmed and have large green leaves. On the ends of some of the stems are round squash that appear almost ripe.

Loretta's heart skips a beat as she realizes that the squash look like the ones her mother grows in the garden. She thinks of the way her mom cooked squash and eggs on a summer evening and how tender and buttery it tasted. Her thoughts make her mouth water, so she grabs a squash from the field. By taking a flat rock she cuts the end off. She begins scooping out the flesh with her fingers and devouring it.

As she eats, a familiar smell hits her nose. It's the smell of wood smoke. She remembers the smell from the many campfires her family used to have in the fall when the air was cool and jack-o'-lanterns flickered in the dark night. She scans the clearing for the source of the smoke. It seems to be coming from the far end where the clearing turns into a forest of scattered trees. She picks another squash and starts walking toward the trees.

She pauses at the end of the field to peer into the woods. From a distance, she can see what look like small houses made of logs and grasses. There are about 20-30 houses forming a loose circle around a fire. The fire releases blue smoke which drifts into the treetops before being carried off by the wind.

As she scans the houses, something black catches her eye. *Oh no, another bear!* She looks closer and sees hair instead of fur. The hair surrounds a tan face with black eyes that peer at Loretta. "It's a girl!" she says in surprise. The girl is hidden behind a large clump of bushes, their green leaves hiding everything but her head. Loretta and the girl stare at each other. Finally Loretta calls out, "Hello, please help me. I'm lost and I don't know where my family is!" The girl breaks from her hiding spot and runs towards the houses. She wears only a wide piece of leather wrapped around her waist. She runs silently through the woods before disappearing into one of the houses.

Loretta is scared but knows there is only one thing to do. She summons all her courage and slowly but steadily approaches the houses.

Chapter 7

As she approaches, she sees a group of men coming out of one of the larger houses, the one the girl went into. They come close to her but keep their distance, studying her closely. They converse amongst themselves in a language Loretta cannot understand. They stare at the cotton fabric that makes up Loretta's skirt and t-shirt. They note that the little girl looks dirty and unkempt, a result of her two days in the woods.

Loretta stands quietly and stares back at them. She looks at the jet-black hair that hangs well past their shoulders. She notes that their skin is much darker than hers and their faces are smooth, unlike the stubbly face of her father. She studies the buckskin held around their waists by a leather strap. The men continue talking to each other, their voices growing louder and more heated. All at once they stop talking and Loretta knows they have decided what to do with her.

A man in the middle of the group walks up to Loretta. With his black eyes, he peers deep into hers. His face is creased with deep lines, but his eyes look steady and sharp. Across his face are strange dark lines that remind Loretta of tattoos. He is so close that Loretta can smell the scent of wood smoke coming from his hair. The man begins to speak, pausing after each sentence as if waiting for Loretta to respond.

Loretta has no idea what he is saying. "I've lost my family and my home," she says. "Please help me. I'm hungry and alone and I want to go home."

The man stands silently after Loretta finishes. He cannot comprehend what this girl means. Where did she come from? Where did she get the strange clothes she's wearing? And what does the sign of her coming mean for his village?

The man steps forward and grabs Loretta by the arm. "Please let me go! Please, help me!" Loretta yells, but the man says nothing. He walks into the village gripping Loretta's arm tightly. As she's taken through the village, people gather around to touch her hair and feel the fabric of her

42

clothing. The man draws Loretta to the front of a low hut, opens a door made of animal skin and throws her inside. She hits the floor with a thud landing flat on her back. As the flap is let down, she catches a glimpse of the girl from the field. She stands with her eyes fixed on Loretta. The last thing Loretta sees before the hut goes dark is the watchful face of the girl.

Chapter 8

Inside the hut the air smells of animal skins and wood smoke. Only small traces of light filter through the thick stick and bark walls. Loretta studies the door. The hide is lashed tightly to the hut, held secure by several large rocks along its bottom. The walls are made of tightly woven branches. The floor is made up of well-packed dirt. The only furnishing in the hut is a deer skin lying on the floor. Loretta pulls on a corner of the skin and sees that it is stiff and hard. It's much rougher than the hides at the rendezvous she'd attended with her dad. Those were soft and could easily be used as a blanket. The hide in the hut was suitable only as something to lie on.

Loretta sits on the hide feeling the coarse deer hair against her bare legs. Outside she can still hear voices mixed with chopping and grinding sounds and the sounds of firewood being broken. The light through the cracks is beginning to soften and Loretta knows day is fading to night. Now the wood smoke that lingers in the hut has a new smell to it. It smells of roasted meat and vegetables. It reminds Loretta of fall nights with her family spent around a campfire, cooking sausage and potatoes over the open fire. Loretta's mouth waters at the memory, but her stomach feels empty and dry.

Outside Loretta can hear voices coming closer to the hut. She hears the large stones that hold the skin door being moved away. Then a brown arm and hand appear from the bottom corner and set a large wooden bowl on the floor. The hand retreats and comes back with a small piece of roasted meat and a handful of steamed squash. The hand also places a hollow squash full of water on the floor. Loretta hears the rocks being placed back and waits until the voices grow quiet before moving over to the food and water. She drinks deeply and immediately feels better. Next, she examines the meat. It's greasy on the outside and she has to wipe away dirt and ash before she can tell what it is. She knows it's not deer by its texture and guesses that it's probably bear meat. She thinks of the bear in the clearing and wonders if it's him she is about to eat. She takes a big bite and hot juices run down the corners of her mouth. The meat is rich and she finishes the piece without pausing between bites. Next, she scoops the squash out of the bowl. The squash is moist and tender and its rich flavor mixes well with the bear meat.

When Loretta is done eating, she can tell that night has settled on the village. A new light creeps through the cracks of the hut. This is a yellow light that flickers along the walls and floor. Loretta begins to hear what she thinks is singing. She moves over to the far wall and finds a small opening. Through the opening she peers into the night. Towards the center of the village, Loretta can see a large fire throwing long licking flames and orange sparks into the night air. Around the fire men and women dance and sing. Loretta hears shrill cries and yelps which pierce the night air. The singing and dancing last for several hours until one by one people leave the circle and enter their houses to sleep. Soon the fire ring is empty and the fire burns down to a pile of large red coals that flicker with small blue and orange flames.

Loretta's eyes become heavy and she lies down on the deer rug. Tonight she will sleep on a crude bed in a crude shelter. She will also share the night with other humans nearby. But in her heart she feels just as alone as she did on her first night in the woods. She prays to her Creator, thinks about her family one last time, and drifts off to sleep.

Chapter 9

Loretta awakens to the stone being drug away from the hut's door. Again, the deer skin is opened and the brown hand appears and deposits water and some steamed squash. Loretta sits up and blinks a few times in the morning darkness. She reaches to her face and brushes her hair back. She notices her fine blond strands feel heavy and dirty. Her clothes are stiff from a thick layer of dried dirt. They are also stained with raspberry juice. Her hands are dark purple from raspberries too and she sees dark lines of dirt under her fingernails. She looks very different from a few days ago when she was at home, her skin and clothes clean and her freshly washed hair shiny and light.

After eating, Loretta lies back down on the deer skin and thinks about her situation. *What will happen next? What will they do with me? Will they keep me prisoner here forever? Will I get a chance to plead my case to them, to explain what has happened and ask them one more time to help me?*

Suddenly the door of the hut flies open. Loretta blinks weakly in the bright light. A dark figure silhouetted in the light of the door approaches her. It is the man who drug Loretta to the hut. He grabs her by the arm with an iron grip and pulls her into the light.

Many people stand around staring at her and talking with hushed voices. Their skin is deep brown and their black hair matches their black eyes. Many of the adults wear tanned animal skins over their lower bodies while the children are naked. Some of the women's hair is braided and held in place by small bands of leather and pieces of bone. Many of the villagers wear adornments over their upper bodies which remind Loretta of sashes. Loretta looks at them with as much curiosity as they look at her.

The man stands Loretta in front of him and examines her. He looks at her blond hair and at her pale skin. He once more feels the soft cloth of her clothing. He brings his dark eyes down to hers and holds them there. Loretta stares back and feels for a moment that the man is concerned for her safety.

After a long pause, the man leads Loretta away from the village. He releases his grip so that she is able to walk on her own. They make their way towards a clearing with a raised mound in the middle. The mound is large, about as large as the playground of her school and slowly rises about 10 feet above the surrounding terrain. In the middle of the mound is a small platform made of logs. The man leads Loretta to the platform. He stands Loretta on the platform and begins to walk away. "What are you doing?" Loretta yells in fear.

The man makes no response but keeps walking away. "I'm leaving here," Loretta shouts before jumping from the platform. The man turns around and grabs her by the arms again and forcefully places her back on the platform. Taking a leather strap from his belt he roughly ties her hands behind her back. Loretta tries to sit down but the man lifts her back to her feet. He says a word that Loretta can guess means "stay." Loretta stays standing as the man again walks away. Two or three villagers stand on the edges of the mound making sure Loretta doesn't leave. Other villagers watch closely, talking quietly amongst themselves. Loretta can't understand what they say but senses they are trying to make sense of her appearance in their village.

One by one, people begin to leave the mound, some making their way back to their houses while others walk towards the squash field. Only the three men watching her remain. Loretta's platform is directly in the sun which by this time is shining brightly. Her pale skin and blond hair offer little protection from its rays and soon she begins to sweat.

As the day wears on, Loretta's legs begin to ache from standing on the hard platform. The skin of her wrists is breaking open from the chafing of the leather strap. She wishes she was back in the hut with a dipper full of water. She still sees the villagers coming and going from the village but they pay little attention to her. As the sun finally begins to sink towards the tops of the trees, Loretta lowers her head and rests it on her chest. She feels like crying but she has no emotion left to devote to tears. She looks down at her dirty feet resting on the rough surface of the platform and feels her hopes of finding help slowly slipping away.

Chapter 10

As night settles on the village, people are busy preparing for an evening meal. Loretta watches women with stone knives slicing up squash before roasting it over small fires in front of their houses. She also watches men slicing large hunks of meat from a deer that hangs from a pole. Villagers sit together in small family groups eating and talking. After eating, the families sit together or stretch out on the earth to let their food settle.

Off to her right, Loretta can see young boys gathering small branches and twigs. They carry the wood to the mound and lay it in a circle around her. They look at Loretta from time to time but keep their voices low. One by one, villagers come out of their houses and start gathering on the mound. When the brush and twigs fully circle Loretta's platform one of the boys brings a flaming log from a nearby cooking fire. The boy starts lighting the brush. By this time a large crowd has gathered. In the middle of the crowd is the man that put Loretta on the platform. He is by far the tallest villager and the other villagers are timid and respectful when they address him. The man carefully watches Loretta with his dark eyes. The boy with the flaming log has made it all the way around the circle and soon long flames emerge from the brush.

As flames rise higher, Loretta feels the heat against her skin. An occasional puff of wind sends heavy smoke into her eyes. She puts her head down and shuts her eyes. *What are they doing now? Do they intend to burn me? Will I die here never to see my family again?* She thinks about what her dad would do in this situation. She remembers the many times he told her to stay calm and think in a difficult situation. She remembers him telling her to pray when something stressful happens. And so, as the flames and heat become intense, Loretta prays with all her heart that her Creator will give her strength and wisdom.

After she finishes praying, she feels a warmness building in her heart. She is filled with courage and can feel her Creator's love almost as if a warm hand presses gently on her chest. She raises her head and straightens her back against the pole. She turns toward the man and lets the strength and courage she feels inside of her pour out of her blue eyes. Loretta and the man lock eyes. A sudden hush falls over the villagers. The man holds her gaze for what seems like several minutes. The silence is broken when the man calls out to the boys, his words piercing the stillness of the night air. The boys clear away some of the burning branches creating a hole in the circle. The man steps through this gap still holding his eyes on Loretta's. As he approaches, he draws a stone knife from a pouch. He stands inches from her face, holding the knife firmly in his muscled arm. Loretta's heart races and pounds at the base of her throat but she holds his gaze.

The man begins talking in a loud voice. As he talks, he looks up at the sky which glistens with bright stars. Slowly the intensity of his voice builds and he holds both of his arms wide above his head. Suddenly his voice quiets and the man bows his head and whispers.

The man looks up at Loretta. His eyes pierce her to the depths of her heart. She stares back, determined to meet his gaze. After several minutes his facial expressions begin to change. Slowly, like ice melting from a sidewalk on a warm winter day, he begins to relax. The corners of his mouth seem to rise a little into a slight smile giving the cold hardness of his eyes a hint of warmth Loretta has never seen before. He reaches around behind her and cuts her hands free. Loretta feels a wave of relief wash over her. She bends her head, and feels large tears rolling down her face. Her legs weaken and the fire, the man, and the onlooking villagers all start to fade to black. She feels her body falling but can do nothing to stop it.

As she falls, the man steps forward and scoops her into his arms. Her long blond hair dangles from one of his arms while her legs dangle from the other. The man takes Loretta from the fire as the villagers look on in silence. He brings her to a house and places her inside. A woman covers the sleeping girl with a blanket of soft buckskin.

That night as Loretta sleeps, the villagers build the fire up until its flames flicker high into the night air. They sing and dance with abandon around the glowing blaze. The moon, which is full, looks down on the villagers and their lively fire as the platform that Loretta stood on erupts into flames. It burns brightly before collapsing into the fire as sparks explode into the night air.

Chapter 11

The next morning Loretta wakes as the sun rises over the village. The house is much nicer than the hut. The walls are made of poles lashed together with rope. It has a pitched roof that looks to be about 15 feet high at the center. The roof is covered in a thick layer of thatching. The house measures about 25 feet by 25 feet. A bench standing against one wall holds clay pots and other cooking utensils and is covered in a finely woven mat of cattails. The floor is made of hard packed dirt. From the rafters, a large chunk of smoked meat and several bundles of herbs and leaves hang tied in small bundles. The house is airy and smells of freshcut wood.

On a high shelf, Loretta notices the figurine she found in the sycamore tree. *They must have taken it while I was sleeping* she thinks. Next to Loretta's figurine are several others, each neatly painted with bright colors. The woman catches Loretta looking at the figurines and Loretta looks away.

Loretta lies on the floor on a thick cattail mat. A soft blanket of deerskin covers her. Loretta looks under the blanket to discover that her shirt and shorts are gone, replaced by soft buckskin that is held around her waist by a leather strap. Her hair is hanging on either side of her face in two tightly woven braids. Her face and hands are no longer caked in dirt and feel soft and smooth again.

In the middle of the house is a small fire. Loretta watches as the woman cooks squash over it. Next to the woman is a young girl who looks to be the same age as Loretta. Loretta sits up and pulls the deer blanket over her shoulders. The woman and the girl look at her and then go back to cooking the squash. When the squash is done, the girl comes over to Loretta and repeats a word several times while motioning towards her mouth. Loretta eagerly accepts and is soon using her fingers to eat from a small clay bowl. As she eats, she thinks about the word the girl used. Loretta pauses and repeats the word aloud softly to herself. When it sounds right, she says it loudly while looking at the girl and woman. They both look at Loretta. The woman nods her head and makes a motion of putting food to her mouth. Loretta knows the word will come in handy the next time she wants something to eat.

After breakfast Loretta lies down on her bed. Her body is sore from yesterday's ordeal and her mind is still trying to come to terms with her new situation. She is no longer treated like a prisoner, although the woman and girl seem to keep a close watch on her. Loretta knows it would be a lot easier to escape now that she is not locked in the hut. But if she did escape where would she go? If she continued up the river alone, she might come across more bears or be captured by another village that may not be as nice to her. Loretta decides she will stay at the village and learn more about the villagers and their way of life.

When the girl and the woman are finished cooking, they look at Loretta and speak another word while motioning with their hands for Loretta to come with them outside. Loretta repeats this word also and follows them outside. The day is bright and the air feels light and cool. As Loretta follows the woman and girl through the village, she sees many children playing together in small groups. They laugh and scream as they run fast between the houses. When their game playing gets close to a house, a woman appears brandishing a stick chasing them away.

Loretta also notices men sitting in small groups talking and working on stone tools or long thin sticks that look like arrow shafts. She also sees a woman shaping a lump of clay into a large bowl.

Loretta follows the girl and woman to the outskirts of the village and then down a well-worn trail towards a clearing. In the clearing, several women are stooped over picking squash and corn and putting them into leather bags. The women sing songs as they work. The songs mix with the songs of the many birds that call from the edges of the clearing. Loretta smells the strong odor of plants that is stirred by the women's work. It reminds her of the smell of her mother's tomato plants in summer.

The woman and girl stop near a clump of squash and corn and look at Loretta. The woman shows Loretta how to pick the vegetables. She pauses for Loretta to try. Watching, she nods her head in approval and speaks a word that Loretta recognizes as "good." The woman gives Loretta and the girl a bag to put their harvest in and leaves them to pick on their own.

Loretta and the girl start picking. They work side by side without looking at each other. The girl holds the bag and Loretta puts the squash and corn inside. As Loretta reaches to put a big squash into the bag it slips and rolls onto the ground towards her foot. Loretta pulls her foot back to avoid the squash but she catches her other foot in a vine and falls to the ground with a crash. She lies flat on her back for a moment looking up at the sun. The sun is eclipsed by the face of the girl as she bends over Loretta. A smile appears on her face and Loretta smiles back. The girl lets loose a laugh as she helps Loretta to her feet. The woman, who is picking nearby, sees the two girls laughing and a smile creeps across her face.

The girls and the woman spend the rest of the day picking in the field. When they get back home, Loretta is tired but feels good about spending the day working. That evening they eat a simple meal of corn and deer meat cooked over the fire. The food tastes good to Loretta after a hard day's work. When the sun finally sets on the village, Loretta lies on her bed. The girl lies next to her quietly for a few moments before her breathing slows down and Loretta can tell she is asleep. Outside the village is quiet, no fire burns in the fire pit tonight. From the darkness Loretta hears the call of a barred owl pierce the night air. She thinks of the many nights from her cabin bedroom she heard barred owls calling. She thinks of her family and how she misses them deeply until her heart feels like it will burst. She wonders what tomorrow has in store for her as she slowly drifts off to sleep.

Chapter 12

The next morning Loretta rises early, and after a quick breakfast returns to the crop field with the girl and woman. She spends the whole day picking, only stopping to take breaks for water. When they get back to the house, they enjoy a meal of steamed squash and sit around the fire until Loretta's eyelids grow heavy. She's soon asleep on her deer rug, exhausted from the day's work.

The next several days pass in the same fashion. Always Loretta rises early and always she works in the farm field until evening. As the days pass, Loretta slowly learns the language the woman and girl speak. With each new day she is able to understand and speak several new words, and soon begins to talk easily with the girl and woman. Loretta notices that the woman refers to the daughter as Nammi and the girl refers to the woman as Waimpe and begins calling them by these names too.

As the days wear on, Loretta notices that the nights and mornings are getting colder. When she wakes in the morning and steps outside, she can see her breath in the frosty air. Waimpe puts plenty of wood on the fire in the mornings to drive the chill away. Instead of a buckskin blanket, the girls now sleep under a heavy bearskin blanket. The squash and corn in the farm field are now almost all picked. Waimpe has dried and stored much of the harvest. She wraps them securely in animal hides and buries them in the floor of the house.

The leaves in the forest are beginning to turn shades of brown, red and yellow. Loretta loves to look at the leaves especially in the evening when the setting sun makes their colors glow. The air is crisp and dry and the leaves on the ground are crunchy. The cicadas that have called all summer are now replaced by a low chorus of crickets.

One morning Loretta wakes to the sound of men talking outside the hut. She sits up and looks around. A low fire burns in the fire pit but Waimpe is not there. Nammi is sleeping next to her, her long black hair splayed across the brown and white deer hide. Loretta nudges Nammi.

"Wake up," she says. "Waimpe is gone and something is going on outside." Nammi pulls the bearskin blanket over her head.

Loretta yanks the blanket back and Nammi sits up from the sudden rush of cold. She shoves Loretta. "Don't do that!" she says. Wiping the sleep from her eyes, she looks around.

"Something is going on," Loretta says. "Listen."

Nammi listens to the voices outside. "The men have come back from a hunting trip and they have three deer and a bear. There will be lots of work for us. We will have to remove the meat and hides from the animals and begin the smoking process. But when we are done, I think there will be a big feast and a big fire to celebrate the fall harvest."

Loretta and Nammi put on the buckskin dresses that Waimpe made them. The dresses are soft and fit each girl perfectly. Across the front of each dress small red beads are woven into the leather.

After eating some leftover fish, the two girls pull back the buckskin door and step into the morning air. The fallen leaves strewn around the village are covered in a light frost, twinkling in the early morning light. Their house is also covered in frost except for the edges of the hole that lets blue smoke drift up and into the sky.

Near the center of the village, the girls see men hoisting the deer and bear off the ground. The men hang them from the limb of a large hickory tree. Waimpe is there holding a stone knife watching the men work. Several other women are there too, each holding a knife or stone ax. Loretta and Nammi walk over and stand silently next to Waimpe.

When the animals are all hung by their feet with their heads off the ground, the women step forward and begin to work. Waimpe motions for the girls to bring two large clay bowls and place them near a deer. She looks closely at the deer's eyes and feels the muscles in its front and back legs. She closes her eyes, and in a soft voice says, "Thank you, Creator."

After she prays, she begins pulling hair from the deer's belly. Once she has a bare spot, she takes her knife and slits upwards. When she reaches the backside, she repeats the slitting forward towards the deer's chest. As she cuts, steam escapes in long wisps that curl upward before disappearing among the leafy branches of the hickory. When she gets to the rib cage, the stomach and intestines are bulging out from the slit. Waimpe reaches down and positions one of the large bowls directly under the deer. Small trickles of blood run down the deer's neck and into the bowl. Loretta can hear the sound of bones being cut as Waimpe works the knife through the center of the rib cage. Now the slit is bulging in the middle and the stomach and intestines are hanging low. Waimpe reaches up into the rib cage and, taking her knife, makes one final cut. The stomach and intestines fall into the bowl in a heap, splashing small drops of blood high into the air. Loretta and Nammi jump back but still get small spatters on their dresses and faces. Waimpe reaches her hand up further into the deer's rib cage and retrieves its heart. She holds the heart out for the girls to see. Loretta looks at the heart with its blue and white veins lying in the blood-stained hands of Waimpe. She puts the heart in a separate bowl and tells the girls to take it back to the house. Other women come and get the bowl full of internal organs and take them for preparation for tonight's feast.

Now Waimpe takes her knife and works around the base of the deer's head just above the jaw line. With one motion she finishes the cut through the spinal cord, letting it fall to the ground. Taking a stone ax, she splits the deer's skull open and scoops its brains into a bowl. These will be used for softening animal skins to make clothing. When she is done with the head, she starts skinning the deer. She begins from the hind legs and works her way down. Loretta and Nammi help pull the hide from the deer as Waimpe cuts. When she is finished, she has the girls put it into the house to be processed into buckskin.

Next Waimpe begins cutting meat from the bone. She works until several bowls are piled high. The carcass is now bare, with only the smallest specks of red meat clinging to the pearly bone. Some of the deer meat will be used for tonight's feast, but much of it will be stored until tomorrow when it can be cut into small strips and smoked.

By the time Waimpe and the girls are done, the sun is midway in the sky. After rinsing the blood from their hands, the girls lie in a pile of leaves staring up at the puffy white clouds above them. "I'm sleepy," Loretta says.

"Go to sleep then," Nammi replies. "I'm sure the singing and the dancing after the feast will drag long into the night." Loretta is excited about the feast but soon the warm rays of the sun lull her into a peaceful noontime nap.

Chapter 13

When Loretta wakes from her nap Nammi is gone. Rising to her elbows she sees the village is busy with activity. Pulling a red leaf out of her blond hair, she rises and walks toward the village. She can see that the wood for the center fire is already gathered. In front of each house, groups of women are busy cooking over fires. There are large clay bowls that simmer with stew mixtures. Loretta can smell the rich scent of deer meat coming from the stew. There are large cooking rocks with piles of squash on them. In front of one house a large deer leg is roasting high above a smoky fire.

Loretta sees Nammi running with a group of kids and runs to catch up with them. Her blond hair blows in the breeze as the ground zips by under her bare feet. When she catches up to the girl, the group stops.

"We are playing a game," Nammi says.

"How do you play?" Loretta asks.

"Well it's called the wolf game. One of us plays the wolf and the rest of us are rabbits. If the wolf catches you, you are out of the game. We keep playing until the wolf catches all the rabbits and then we pick someone else to be the wolf. You see that boy over there?" Nammi asks pointing to a boy a little older than the girls with long black hair. "He is the wolf."

The boy growls and all the kids laugh. "Now, let's play!" Nammi yells. The wolf runs toward them and the whole group scatters into the woods.

Loretta veers off from the group and runs hard, leaves and branches whipping her face and body. She spots a large log and flops down tight against it. Lying down on her stomach she holds her head just over the top to watch for the wolf.

The breeze that has blown all day has quit and the leaves hang perfectly still. Loretta can't see the other kids but can hear them yelling and laughing through the trees. She lies still for several minutes in the quiet woods until she wonders if the wolf has forgotten about her.

Suddenly she hears crunching in the leaves — crunch...crunch, crunch... crunch. Loretta strains all her senses in the direction of the crunching, her body tense. The crunching stops and she holds her breath. And then she sees something brown and furry. "A fox squirrel," she says when the squirrel begins moving again. Its dense fur is the color of rusted metal and the sun makes the reds in its tail glow. The squirrel takes a couple more hops before jumping onto Loretta's log. It gets so close, Loretta could reach out and grab it. It freezes and stares at Loretta. Its eyes look like the surface of a deep lake on a moonlit night. All at once it lets out several loud barks breaking the silence of the woods. Loretta waves her arm at the squirrel and it leaps from the log onto the trunk of a tree. The squirrel runs up the tree and then stops to continue its barking. Loretta picks up an acorn and throws it at the squirrel sending it scurrying high into the tree.

The woods go quiet again. Loretta watches a small bird climb the trunk of a shagbark hickory. While she watches, she hears rustling in the leaves behind her again. She turns quickly but doesn't see anything. She continues watching the bird as it climbs higher. But then she hears the noise again, and this time she sees something move. She can't be sure what she saw and doesn't want to give up her hiding place so she goes back to watching the bird. It moves in small hops probing with its bill under the tree's bark for bugs.

All at once Loretta hears the crunching again, and the bird suddenly flies away. As she turns, the leaves explode with crunching. A blur rushes towards her. She screams, scrambling to her feet. "Got ya!" the wolf cries.

"You scared me!" Loretta screams.

The smile on the boy's face fades and he looks concerned. "Just kidding," she says. "I wasn't that scared." The boy's smile returns and he leaps off through the woods looking for another rabbit.

Loretta takes her time walking back to the village, stopping to watch small birds as they fly from branch to branch. There are yellow and black butterflies too that flutter lightly in the open spaces of the forest. They fly in circular patterns rising and lowering but never leaving their treetop sanctuary.

When Loretta gets back, the sun is close to going below the treetops and a hint of night air hangs in the village. Women are gathered near the central fire, laying their food dishes on several wooden tables. Loretta finds Nammi and they watch as stews, squash and roasted corn are all brought forth. The deer heart that Waimpe has saved is there too, steaming hot in a wooden bowl with a small pool of dark blood surrounding it. There is so much food that Loretta wonders how they can eat it all in one night.

When the food is laid out, the men of the village join the women and stand silently looking at the feast. The villagers part when the man from Loretta's first day walks through them. The man stands and looks at the feast. He turns towards the villagers and lifting his hands towards the sky begins to speak. "O Great One, you have given us this harvest. Bring us through the coming winter that we may live to see a new spring and a new harvest." After he finishes, several women begin handing out food. Loretta and Nammi each grab a large chunk of venison and some steamed corn. The meat has a rich smoky taste and the first few bites steam in her mouth. The corn is tender and it reminds Loretta of her many days spent in the farm field. Loretta and Nammi make several trips to the food table and each time Loretta notes that the food is dwindling.

When the food is all gone, a boy brings a large handful of grass and lays it at the base of the central fire. Another boy brings a flaming log and soon the flames of the fire are rising above the heads of the people. By this time the sky has darkened and Loretta can see the beginnings of a large orange moon rising over the village. The boys keep adding sticks and logs to the fire until the people have to stand several feet back because it's so hot.

From somewhere beyond the light of the fire, Loretta hears a woman's voice break into song. The song becomes louder as the woman steps into the ring of firelight. Loretta sees that although the woman's hair is gray, her eyes shine brightly in the firelight. Her buckskin dress has some of the prettiest beadwork Loretta has ever seen. Her voice builds in power and emotion, piercing the night air with its wavering cry. All of the villagers watch her as her song ends. There is a brief moment of silence when the only sound is the popping and crackling of the fire. Another villager takes up the song and a few more join in. Soon all the villagers are singing and Loretta imagines that even the squirrels tucked away in their leafy nests can hear the noise. One by one the villagers begin circling the central fire, moving in rhythm with the song.

In the middle of the mass of people is Loretta, who only months before had never known such a night like this could exist. Now her blond hair and fair skin mean nothing to the people. To them it is as black and brown as their own. The mass of moving, singing people has only one soul and one united spirit on this night. And that spirit dances and sings around the blazing fire until the orange moon sinks and the sky is overtaken by star-studded blackness.

Chapter 14

The next morning Loretta wakes from a heavy sleep. The singing from the night before still rings in her head. Waimpe has a large fire in the house and Loretta pulls her bearskin over her shoulders to ward off the morning chill. "Good morning," Waimpe says.

"Good morning," Loretta replies. "What are we going to do today?"

"Today we must begin preparing for winter. The roof of the house must be re-thatched. Seeds must be put away for spring and firewood needs to be drug close to the house in case we get snow. Here, eat this," Waimpe tells her. Waimpe hands her a small bowl full of steaming corn mush.

Outside, a steady cold wind blows away much of the yellow and red leaves from the trees. Loretta notices that the mood around the village is much quieter than the days leading up to the feast. The women work hard drying and storing food for the coming winter. Many of the men leave early in the morning to hunt the salt licks that lay far south of the village. Loretta spends the day helping Waimpe and Nammi dry and store food.

She spends the next several weeks much the same way, helping prepare for winter. She dries and stores food. She helps tan deer, bear and buffalo hides. Waimpe makes moccasins for the girls to wear and they each have a small buckskin blanket they drape across their shoulders to keep warm.

One morning Loretta wakes to find the village blanketed in a light dusting of snow. "Winter has come," Waimpe tells them. "Our days of preparing are over, now we must endure."

As winter sets in, Loretta and Nammi leave the house less and less. When the big snows come, they only go out to gather firewood and to get snow to melt for water. When they need food, Waimpe digs up dried corn from the floor of the house. Each day, Mother makes hot stew which helps fight off the cold.

During the long winter nights, Loretta can hear the wind blowing outside the house. Each girl has a thick bear blanket. Before they go to bed Mother covers them both with a large buffalo blanket in addition to the bear blankets. The blanket smells of hide and dust but keeps the girls warm on the coldest nights. Some nights Mother stays up feeding the fire with large chunks of oak and hickory. The wood produces orange coals the size of apples. Loretta likes to lie under her blankets and stare at the blue and purple flames that flicker over the hot coals. Watching the coals makes her feel warm, but she can only watch them for a few minutes before drifting off to sleep.

As the winter wears on, the importance of the corn, squash and beans that have been dried become apparent. The men of the village can be counted on to bring fresh meat from their winter hunting grounds, but the villagers cannot survive on meat alone. They need the fiber and fat they get from their crops. The food is not as plentiful as in the fall, but it is enough to keep the villagers strong.

One morning after a big snow, Waimpe tells the girls to go outside and find some firewood. Waimpe helps them put their moccasins on and wraps buckskins around their legs. They wrap their bear blankets tightly around their shoulders and step out into the snowy morning. The village is draped in a thick blanket of snow. The snow covers the houses except for the tops of the roofs where heat from the morning fires melts it. The sun is beginning to rise in the east making the white snow sparkle.

When they begin walking, the snow is well above their knees. Their buckskin leggings keep the snow out but Loretta can still feel its coldness creeping through the animal skin. Pushing hard against the snow, they plow their way through the village and into the woods. They take turns leading, one girl breaking the path while the other walks more easily behind. The snow seems to wrap the woods in a hushed silence. The cold winter wind that blew all night is gone. Nothing stirs but the bear-skin-covered girls, and even they make little noise in the snow.

"How far do you want to go?" Loretta asks the girl, her breath curling into the frosty air in short wisps.

"I don't care. What if we go to the pines?" replies the girl.

"OK," Loretta says, "we can pick up our firewood on the way back." As they continue walking Loretta notices the songbirds that flit here and there across the snow. They feed on small seeds that lay scattered under the trees. Their feet make tiny prints in the snow.

When they arrive at the pines, they seek shelter from the snow under the bows of the big trees. The pine limbs droop low from the weight of the snow. "Let's crawl under this tree," Nammi says as she stoops to go under the limbs. Loretta follows and soon the girls are in the dark, quiet shelter of the tree.

"It smells good in here," Loretta says.

"Yes," says the girl, "and it's like our own little house." The girls wipe the snow from their leggings and sit down. Loretta pulls out a piece of smoked deer meat from her leather pouch. She breaks it in half and the two girls sit quietly chewing the deer meat.

"Let's make beds out of pine needles." Loretta says. They make bird-nest-shaped beds and pretend to sleep for a while.

But soon Nammi asks, "Are you ready to go back?"

"Yes, Waimpe will wonder where we are," Loretta replies and the two girls leave their pine needle hut and begin walking toward home. As they walk, they find several pieces of dry firewood until they each have an armful.

When they arrive at the village, a few people are out and about collecting firewood. Other than that, the village is quiet. Back inside the house the girls take off their buckskin leggings and moccasins and huddle close to the fire.

Waimpe looks up from the fire and asks, "Did you get the firewood?"

"Yes," the girls reply as they plop down next to the fire letting its heat soak into their skin.

The rest of the day they spend helping Waimpe prepare a stew for supper. First they melt snow in a large clay pot. Then they put strips of smoked deer meat in. Next, Waimpe digs up some corn and drops it into the stew. Last to go in are sunflower seeds. They heat and stir the stew until it is simmering hot and fills the hut with tasty smells.

That night they sit around the fire eating the stew. Loretta likes the way the hot broth warms her belly. Waimpe lets the fire burn down to large coals that glow orange in the darkness of the house. Since there is very little smoke going through the hole in the roof of the house, Loretta can look up and see stars gleaming in the cold winter sky.

Waimpe sees Loretta looking at the stars and asks in a low voice, "Do you know why the stars shine the brightest in the wintertime? It's because the sun becomes weak in winter, and the stars become stronger. But the light from the stars is a cold light that pricks the night sky but can never make it go away like the strong sun can." Waimpe's voice trails off and she stares into the fire.

Loretta pulls her head under her buffalo blanket snuggling close to Nammi who is already asleep. Outside in the darkness, Loretta hears a group of coyotes calling in a series of yelps and yips that pierce the night air. She thinks about what it would be like to be a coyote howling under a star-filled sky and soon she too is asleep.

Chapter 15

The long winter days soon turn into long winter months. Loretta's daily routine consists of gathering firewood, helping Waimpe cook food, and talking to Nammi in the spaces between. Sometimes she helps Waimpe turn animal hides into clothing which requires long hours of hard work. Their days are filled with work but Loretta likes the feeling of accomplishment she gets at the end of each day. Sometimes when the men return from a good hunting trip a tribal fire is lit. The fires are not as big as the ones held in fall and don't last nearly as long. By the time the moon rises high in the night sky, most of the villagers retreat to the warmth and comfort of their houses.

At night they sit in their house and talk quietly or listen to Waimpe tell stories. One night, Waimpe gets down one of the figurines from the high shelf. "Where did you find this?" she asks Loretta.

"I found it in a big sycamore tree," Loretta replies.

"What did the tree look like?" Waimpe asks.

"It was very large and in the middle it was hollow. Also, a vine with large red vines grew from it," Loretta says. Waimpe looks away from the fire, slowly turning the figurine over in her hands.

"Do you know what this figurine represents?" Waimpe asks her.

"No," Loretta replies.

"It represents the spirit of the person it was made for. Because you found it, the figurine now represents your spirit. The place where you found it must have been special to its previous owner," Waimpe tells her.

Waimpe hands the figurine to Loretta and says, "It is now yours; protect it carefully." Loretta takes the figurine and carefully tucks it under her sleeping mat in a small hole in the floor. That night as she falls asleep, Loretta feels good with an object that connects her to her previous homestead close to her. She also feels good Waimpe is finally entrusting her with it.

After several hard months of winter, Loretta wakes one morning to the sound of rain falling on the roof of the house. All that day it rains steadily and the air is warm. Loretta knows that soon all of the snow will melt and the birds and animals that have slept through winter will soon fill the forest with their presence again. Most of the day Loretta and Nammi spend in the house, huddled away from the damp rain.

"Can you smell spring in this rain?" Loretta asks the girl.

She smiles and nods her head. "Soon, girls, we will be out in the fields and woods again," Waimpe says smiling at them both.

After several weeks of warmer temperatures, the village comes to life again. Almost all of the snow is melted and green things have begun appearing from the brown earth. The nights are much warmer and the girls no longer need to wear leggings and moccasins. They are free to feel the warm earth beneath their bare feet once again. The central fire is lit on a warm clear night to celebrate the coming of spring. Loretta spends her mornings and afternoons helping Waimpe prepare food and make clothing.

In the evenings Loretta and Nammi are free to explore the spring woods around the village. They examine the many kinds of spring wildflowers that grow in the deep woods. There are yellow tiger lilies with a single flower hanging daintily from a smooth green stem. There are Dutchman's britches with their many white flowers gracing finely toothed leaves. Loretta examines each different type of flower, smelling their blooms closely.

She also carefully digs the roots of each flower to smell and examine them as well. The roots of the Dutchman's britches are small and a cloudy white resembling small pearls. She particularly likes to dig the roots of bloodroot. "Come here," she'd call to Nammi after digging one, "hold still." Nammi would hold perfectly still as Loretta took a root and painted circles and squiggly lines on the girl's face. "Now you paint me," and Nammi would grab the root and go to work on Loretta's face. When they'd finish they'd examine each other.

"Oh pretty," Loretta would tell the girl.

"You look like a warrior," Nammi would say. Laughing, they'd look for another plant to dig. They also liked the roots of golden-seal which yielded a yellow sap that was equally suited for face painting.

When they grew tired of wandering, they'd find a sunny clearing and lay among the green forest plants soaking in the rays of the warm spring sun. Loretta loves the way the forest smells in spring. She loves the warm rays of the sun against her skin. She loves the small songbirds whose arrival coincided with the coming of spring. The birds' feathers and songs are much brighter than the birds that live in the woods in the wintertime. Their beaks are finer and their flight is delicate and spirited. Loretta loves their songs too, which seem to bubble and flow like a child playing a small flute.

One morning Loretta wakes to the sound of digging. She watches as Waimpe uses a small stone tool to dig down into the floor of the house. With both hands she reaches into the hole and pulls out a small bundle. She unwraps the bundle and in the pale morning light Loretta sees the bundle is full of corn seed. "Tomorrow we will plant the field," Waimpe says, "but first the men must burn it to clear away the dead grasses."

After a quick breakfast of cornmeal cakes, Loretta and Nammi emerge from the house. All around the village, people are clearing dried leaves and grasses away from their houses. "They're getting ready for the fire," Nammi says. "If there are too many leaves around the houses they could catch fire." The two girls walk through the village and into the field. The sun feels warm and the tall grasses in the field move back and forth from a strong wind. Occasionally the wind gusts, pushing leaves and dried grasses high into the air. Scattered about the field, men stand waiting. Loretta and Nammi pick a spot at the edge of the field next to a big oak tree.

"Are you ready?" one of the men calls to another man.

"Yes," the man calls back. The man goes to the village and brings a smoking branch back to the field. With the wind to his back, he bends down in front of a large clump of dead grasses. He blows on the stick until dark gray smoke begins streaming into the air. The smoke is followed by large yellow flames. The man gives a loud yell and springs away from the heat and flame. Loretta watches the fire as it grows. The crackling of the flames fills the air with popping sounds. The thick gray smoke clings to the insides of her nose. The fire is growing and spreading rapidly like a bucket of muddy water poured over a flat rock. Every time the wind gusts, the crackling of the fire turns into a roar and large flames leap and jump into the air in bursts of orange and black. Loretta watches the tips of the flames which seem to shoot small wisps of fire high into the air. The fire is bright orange at the top but its base is black. Many of the villagers have gathered at the edge of the village to watch.

As the fire grows closer to the oak tree, its heat stings Loretta's skin. The smoke overwhelms her sense of smell with its heavy oily sent. "We must move," Nammi says when the heat becomes so strong that both girls turn their backs to protect their faces. Nammi grabs Loretta's hand and they run out in front of the fire.

Suddenly a large wind gust catches the fire and it roars so loud and hot that Loretta can't hear her own scream or feel her own tears as they roll down her hot face. The tears mix with sweat creating small rivers that flow down her soot-covered face. The sweat stings Loretta's eyes. She runs with all her might but the thick grasses and vines slow her down. "Run faster!" Nammi cries.

Loretta takes one more bound and falls to the ground, her leg caught in a large vine. She looks behind her and sees the fire swelled by another wind gust, looming above her like an orange and black giant. She looks for Nammi but she is gone. *She must not have seen me fall!* she thinks. Pulling with all her might she rips the vine loose from her foot and begins to run again. Loretta's lungs feel like they will burst from the running. All around her she can see the fire burning. She knows she can't go back and that she's not running fast enough to outrun the fire.

"Over here!" she hears a voice scream above the roar of the fire. She looks to her left and can see Nammi standing in the edge of the woods, her face barely visible through the flames.

Loretta veers towards her and Nammi screams, "Jump through the flames!" Loretta hesitates but decides it's her only option. She closes her eyes and jumps. She feels a hot flash of heat pierce her body and all of the air in her lungs is sucked out as if someone hit her in the stomach. For a moment she thinks she is dead.

She hits the ground on the other side with a thud. All around her the ground is black and smoking. Nammi rushes to her side and pulls her further back into the blackened ground and away from the flame.

"The fire has already burned through here. We are safe now," Nammi says.

Loretta looks up at her and sees a large tear rolling down the side of her soot-blackened face.

"I thought the fire was going to take you," Nammi says.

Loretta takes a deep breath filling her lungs again with cool air and smiles at the girl. "Not with you around to watch over me," she says.

Both girls sit in the blackened earth and watch the fire as it roars away from the village. Loretta doesn't know for how long or for how far the fire will burn, but she is glad it is leaving her and the village far behind.

Chapter 16

The next morning the girls get up early to help Waimpe plant the field. They join a large group of women and children in the field working side by side, singing as they plant their seed. The field is black and sooty and smells like smoke. Loretta watches as Waimpe shows her how to make a small opening with a stone tool, drop a seed in and then carefully cover it with dirt. All through the day Loretta works in the field. At the end of the day she is tired but stays up late, dancing and singing with the other villagers around the tribal fire that marks the beginning of the growing season.

Loretta's next few weeks are spent looking after the crops that have begun growing in the field. She watches the small green sprouts of corn, squash and sunflowers poke through the blackened earth. Loretta and Nammi tend the sprouts carefully, pulling weeds and scaring the small birds and squirrels that come to eat the tender plants. Loretta loves the feel of soft earth under her feet as she works. Her feet are now blackened and hard on the bottom from going barefoot all the time. She loves the way the field smells in the morning when the dew clings to the crops and makes the world seem fresh and alive.

Village life in summer is easy. Loretta and Nammi are expected to help with the fields in the mornings, but in the evenings they can do as they please. They spend many afternoons playing in a small creek that runs through the woods behind the village. There, in the deep shade of tall oaks and hickories, they splash in cool waters. They lift large rocks and catch crayfish. When the crayfish are big enough, they take them home for Waimpe to cook. The girls love the way the crayfish taste steamed over the fire on a flat rock. In the evenings Loretta and Nammi stay up late catching fireflies. On some nights they take their deer rugs outside and sleep under the stars.

Lying on their backs they look up at the tiny dots of bright white light. "Look, a shooting star," Loretta says, as they both watch a flaming meteor streak across the sky.

One evening as Loretta and Nammi sit and talk by the house, cicadas start to call. Loretta stops talking and listens. The creaking sound of each cicada rises to a high point before trailing off like a top winding down. In all her time in the village Loretta has tried not to think of her past life. But hearing the cicadas calling on a quiet summer evening makes the memories of her past life come flooding back. Loretta thinks of her family and all her favorite moments spent with them. She remembers the way her mother smiles and the sound of her dad's laugh. She remembers the sparkle in her little sister's eyes when they looked at each other on Christmas morning. She remembers the way her brother held her hand when he was scared and how in the summertime he stopped to show her a toad or a robin's egg he found. She misses them all and while she has grown to love Waimpe and the girl, in her heart she can never really feel at home here in the village.

Loretta thinks of her last night at the cabin. She thinks of the last conversations she had with her mom and dad. She thinks of how she fought with her brother and sister. She thinks about walking down to the river and the way the woods looked on that night. "What happened to them?" Loretta asks out loud. "Where did they go?" Nammi looks at her but then looks away knowing not to ask about her past because it makes Loretta sad. Loretta still cannot come to terms with what happened that night. What made her sleep through the night in the tree? Where did that storm come from? Loretta's mind keeps going back to the tree. Many nights she has dreamed about the tree and the strange way it looked that night. "It's the tree," Loretta says. Again Nammi looks at her and looks away. "I've got to get back to that tree."

That night Loretta falls asleep knowing she must leave the village and make it back to the tree. She wants Waimpe and Nammi to know how much she loves them, but she is afraid to tell them because they will make her stay. *Tomorrow night I will leave* she thinks as she drifts off to sleep.

Chapter 17

The next morning Loretta wakes to the sound of Waimpe cooking corn cakes over the fire. She blinks the sleep from her eyes and lies watching her work. Waimpe's long black hair is braided. A long piece of brown leather is woven through the braids. She works hard, focused on making the corn cakes. Around her waist is a piece of finely worked buckskin. Her worn brown hands are covered in the light yellow powder of the ground corn.

Waimpe looks at Loretta and smiles. "Good morning," Loretta says in English. After months of speaking another language the words feel awkward to her. Waimpe returns the greeting imitating the English words as best as she can before returning to her work. Loretta thinks back to the day she first came to Waimpe's house. She remembers the way Waimpe washed her and gave her a warm and dry place to sleep. She remembers how she made a pouch for her. The pouch has a long shoulder strap and is made of finely worked buckskin. Waimpe wove a string of beads across the front edge of the flap.

She remembers the stern way Waimpe looks at her and Nammi when they do something wrong and the gentle smile when the girls are by her side helping grind corn or tend crops.

Loretta rises from her rug and walks over to Waimpe. She stoops down and hugs her taking in the smell of her skin and the feel of her hair. Waimpe stops working and asks, "Is something wrong, Girl?"

"No Waimpe," Loretta replies as she lies back down on her deer rug. Loretta thinks of leaving Waimpe and turns her head away as tears begin to flow.

Nammi wakes too and rises to stretch. Loretta watches Nammi as she strides over to Waimpe to get a corn cake. Nammi takes a cake and begins eating.

Nammi has changed some since Loretta first came to the village. Her legs and hair are longer and her dark eyes show more wisdom. Loretta taught Nammi a few English words and a few games, but Nammi has taught Loretta much, much more. She taught her how to stay out of the adult's way enough to avoid attention, but also how to get what she needs when she needs it. She taught Loretta how to stay warm on a cold winter's night and how to survive a wildfire. And she taught Loretta how to love a culture and a people not her own.

Nammi looks at Loretta and sees that she is crying. She drops the corn cake and sits down. Putting her arm on Loretta's arm she looks her in the eye. "It's nothing," Loretta says. "I've just had a bad dream."

Nammi nods and goes back to her corn cake. The two girls have lived together long enough to be able to tell what the other is thinking. Loretta knows that she must be careful today in order to keep Nammi from knowing what she has planned for the night.

That day the girls help Waimpe tend the crop field. Several men in the village come back from hunting and the girls help process their harvest and smoke the meat. The girls spend the afternoon walking slowly through the woods of the village.

"Soon we will be picking the fields," Nammi says.

"Yes, I know," Loretta replies. "It looks like a good harvest, which means we will get through the winter easily."

"I can't wait till harvest season," Nammi says.

"Yeah, me too," Loretta replies.

"Do you see that boy over there, the one with the necklace?" Loretta looks in the direction Nammi points.

"He came over to our house yesterday and asked Waimpe to see me," Nammi says.

"What did you do?"

"I hid under my blanket until he left."

Both girls break into laughter.

When they get back to the village, they sit in front of the house together. Waimpe cooks venison and a fresh-picked squash that is the first of the season. Loretta eats the food enjoying the fresh and rich flavors. As evening approaches, she hears the cicadas start to call. Her mind drifts from the conversation of Nammi and Waimpe to her plans for the night.

She will lie in the house and pretend to sleep until she's sure Waimpe and Nammi are asleep. She knows where the smoked meat is kept and she will put enough into her pouch for three or four days. She will make her way through the crop field stopping to pick a squash or two before putting her back to the village and heading for the river. Once she finds the river, she will follow it downstream until she comes to the place where her cabin used to be and find the sycamore tree.

That night after eating and sitting around a small fire, Loretta and Nammi lie down to sleep. "I love you," Loretta says.

"I know," says Nammi and soon by the sound of her breathing Loretta can tell she is asleep. Waimpe comes into the house and silently lies down. Shortly after, Loretta hears her breathing and can tell she is asleep too. Loretta's heart races as she waits for the right time to leave. She snuggles close to Nammi and thinks of the many days they have spent together. Loretta has come to know her as a sister. She would love to tell Nammi how much she loves her and how much she is going to miss her. But she knows if Nammi finds out she is leaving she will try to stop her. Outside the house the calls of the cicadas are giving way to the soft chirp of crickets. Loretta knows it's time to leave.

She rises to her knees and looks at the girl. Tears swell in her eyes as she bends down to kiss her one last time. A big tear runs from Loretta's eyes and falls on the girl's cheek. Nammi stirs slightly and brushes the tear away without opening her eyes. Loretta freezes momentarily until everything is quiet before standing up to leave. She looks at Nammi and Waimpe one last time before quietly opening the flap and stepping out into the darkness.

Chapter 18

Outside, the village is shrouded in darkness. Loretta makes her way through the houses and out into the crop field. She looks for a big yellow squash to put in her pouch. She finds one and breaks it free from its green vine and puts it in her pouch. A barred owl calls loudly from the woods as Loretta leaves the crop field and heads towards the river. She has not taken moccasins with her and wears only leather buckskin around her waist. Tucked away securely in the bottom of her pouch is her figurine.

Trying not to think of the Mother and sister she is leaving behind, she walks with hurried step through the woods. When she reaches the river, she stoops on her hands and knees and drinks deeply from its waters. She wants to rest but she needs to get as far away from the village as possible in case the villagers come looking for her tomorrow morning. She sticks to the edge of the river, splashing through its shallow waters. Every once in a while, Loretta can hear a deer or some other animal take off through the dark woods, spooked by her presence.

After living in the village for almost a year, Loretta is no longer scared of being in the woods by herself. She has learned to listen and watch for signs of movement and to pause often. She knows that while bears and wolves are a threat, they were few and far between.

She keeps moving along the riverbank until the first signs of daylight filter through the treetops. The oranges and purples of the morning light are a welcome sight to Loretta's mind and body. Once the sun has fully risen and daylight illuminates the river, Loretta looks for a good place to rest. She finds a downed tree next to the river with a dry spot beneath it. Loretta sits with her back to the tree and reaches into her pouch for some deer meat. She eats the meat then curls up under the tree to rest.

When she awakes, day is slipping into evening. Lying quietly for several minutes she listens for any sign of movement. When she's sure she is alone she rises and stretches her arms. Walking back to the river she takes a big drink and sets on her way again. Loretta knows that she can't be far from her destination. She figures one more night of hard walking and she will be close to where the tree is.

That night Loretta pushes ahead splashing through the shallow waters of the river. She shares the night with the raccoons who feed along the water's edge, running into the woods when they hear Loretta. The next morning, she finds another hiding spot along the edge of a bluff. Loretta recognizes the bluff as the same bluff that her cabin used to be on. "I'm getting close," she says as she closes her eyes to sleep.

It is midday when Loretta wakes. She takes a large rock and breaks open the squash she brought along. She scoops handfuls of the yellow flesh into her mouth. *Not as good as the way mother cooked it,* she thinks. She also eats the last of the deer meat in her pouch. Now she must find the tree. She cannot go back to the village and she knows that she cannot survive on her own. She rises and begins walking along the edge of the bluff, her heart and eyes searching intently for the tree.

As the day wears on, the course of the river and the shape of the bluff become familiar to her. She has the sense that she is getting closer to her home site. When she comes to a sweeping bend in the river she knows she is close. She remembers the days when Dad paddled the family upriver to this spot in their canoe. Here they would beach the canoe and spend the day playing on the sand bar. They wouldn't be on the bar long before Dad would pull out a bag of candy and ask, "Who wants some candy!" Loretta remembers the way her front teeth cut through sugar-coated fruit slices and the thought makes her mouth water.

She gets on her knees and stoops to the river for a drink. She catches a glimpse of her reflection in the river. Her hair is still braided in the tight weave Waimpe made many weeks ago. Her face is dirty and her skin is browned from her time in the summer sun working in the village field. "If I make it home, my family may not recognize me," she says to herself. She thinks of the changes that have taken place inside of her too. She is more mature now and holds a greater appreciation for the things she used to take for granted. She thinks of taking a bath in clean warm water, or eating a hamburger and french fries. She thinks of staying dry and snug inside the family's cabin. With these thoughts in her mind, she rises and walks boldly along the riverbank keeping her eyes peeled for the sycamore.

By now the day is beginning to wear on. The sun is slipping away to the west and Loretta can feel the cool night air creeping into the forest. Loretta suddenly stops in her tracks. This is the spot. Here in a life that seems lost in the distant past, a set of steps led up to a log cabin. Here Loretta and her family spent many nights around a campfire, looking out over the river and enjoying each other's company. Loretta's heart beats fast as she looks to the spot where the tree must be. And it is there, standing with its white bark gleaming in the last golden rays of daylight. Loretta breaks into a run, the touch-me-nots and winged sunflowers whipping at her face and body. When she gets to the tree it is exactly like she left it. The strange vine, the scaly bark clinging to its white trunk and the gaping hole that beckoned her inside are all there. Loretta's heart leaps with joy. She rushes headlong into the tree and collapses in the cradle of its trunk. She is too exhausted and hungry from the long journey for her mind to dwell on much more than the thought of finding the tree. She carefully removes the figurine from its pouch. Kissing it once, she buries it in the place where she found it so many nights ago. As the last rays of daylight fade Loretta begins to cry, letting go of all the worry and stress from the past few days. She prays to her Creator with all her heart and mind thanking Him for her deliverance back to the tree. Outside, a heavy chorus of cicadas ebbs and flows in the cool summer night as Loretta drifts into a deep sleep.

The next morning Loretta wakes to the sound of a wren calling. She sits up and wipes the sleep from her eyes. For a moment she thinks she is back in her house with Waimpe and Nammi, but the rich smell of decaying sycamore wood brings her to reality. She springs from the tree. Outside the morning sun is casting long rays through the misty forest. The woods are lush with heavy dew. Loretta walks slowly and anxiously away from the tree, the touch-me-nots soaking her buckskin skirt with dew. She is making her way toward where she hopes to find the wooden stairs.

And then she sees him. He is standing with his back to her looking out over the river. Loretta can see that his head is bent in prayer. The woods are quiet except for the sound of the small shortened breaths of the girl. Tears swell up in Loretta's eyes. When she can't contain her emotions any longer, she lets go a cry and begins running toward the man. He turns at the noise, and dropping to his knees, raises his arms to heaven to give thanks before wrapping them around his daughter.

The End

Part 2

Non-Fiction Stories

Crew Chief

Iraq

The engine comes to life with heavy noise and vibration. Yellow flame shoots from the exhaust. The jet begins moving down the runway and the yellow flame soon turns to shades of red and purple as the pilot pushes the throttle forward. The flames group in circles of intensity and soon the jet takes off, flying low over the runway while the landing gear retracts. The pilot pulls straight up on the control stick and the jet launches into blue sky and out of sight.

I take off my headset and wipe the sweat from around the ear pieces before putting it in my gear bag. As I walk towards the hangar I look out over the sands of Iraq. They look brown and barren compared to the blue expanse of big desert sky sprawling above me. Over to the south I see the fence that runs along the perimeter of the base. When my unit first arrived here, one of the Staff Sergeants, accustomed to running along the perimeters of other bases, decided to take a run along the fence. About midway through the run he was confronted by an Iraqi woman and her three small children. They were clinging to the fence and frantically pleading in broken English to be taken onto the base. He ran on past without speaking to them. From that point on he quit running the perimeter, sticking instead to the internal roads on the base.

Beyond the fence is a small town with a tall gray Mosque tower at its center. When we got here, we were warned against climbing on top of the hangars where our aircraft were kept. It was possible to be shot at by a sniper from the town. One day I climbed to the top of the hangar that was closest to the fence, unconcerned by such small odds of getting shot and urged on by the gently sloped roofs that begged to be climbed on. I had an excellent bird's-eye view of the massive base and a closer look at the town with its squat dark buildings and the tall Mosque tower. I didn't stay long, however, and soon was sliding my way back towards the relative safety of the ground.

To the east I see the burn pile where third-party nationals use bulldozers to push heaps of Styrofoam and plastic trash into a burn pit. I watch which direction the black smoke drifts and note that today it's going away from the hangar. I won't have to worry about the sore throat and runny nose that comes from breathing the toxic smoke.

To the west stands the control tower where the chaotic airspace of the base is somehow managed. Beyond the control tower are the hangars where the predator drones are kept. I had a face-to-face encounter with one a few weeks prior. Another airman and I were driving down the taxi-way to work on a jet when we noticed a drone taxiing straight for us. We stopped; the drone stopped. The weaponry of a drone, which is a remotely controlled aircraft, consists of two hell-fire missiles positioned on each wing tip. As we faced the drone, the two hell-fires were pointed directly at us. It remained motionless except for the rapid turning of its propeller. "What should we do?" the airman who was driving asked.

"I think we should pull off the taxi-way," I quickly responded and he promptly pulled over, letting the drone move safely past us.

To the north sprawl the tents, trailers and dining facilities that feed and shelter the thousands of troops that are stationed here. In one of the tents lies my sleeping bag which resides on a small mattress perched atop a cot. The tent is situated close to the runway but far away from the dining facility. The location features the non-stop noise of an active military runway and a 15-minute walk each way to get something to eat. I often sit on the sandbag walls surrounding the tent and eat an MRE (meal, ready-to-eat) instead of taking 30 minutes from my busy schedule to walk to the facility. Another deterrent is my knowledge of a recent dining facility suicide bombing at a nearby base. Troops were killed and wounded as they ate and carried on conversation.

When I reach the hangar, it's shaded inside and I can feel a cool breeze upon my face. A few desert pigeons fly past the hangar door. When I look up to watch the birds, I notice a desert falcon perched above the door. The bird's head is masked with black feathers and its breast is buff red. It sits proudly above the hangar, scanning with its large black eyes for movement. The poise and seriousness of the bird reminds me of some of the more noble Arabs I have met. It pauses to study me before lifting its wings and dropping gracefully into the blue desert sky.

I walk to the middle of the hangar and step inside the crew room. The crew room serves as a break room for crew chiefs (aircraft maintainers) and as the center of operations for our hangar. The concrete walls are pock-marked and spotted with black burn marks. Here and there are twisted pieces of metal protruding from the walls.

In the initial push to seize control of Iraq the hangar was bombed by American planes. A "bunker buster" bomb was used, which penetrated through the four-foot-thick walls and detonated inside the center of the hangar. The Iraqi airmen who sought protection there were all killed. Later the room was cleaned of rubble and human remains, the hole in the ceiling was repaired and the room was converted into our crew room.

I quickly check the schedule and see that my jet will return after I get off duty and will be "caught" by another crew chief. Catching a jet consists of guiding the jet back to its parking area, helping shut down the engine and helping the pilot out of the cockpit. Once the jet is caught it must be made ready again for its next flight by refueling, inspecting and updating the jet's forms.

When it's time for the jet to fly again it must be "launched." Launching a jet consists of helping the pilot into the cockpit, conducting a preflight inspection while the jet is running, and guiding the jet out of the parking space.

In general, the main objective of the crew chief is to keep a jet in good flying condition at all times. The more flight time a plane receives, the harder a crew chief has to work. Routine maintenance happens more often and turnaround time between flights is often short, leaving little time for refueling and inspections. Sometimes your plane would have the most flight time and your supervisor would stop as he walked down the flight line to say, "Hey, by the way, your jet flew the most hours last month...good job." And you would smile inside and think of all the other guys who couldn't keep their plane up as long as you could and how they weren't nearly as good, although your gut told you it was just luck that kept your plane from breaking down that month.

On the long deployments you worked your jet with pride, sweating and freezing as you labored on the gray flight line, checking oil levels, servicing hydraulic fluid, crawling into the intake to do an inspection and dealing with arrogant pilots who knew you had to do your task regardless of how much respect they paid you.

But I liked the work. I liked that I was where the action was instead of some back-shop working on jet parts and pieces. I liked talking with the pilots and being the first one on the flight line to know that bombs were dropped. I liked the smell of jet exhaust and the way a freshly cleaned canopy shined in the sun. At the end of the day your bones were tired but you felt good because you knew your jet was in the sky all day doing some good for the troops on the ground.

I grab my flak jacket and walk outside to wait on the bus that will take us back to the tents. With my back against the hangar wall I take in the warmth of the desert sun. I reach into my front shirt pocket and take a Camel cigarette out of a zip-lock bag. I light it and pull the smooth smoke into my lungs exhaling into the light desert air. I look over at the hospital that's positioned a short distance from the hangar. A Black Hawk helicopter with a red cross on the side approaches and slowly lands behind the protective wall.

One of the crew chiefs from our base volunteered at the hospital. He spent the afternoon helping unload the wounded from the helicopters. He was kept fairly busy and told us that one of the wounded that came in was an enemy soldier. Medical personnel had the man duct-taped to the stretcher to keep him from hurting himself or medical personnel, which sometimes happened. I wanted to volunteer at the hospital, but never committed to sacrificing sleep since the work would have been on top of my crew chief duties. Looking back, I wish I had. I could have given a little more to help those less fortunate than me.

When I arrive back at my tent, I walk to the shower house and take a shower before plopping on my cot in a t-shirt and shorts to read a magazine. I feel clean and relieved to be off the flight line for the day.

And then it happens. The first explosion sends me to my feet with all my senses alerted. When the second explosion happens, I realize it must be a mortar attack and begin putting on my flak jacket and helmet. When a mortar round explodes, shrapnel flies up and out. The best thing to do during an attack is lay flat on your stomach. When the third explosion happens, I'm lying face down staring at the plywood floor of my tent. My heart rate triples in pace and intensity. The explosions are loud and close and seem to pound the air for the brief seconds they move through it.

After lying there for a minute, nothing else happens so I walk outside. I scan the surrounding tents for signs of damage. I think of the military first aide training I've received and that I may have to put it to use on a fellow airman. None of the tents are damaged and everything appears to be normal. I walk over to the smoke shack which is where crew chiefs gather to smoke and talk. I ask what happened and they tell me a munitions team exploded some dud mortar rounds that must have come in during the night but didn't go off. They tell me how everyone scrambled from the smoke shack to seek shelter when the explosions went off. Apparently, the munitions team didn't bother to tell anyone of their plans.

Qatar

My first deployment was to a base in Qatar called Al Udied Air Base. Qatar is a small country located on a peninsula off the coast of Saudi Arabia. The country is cooperative towards America's goals in the Middle East and unlike the base in Iraq, seldom came under attack.

In Qatar our jets flew 6-hour missions to Iraq and dropped bombs on a daily basis. When a pilot had a successful drop, you knew it because the other pilots would gather around the plane to greet him as he climbed out of the cockpit. Our pilots had trained their whole careers for these missions and were happy to put their training to good use. I liked that we were dropping lots of bombs. If I had to come all the way over here and work in blazing temperatures 12 hours a day, I wanted bad guys to die. And I was putting my jet in the air in a country that was out of harm's way, which was icing on the cake.

On the flight line in Qatar you could look out in any direction and see nothing but flat, white, hard-packed sand that stretched for miles. When the sun was high the whiteness was almost blinding, the heat shimmering off the sand in waves of blurry gray and black.

When I walked out to my jet, I had to cross a small stretch of sand that was between the hangar and the flight line. I would always stop to look at what little plant life lived there. Small hard berries grew from plants with hardened light green leaves that grew close to the ground, almost unnoticeable. Their only water source was the dew that gathered in the mornings. And that was it for plant life.

In the early morning hours, I made sure I was on the flight line so I could watch the sun come up over the desert flats. The sun was as fiery red and as big as I have ever seen it as it slowly rose. Due to our close proximity to the Persian Gulf, the morning dew was heavy. It would bead up in big drops and then drip off the jet canopies onto the concrete of the flight line as the sun came up.

The barracks at Qatar were composed of rows of double-wide trailers. A narrow hall ran the length, and on either side were the small bunk rooms where we slept. My trailer smelled of new carpet and fresh plywood. The air conditioner that hung in the window kept it cold while you slept and covered over the noise of jets taking off.

Since I worked a 12-hour shift that started each day at midnight and ended at noon, I slept during the hottest part of the day. The latrine building was separate from the bunk houses and was located a couple of buildings down. I made frequent trips to the latrine, since working in the desert heat required drinking lots of water.

When you opened the door of the trailer to get to the latrine, the desert heat would hit you in the face the same way the heat from a hot oven hits you when you open the door to check your biscuits. Inside the latrine I could see in the mirror that my ears were red from the heat. The temperatures could climb as high as 129 Fahrenheit during the hottest parts of the day.

Since all of the water was trucked to the base and stored in large tanks that sat outside in the sun, the water in the latrine was always warm. When you sat down on a toilet you could feel the heat from the water against your bare skin.

Scratched and scrawled on the stalls of the bathrooms were short poems and pictures. Most of the "artwork" was explicit in nature. Looking at the pictures made me wonder what kind of soldier would take the time to draw them. While his family tells their neighbors about how he is in the Middle East fighting for his country, he is sitting on a toilet using a pocket knife to engrave a giant penis. I tried to understand him but couldn't.

When we weren't sleeping or working, we would go to a gigantic white tent located in the center of the base. It was always shady and usually a breeze stirred which made it a decent place to seek respite. Troops would sit in small groups talking and sipping beer. I liked it here because you could look out over the white flatness of the desert from the comfort of the tent.

The club, which was next to the tent, served European beer. Some of the beer cans had widgets in them which were designed to mix the beer upon opening. The first couple of these we drank, someone pulled out a pocket knife and cut the can open producing a small ping-pong-like ball. Beer cans with widgets in them were an oddity for us Midwesterners.

Since Qatar was relatively friendly towards America, we were allowed to take short trips into the capital city of Doha if so desired. I so desired, and one hot day I piled into a F-250 extended cab pickup truck with a couple of other guys and headed for town. Our guide for the day was a Master Sergeant from my base we called Yackie. Yackie was an older crew chief who was known for his ability to strike up a conversation, hence the name Yackie. He was tall and lanky and wore a neat mustache beneath his glasses. On the flight line, I had seen him on at least one occasion fail to keep his calm under pressure. I felt bad for him but at the same time knew that competence and keeping a cool head was important on the flight line. He made a hell of a tour guide though.

When we pulled onto the highway headed towards Doha, the capital city of Qatar, we became part of a steady flow of semitrucks. The trucks were painted a variety of oranges and reds and inside the cab you could see tassels hanging down along the edges of the windshield and door windows. They resembled a cross between a Mack truck and a gypsy wagon. The drivers were aggressive, but Yackie knew how to be aggressive too and soon we were veering off on the exit to Doha.

Yackie made a wrong turn though, and we ended up in a residential neighborhood. The houses were one story with no doors or windows and looked to be made of mud. As we turned around in a cul-de-sac, I watched a small Qatarian boy dressed in a long white robe standing in a doorway. The whiteness of his robe stood in stark contrast with his black hair and caramel-colored skin. He stared blankly at the truckload of Americans that had momentarily invaded his neighborhood as we pulled back onto the main road.

Soon, we were in the thick of Doha traffic. Yackie mixed into the quagmire of old Mercedes Benzes and banged-up taxi cabs like a pro. He spun us around several chaotic roundabouts before we hit the main road that runs along the Gulf and into downtown. The sun had reached its peak in the hot sky as we drove along the Gulf. I noticed a woman clad in black from head to toe walking along the side of the road in the midst of the intolerable heat. When I considered how hot and uncomfortable she must be enveloped in her blackness, I quickly realized that the only reason a man would require such a thing was for control and suppression.

We passed a prominent building that Yackie pointed out as belonging to the prince of Qatar. The building was long and white with several imposing spires. In the front was a green lawn which stood in stark contrast with the harsh whiteness of the desert. This was the seat of power in Qatar, an Arabic White House.

After passing the palace we plunged into the heart of Doha. The streets thronged with men wearing black mustaches and light-colored clothing. Some wore turbans wrapped with red cords while others were bareheaded, their thick black hair all the protection from the hot sun they needed. Many of the men held hands, a common custom among Arabic friends who are male. Like the widgets, this was a hard concept for a Midwesterner's mind to grasp.

We pulled off the main road and parked. Yackie told us to check the truck for explosives. Each time we either exited or entered the truck we all got on our hands and knees on the hot pavement and looked under the truck for bombs.

Satisfied our truck wasn't going to explode, we hit the sidewalk headed for the shakes (a grouping of merchant stalls). They were dominated by jewelry stores and electronic dealers that sold bootleg DVDs for two bucks a pop. I scanned the items for sale in the shops but mostly watched the men and women of Doha as they went about their daily routines.

Later in the day we visited a gigantic three-level mall that was full of fancy European clothing stores and other upscale retailers. The air was rich with the smell of exotic perfumes and oils. As we walked through the mall, I studied the sheiks that strode past us. Many wore the traditional robes and headdress that their fathers and their grandfathers had worn. But they talked on fancy gem-encrusted cell phones and wore gaudy Armani watches. The watches glinted in the light that came in from the big windows that ran along the very top of the mall.

In one of the stores I found a wooden jewelry box with a painted picture of an Arabic woman carrying a vase on her head. This I purchased for the woman I had just begun dating. It now resides on the top of her dresser in our bedroom.

As night approached, we made our way towards a pearl shop that was a regular stop on Yackie's tour. He was on friendly terms with the owner who I'm sure appreciated Yackie's company for the business he brought to the store. The shop was part of a group of businesses located below ground level that had an open-air courtyard running down the middle. Darkness crept over Doha as we walked down the steps to the shops. The evening call to prayer drifted to my ears and echoed gently through the courtyard.

We walked into the pearl shop which consisted of two small rooms, the first with a counter full of pearl earrings and necklaces. Standing behind the counter the friendly proprietor greeted us in English. Yackie returned the greetings and performed a sort of half bow several times saying hello in Arabic as he did so. I felt a little embarrassed at Yackie's over-enthusiastic salutations.

Yackie told us that the shop owner was a descendent of a Qatarian prince. He was dressed in a clean white robe with headdress. His mustache was neatly trimmed against the tanned skin of his face and dark eyes. I was impressed by the shopkeeper's manners and appearance and believed Yackie's story might be true.

Since the other airmen were married, they quickly began conversing with the shopkeeper about the pearls in the display case. I wandered away from the counter into the second room. The walls of this room were covered with Arabic paintings. A couple of low-sitting couches were situated against the walls beneath the paintings.

I studied the striking colors of the paintings. Some displayed deep black and purple tones of desert night skies studded with white sparkling stars. Others had rich tan tones of desert sand dunes set against deep blue skies. The clean whiteness of the coat of an Arabian stallion and the robes of the prince who rode him were especially striking when set against blue desert skies. The black skies of night seemed to hold mystery and enchantment while the whiteness of the Arabian stallion's coat spoke of nobility and pride.

Seated on one of the couches was a man named Muhammad. Muhammad was wearing traditional Arabic garb and wore a long jet-black beard. He reminded me of the many pictures I had seen of Osama bin Laden. I asked if I could sit on the couch next to his and he nodded and offered me a Camel cigarette.

We began to converse. Muhammad was very interested in my family status. When I told him I was not married and had no children he frowned and shook his head. "I have a wife and six children," he told me. He was very proud of his family. As we talked, the smoke from the Camel cigarettes hung in the room and I wondered if it could somehow fade the deep tones of the paintings.

The shopkeeper was very polite to us and at one point brought around a tray with little cups of coffee. When he offered me a cup I declined, which I think offended him. I was secretly worried that the coffee might be poisoned. It was a foolish thought and I wish I had tried some.

As I sat in the back seat of the truck on the way home riding through the desert night, I thought of the day's events. I recalled the way it felt to walk amongst a throng of Qatarians looking for deals in the Shakes. I wondered at the splendor of the mall and the richness of the fine perfumes it smelled of. And I thought about the time I spent smoking with Muhammad while noble princes and proud Arabian stallions looked down upon us.

Training

I joined the Air National Guard when I was 20. I felt compelled to serve by the patriotic need to do my part to protect my country. I also realized the value of ample college assistance that was offered at the time. I remember telling my dad of my intentions to join the guard as we stood in the driveway of the family home on a warm summer evening. Pop had just come up out of the barn from working on the hay bailer and stood listening in his cut-off-sleeved t-shirt and jeans that had bailer grease on them. The sun was beginning to set and the world was quietly easing into night except for the occasional car with exhaust issues that passed on its way to the nearby trailer park. "Make sure you think about what you're doing first, Son. Six years is a long time." I could tell he didn't want me to join. I guessed that like any father he was concerned about how it might affect my college career and where it might put me if conflict broke out overseas.

After I joined, I had to go to the Fort Wayne air base once a month for guard drill. At that time, I was enrolled as an undergrad at Purdue. My days were filled with lectures, labs and college fun except for the one weekend a month when I drove my 1982 Ford F-150 back to Fort Wayne for drill. The truck was old and the valves made a ticking noise as you drove because the oil pressure was always low. Pop and I had painted the truck in the barn next to the haystack. I was proud of the truck and it looked good for its age with its chrome wheels and new paint.

At Purdue I had an Indian friend named Shitaj who lived in the same dormitory. Shitaj and his friends liked to sit on the steps in front of the dorm and smoke clove cigarettes. I met him one evening when I bummed a clove cigarette and asked him what his name was. "Shitaj," he said.

"Uh...Shitig?" I asked. "

"*No*, Shi-taaj." I nodded and made every effort to call him Shitaj instead of Shitig, although sometimes I couldn't help myself. He had shoulder-length black hair and wore a hoop earring in his left ear. He had an edgy look about him that reminded me of an Indian version of Johnny Depp.

Shitaj would introduce me to his Indian friends usually by stating in his thick Indian accent, "This is Sam. He has a truck." The fact that I owned a truck usually generated a buzz of excitement amongst the group. The excitement would build into a frenzied pitch that would end with me driving to the nearest bar with Shitaj and four or five of his friends in the bed of my truck talking and laughing and having a general good time of it.

I spent most of my first year of guard drill at the base hanging around the sheet metal shop which was my original job assignment, not really doing much of anything because I wasn't trained yet. I hated not being useful and felt nervous around the older more experienced guardsmen. But I showed up every weekend and wore my uniform that had no rank on it the best way I knew how. I had not been to basic training yet so I had yet to learn about military customs, which in all practicality at a guard base didn't amount to much. There were overweight men in their late 50s who wore untrimmed mustaches and complained bitterly when the chow hall wasn't serving cheeseburgers for lunch. Their uniforms were loose and wrinkly and the browns, blacks and greens of the camouflage patterns were faded a mushy gray. Even with these troops lingering around smoking cigarettes and digesting cheeseburgers, I still felt obligated to swing a nervous salute when my paths crossed with those of a pilot or officer.

The following summer I enlisted. I was finally scheduled to attend basic training at Lackland Air Force Base in San Antonio, Texas. I arrived at the base on a bus full of new recruits. There was little conversation on the bus ride as most recruits sat and thought about what awaited them at Lackland. After completing in-processing paperwork, we lined up in rows shoulder to shoulder under an outdoor pavilion. By this time night had fallen and the bug-filled lights above us cast a dull yellow shade on the scene. A couple of drill sergeants came out and began to yell. They wore round black hats with the brims tilted down to just above their eyes. They went from person to person asking questions with no right answers. You stood at attention daring not to flinch a muscle while inside your stress levels were going through the roof. The yelling continued for some time before we were finally herded into our barracks. I climbed into my bunk that night and felt protected from the drill sergeants for the first time since we got off the bus.

In the mornings at 4:30, reveille would sound and all the lights in the barracks would come on. You had to get out of bed, get your physical training uniform on and be down in the pavilion by 4:35. As the rest of the day played out, the drill instructors were constantly on us and loved to find someone they could single out and make an example of. If pressed hard enough, some of the younger recruits would cry, the tears streaming down their face as the drill instructor barked on, his face inches from theirs.

It was a fast-paced and rushed existence. We were constantly busy shining boots, cleaning shower floors, organizing foot lockers, learning how to march, etc., until the moment the lights went out and we were safe again underneath our wool blankets.

We did our physical training in the morning when it was still dark to avoid trainees from falling out in the hot Texas heat. I recall one of the troops in our flight that had an athletic physique like that of a football player. However, when we ran on the track I would easily lap him. I'd pass him in the darkness and notice him gasping for air as he ran. I had heard that he complained of shortness of breath and fluid on his chest, but that each time he went to sick call they never found anything and sent him back to the flight.

A couple of weeks into training we did our physical fitness qualification run. We were required to run two miles in less than 18 minutes. After I had finished my run, I stood stretching and catching my breath. In the early morning darkness I saw the red and white lights of an ambulance approaching the running course. When our flight regrouped, I found out the recruit with the athletic build had attempted to run the course but had collapsed just short of the finish line. I later learned that he died. We all knew that even though he didn't fall on the battle field, he had given his life for his country. I still wonder at the competency of those military doctors who failed to diagnose a health problem the signs of which seemed so obvious to us.

After I completed basic training, I resumed my weekend drill duties working in the sheet metal shop. One drill weekend I went to see the college aid advisor and was informed that I was not eligible for all of the benefits I was promised. I was distraught and knew that I was right about what was promised me but didn't know what to do about it. I explained my situation to Pop. He listened and shook his head but didn't say much. About a month later I got a letter from an Indiana congressman's office that advised they were looking into my situation. Unbeknownst to me, Pop had written them. A couple of days later I got a call from the base and soon Pop and I were sitting in a meeting with base leadership. I was able to produce the document that was given to me by a recruiter which showed all the benefits I was eligible for as a sheet metal troop. Turns out, the document was erroneous and in order to qualify for the benefits I was promised I'd have to switch career fields and become a crew chief.

And so, the summer after I completed basic training, I reported to Sheppard Air Force Base in Wichita Falls, Texas to learn how to be a crew chief. The adjustment back to military life after a semester at Purdue was not easy. When I first arrived and presented myself to the sergeant in charge, he scolded me for not standing at attention and not addressing him with the proper military greeting. I soon fell into the swing of things though and tried to enjoy my time at Wichita Falls as much as possible.

On weekends, we were able to leave the base and often went to a club in town where you could hang out in a real Texas dance hall. The local men wore cowboy hats and western shirts and two-stepped with pretty Texas women across the dance floor. These men were the real deal and actually worked on ranches and rode in rodeos, unlike many of the cowboys I had come across in Indiana whose only claim to being a cowboy was a rusted truck and a Travis Tritt CD.

One weekend my roommate and I rented a car and drove to Dallas. We went downtown and watched Texas Longhorns roam the streets before cowhands herded them into big corrals. Something I would never see in an Indiana city.

We went to the spot where JFK was shot. I examined the book depository, the grassy knoll and the fence to get my own impression of how things went down. Here were men dressed in dirty slacks and faded t-shirts selling conspiracy theory books and newspapers. How lonesome it must be to hang around a spot where a man was shot years ago trying to make a living from the tragedy.

While at tech school, I befriended a Bahraini airman who was sent to America to learn how to work on F-16s. His name was Shakar pronounced Sha car but everyone called him Shocker. Shakar had close-cropped hair, a medium build and his brown skin was clean-shaven. He was fairly serious in nature, but if I tried I could get him to laugh and shake his head at me. I learned that Bahrain was a modern Islamic country that had a small air force with F-16 fighter jets.

When Shakar worked on the training jets he never used the tech data like we were taught but instead jumped right in and began tearing things apart. We were quickly scolded by our instructors if we imitated this approach. We were trained to strictly follow step-by-step instructions found in our repair manuals. I suspect that Bahraini squadrons don't have near the safety and flight records that our squadrons do.

Since Shakar was a foreign troop and had more rank than the rest of us, he ate at the chow hall for regular enlisted troops. When we'd return from lunch, I was always curious about what types of American foods he favored. I pictured him eating a cheeseburger with that serious Arabic look on his face. I'd always ask him what he had for lunch and usually ask if he had a cheeseburger before he could reply. His Arabic accent was short and terse when he'd reply, "Come on Whiteleather, I didn't have a cheeseburger. Why do you say this 'did you have a cheeseburger? …'". When he said the last part, he would try to imitate how I talked and he would always end with saying "Whiteleather, no," shaking his head while he made a clicking noise a couple of times.

I once asked Shakar why some Arabs hated Americans so much. He quickly replied "Because you support the Jews, Whiteleather."

After several months at Sheppard we were sent to Luke Air Force Base in Phoenix, Arizona. Luke was a great improvement compared to Sheppard. I was assigned a room of my own, the food was good, you were treated as a regular airman instead of as a trainee and more options were available for weekend trips.

One weekend, a few of us left the base and drove to Las Vegas. At the first casino we came to, I sat down at a slot machine and began to play.

The casino was a massive complex of slot machines that were all ringing and dinging, producing a kind of hypnotic background noise that made it all seem exciting. In contrast to the ringing and dinging were some of the zombie-like players, mostly older women with cigarettes hanging out of their mouths that had long tips of ash dangling capaciously from the ends. When they won, the bells would go off and the ringing became a fevered pitch. They would sit and stare blankly as if nothing were happening and when the machine quit ringing they would simply hit the button and start playing again.

The first machine I played didn't produce after a couple of pulls, so I moved a few machines down. Shortly thereafter a pair of young women sat down and began to play the same machine. After one pull they began to scream and began calling people telling them that Christmas was coming early this year (it was November). They came over and started a conversation with us and all I could say was "I was just on that machine," which they seemed not to hear. Thus began and ended my short gambling career.

Another weekend I went to the Grand Canyon and did some hiking. I went with a male and female troop and we hiked hard down into the canyon until we were low enough to see the river clearly. We paused on an outcropping and looked down at the river which was a green sliver that ran between cliffs of brown and gray. On the way out, the female troop stayed in front of me the whole time we climbed up the switchbacks, no matter how hard I tried to pass her. She was fit and tough and I gained a new respect for female airmen.

Once I completed my training, it was back to weekend guard duties at Fort Wayne. Since I was a full-fledged crew chief, I was put to work on the flight line. Each weekend I'd be assigned a jet which typically flew once in the morning and once in the afternoon. After I launched it, I'd sit around with the other crew chiefs and watch movies or simply converse until my jet came back.

Fort Wayne winter days can be punishing, especially when you're working on the flight line which offers little protection from the wind. In the wintertime, when the cold winds blew and the skies were gray with heavy clouds that threatened snow, you worked your jet with gloved hands and jacketed shoulders. The main defense from the cold was to keep moving, shuffling your combat boots in place and slapping your arms against your sides. When you were launching a jet and it was running, you could stand next to the hot exhaust to stay warm.

Fort Wayne summers, on the other hand, were mild and gentle and times were good on the flight line. If you needed a break you could sit with your back to a jet tire and rest under the shade of a wing, quietly looking out over the flight line.

One weekend at drill we were informed our wing would be deploying to Iraq. The deployment was voluntary as the base did not have the authority to require everyone to go. A sign-up sheet was placed on a table in the crew room.

By this time, I had graduated Purdue and was working full-time as a wildlife biologist. One evening I was invited to my boss's home for dinner. We dined on wild rice and steak smothered with sautéed mushrooms. He lived in a log cabin which had a large stone fireplace. A healthy fire roared and popped casting a pleasant orange glow on the cabin's great room. The TV was on and as I took a sip of wine, I saw American soldiers in an Iraqi city kicking in doors looking for bad guys. The soldiers worked hard in the hot desert heat all the while constantly putting their lives at risk. And here I was leaned back in my chair comfortably sipping wine. I decided then that if I could help those guys by putting a jet in the air, I was going to do it.

And so, when the next guard drill came around, I put my name on the list. A couple of months later my boots hit Iraqi soil as I walked off the back ramp of C-17 cargo jet and onto Balad Air Base.

Leaving Iraq

The next morning, I awake before midnight and begin getting ready for the day. Since my shift runs from midnight to noon, I start my day in darkness. On my way to the shower house my breath steams in the cold night air and here and there I see skim ice forming in mud puddles. Iraqi days in winter are pleasant with low humidity, clear skies and average temps in the 70s. Iraqi nights can get surprisingly cold, not anything like Fort Wayne cold, but cold enough to make it a little harder to work on the flight line at night.

Inside the shower house, I begin brushing my teeth. Another airman a couple of sinks down is doing the same. I hear a distant thud and pause momentarily to listen as does the other airman. One more thud is heard before all is quiet again. We look at each other, I shrug my shoulders and we go back to brushing our teeth. A motor attack, I wonder, or possibly the munitions team up to their old tricks?

Back at the tent I put on my uniform, my helmet and my flak jacket and head for the bus stop. The base's current threat level determined the need for protective gear. If the threat was high enough, everyone on base had to wear a flak vest and helmet when outside. I assume the threat level was based on recent intelligence but often wondered if it was set rather by the whims of a general just to keep us on our toes.

After a short bus ride, I arrive back at the hangar and check the schedule. My jet is due to launch in an hour so I check the forms and do a walkaround to make sure everything is ready. When my pilot comes out, I get him strapped in and soon the jet is taxiing down the runway on its way to another mission.

I pass the time while my jet is flying, helping other crew chiefs work their jets. Since the deployment was voluntary, not all of the Fort Wayne crew chiefs signed up to go and we were short-handed for the duration. This meant that most shifts you were on your feet constantly as something always needed done. We typically sent someone to the chow hall to bring back food since we rarely had time to go. On several occasions I would grab whatever I could hold in my hands and eat my breakfast as I walked through the hangar and onto the flight line.

When my jet comes back, I ask the pilot how things went. He tells me he was up doing reconnaissance of a house the army was raiding. He circled the house from several thousand feet watching his infrared cameras for any bad guys that the army didn't know about. For most of our deployment our jets were occupied with these types of tasks. I know it was probably a big help to the troops on the ground, but I was still a little disappointed we weren't dropping bombs like we did in Qatar.

Noon finally swings around and I get ready to head back to the tents. It's a beautiful sunny day so I decide to join a couple of other airmen and walk across the flight line to the tents instead of riding the bus back. We walk for several minutes discussing the day's activities when we hear a not-so-distant explosion. We pause and I look at the Master Sergeant who is highest ranking in our group. "Probably just something blowing up in the trash heap," he says and we continue walking.

But then a high-pitched descending whistling sound reaches our ears followed closely by another explosion. We all three look at each other and begin running off the flight line. We make our way to a large tent and go inside. Inside the tent several troops sit in darkness watching a movie. We explain to them that a mortar attack is going on. They look at us with a "so what" kind of look on their faces and go back to watching the movie. In the darkness my heart pounds with anxiety as I sit quietly trying to focus on the movie.

When I finally make it back to my tent, I change into my PT uniform, consisting of t-shirt and shorts, grab an MRE and climb to the top of the sandbag wall that surrounds my tent. As I eat, I think about the day's events. The daily mortar attacks put me on edge a little bit, but since the chances of being injured by one are so small I consider it similar to the odds of getting in a car wreck. The closest anyone I knew came to being injured was when a mortar round landed near my friend Lyle while he was launching his jet. Lyle was in the middle of a launch when he heard the alert system, which was broadcast around the base by gigantic speakers, announce, "Incoming! Incoming! Incoming!"

When you heard this you were supposed to lie flat on your stomach with your hands over your head. So Lyle did. The pilot was a little confused when he saw him on the ground since he couldn't hear the announcement speakers inside the cockpit. Luckily the mortar round was a dud and didn't go off. It was found a couple of days later by someone walking next to our hangar. The munitions team came out (this time they let us know) and blew it up.

Another airman called "Spanky" who was a seasoned and highly respected crew chief despite his nickname, saw a mortar round blow up. He heard the explosion and when he looked he saw a cloud of dust and smoke. He was far enough away that shrapnel never reached him.

Mostly I thought about going home. I thought about my wife Rena and what it was going to be like to see her again. I had been able to talk to her a few times by using the telephone room on the base that was always crowded and provided little privacy. You couldn't help overhearing conversations, but you tried not to because some of them were not nearly as cheerful as the conversations Rena and I had.

Other than that, we communicated the old-fashioned way by writing letters. Although being separated was difficult, especially since we had only been married a few months prior to my departure, I enjoyed the letter writing. All the letters we wrote each other are tucked away in a box in our garage.

Days turned into weeks and soon the "X"s on my wall calendar were getting close to my anticipated departure day. When the day finally came, I crammed all of my stuff into my duffle bag and headed for the spot where the buses would pick us up and take us to the out-processing station.

Out-processing the base was a nightmare. The duffle bag I worked so hard to pack was summarily dumped by a grouchy Sergeant and searched for contraband. War souvenirs were strictly prohibited and organic items such as soil or plant material were also a no-no. The only thing I smuggled out was a small bag of sand. I placed the bag in the side pocket of my duffle bag and for some reason the inspector didn't look there. After being shook down, we waited around for several hours in a dark tent before walking out to the tarmac where our plane was waiting in the dark night.

Before we could get on our plane, we had to wait for the new arrivals to get off. As he's walking down the ramp, one of the new arrivals slips on a cargo roller and goes down hard on both knees. I can see the pain in his eyes when he gets back to his feet. *Welcome to Iraq,* I think.

We walk up the ramp and into the bowels of the jet that will lift us high over desert sands and out of harm's way. When it begins to climb I look down one last time at Balad Air Base. Pride wells in my heart at the thought of the troops down there that do their jobs so well. As the plane picks up speed and Balad fades into memory, I feel good inside knowing that I did my job the best I could, holding nothing back, giving all to my jet and the desert flight line.

War Chest

Adescending low-pitched whistle breaks the silence of a snowy gray day in Belgium as men in earthen, could-be tombs duck for cover. Seconds later, the earth trembles like the leaves on an aspen tree as hot shrapnel, smoking tree parts, and dirt rain down with purpose. From the bowels of his foxhole, Max hears a sharp "thwack" and sees a small spot of earth bulge and then swallow a smoldering chunk of metal in the exact location where his helmeted head had been just a few seconds before.

Producing his trench knife from his well-worn and dirt-layered field uniform, he carefully exhumes the golf-ball-sized chunk and examines it thoughtfully as it lies still simmering in his palm. *If I hadn't pulled my head down when I did, I'd be dead. New grave dug in the family cemetery at Larwill, Betty would get the news and weep. The boys wouldn't forget ol' Butch, or would they? Probably go on without me after a while, just as if I hadn't been with 'em at all. Damn Germans. What would Betty do? Probably find another I suppose, and go on just like the boys. Wonder how come I pulled my head down in time but other men don't. The way it goes I suppose, no rhyme or reason just life. Damn Germans. This will make a good story back home. Home ... down by the lake ringed with lily pads in yellow bloom, cool water, warm summer sun, green grass ... lush ... a boy catches a fish, quiet ... And still.*

A wrinkled slightly shaking palm now cradles the German shrapnel. I listen with awe to the story recounted in the basement of my grandfather's home as he drops the chunk into my hand. It's cold and black. Its concentrated density gives it a weight that far exceeds its size. This small piece of metal could have prevented my existence in the wink of an eye.

I lean back on the 1970s era tweed couch; its burlap-like texture provides an edged comfort as grandpa retrieves another firsthand account from his fading memory and I examine another relic from the depths of the red chest. He recalls the time he was strafed by a German fighter plane. "My buddy Mac and I were standing by a pile of rock on an airstrip we were building. I heard something hit the pile and looked at Mac. Mac said, 'I think we're getting shot at.' Then we both dove behind the rock pile. Pretty soon, here came a German fighter plane strafing the construction site. Right behind him was one of our planes that ended up shooting the German down.

"The people in the nearby village were watching everything and when the German went down, they rushed over to the wreck and pulled his body out and then dragged it through town. Somehow, I was able to get his gun. I don't know how I got it, but I did."

The gun, designed to end life as efficiently as possible by one of the evilest government systems in the world, now looks tired and unthreatening with its worn wooden pistol grip and its black barrel turned off-brown by a thin layer of surface rust. Grandpa holds the gun high with barrel pointed to the ceiling pumping it up and down a couple of times. A half smile and a brightness in his eye reassures me that though aged and worn on the outside, the flame of his fighting spirit still burns near the center of his chest beneath the buttons of his plaid button-down shirt.

He unfurls a large Nazi flag. The deep red background sets off the bold blackness of the swastika. I imagine the flag being let down from the window of a Nazi fortress made of neatly trimmed stone by the hands of a proud German officer. The officer, while saluting the Fuhrer on the outside, possibly secretly yearns in his heart for what's best for his beloved Germany.

Grandpa neatly folds the flag and places it back in the chest. "Mac and I went to a French liberation party at a church one evening while we were pushing through France. The locals seemed to be having a pretty good time when suddenly the doors burst open and two French-men were briskly marched into the room. I asked Mac who knew some French what was going on and he said they were accused of being German collaborators, and would soon be shot. Shortly thereafter the two were marched outside."

He pauses, widening his eyes as the corners of his mouth slowly downturn, "I heard the shots."

Item after item is removed and then carefully placed back in the chest. I lean further back into the couch, and pull in a deep breath of basement air, slightly musty and aged like the scent of an antique shop but spiked with hints of cleaning agent, implications of my grandmother's presence here. As my body relaxes so does my mind; black-and-white visions of World War II history play out before me in vivid detail. I see the rich history of Europe: Notre Dame Cathedral, the Arc de Triomphe, rows of grape vines growing in the French countryside, and the Coliseum in Rome — the whole lot of it plunged into an all-destructive war full of death, desolation and despair. And in the middle of it all is Grandpa obediently going about his duties, sent to keep one European nation from killing off the others, all the while collecting and packing around a treasure trove of souvenirs. He plucks them from scenes of intense human drama, scenes of death and courage and fear and hate. When he finally makes it home, he places them in a war chest in the basement of a ranch home at the end of a quiet cul-de-sac in Fort Wayne, Indiana.

Grandpa gently lays the last item back in its place and closes the lid, bringing darkness and peaceful silence once again to its war-borne inhabitants. With his stooped and bent profile, he carefully shuffles back to his recliner placing his knurled and boney hands on its armrests, letting his body slowly down. He looks at me and smiles and I try to think of something to say but don't. The silence of the basement takes over.

Grandson... good boy, means well. Ole Butch did a hell of a job over there. Damn Germans. War chest, worn and faded, like me, but not forgotten, distant past, but not forgotten. Grandson... so young. I was young once, traveled the world for four years, saw and did unbelievable things.

And now all that's left are the soul memories, and those becoming less each day.

War chest... why did I go to so much trouble to bring that stuff back? It resides here like me, worn and faded. We survivors of so much human struggle, living on in a peaceful world. I'll always carry the war memories with me, neatly coiled and tucked away, lying dormant in my breast like the molten core of a volcano veiled by layers of ancient rock.

Soul memories and a war chest, all I've got to show for it ...quiet ... and still.

The Smell of the Place

I sometimes wonder why I duck hunt. Is it the need to rise at an ungodly hour, so early that I can catch the comics on the late-late shows getting in their last punch lines as I pull my wader pants on? Is it the sheer pleasure of walking in ice cold water and then suddenly plunging in over the tops of my waders as I step into a beaver run? Or rather the priceless life experience of possessing fingers so cold and numb that even the simplest tasks like pulling a gun trigger become as difficult as performing brain surgery on a fox squirrel, in the dark with one hand tied behind your back.

And still I love it.

I recall a hunt from a few weeks past. A fellow wildlife biologist, Dan, and I had established ourselves with shotguns in hand, in the middle of a large marsh near where we worked. To get there we had to walk for close to an hour from where we parked the truck. "Hear that?" I asked,

"No," Dan replied.

"Exactly," I say with satisfaction.

Not a truck, car, plane or train to be heard in any direction. You could have dropped us back to the days when bearded Frenchmen roamed the woods plying for new fur trapping grounds; from where we stood we would have never known the difference. And the smell of the place — rotting plants and decaying animal matter, intertwining like the strands of a piece of licorice to form the primordial muck that is the foundation for life here — is the most natural and unaltered smell I've ever known.

In this muck, knee-deep in coffee-brown water we stood. We sometimes heard the ducks before we saw them. Some ducks emitting a low whistling noise, others sounding like the rush of air left in the wake of a fighter jet. They would fly rhythmic circles over the marsh, constantly scanning the water surface with bobbing heads that moved like a marker buoy afloat on a windy day. Finally, they would descend with cupped wings and disappear into some unseen pocket of water concealed by dense thickets of button bush. The thickets gave the marsh a tangled and unkempt appearance.

After several minutes of watching ducks descend into one particular corner of the marsh, Dan and I decided to move in for a closer look. We crept along, carefully cradling our guns, playing an intricate game of cat and mouse with marauding beaver runs and submerged logs which seemed to lie in wait for us like German U-boats. We arrived where we supposed the ducks to be.

"Where are they?" I whispered.

No response from Dan, just a shrugging of shoulders and a quick searching scan of the marsh. We ventured further. Just as we had begun to give up and had decided the ducks had taken a page from Amelia Earhart's flight journal, five drake mallards rose from a clump of button brush with a mad flutter of wing beats. I fired; Dan fired.

Moments later we each stood with a mallard in hand analyzing and critiquing the exciting moments of the chase. By this time the evening sky was beginning to redden as the sun made contact with the horizon. Nightfall began to slowly elbow its way into the marsh. The wind had dropped to all but a whisper and a peaceful stillness permeated the place. We paused to watch the sky fill with hundreds of ducks descending upon their nocturnal roost site as they've done for thousands of years. And I suppose everything else aside, that's why I duck hunt.

O Mother Wabash

The big river slaps the sides of the aluminum boat with a rhythmic thud, its green waters parting begrudgingly as we make our way against its steady current. Tom takes a drag from his cigarette and exhales deeply, the smoke lingering momentarily around his weathered face before fading into the warm summer breeze. "I can't believe we didn't pick up more fish in the deep pool. We normally take a ton from there." I shrug my shoulders and tilt my head slightly to sympathize with his disappointment.

I take a deep breath and savor the smell of the river. It smells of the rich mud and sand that brings new life to fields and woods along its banks. It smells of the lush greenness of the leafy silver maples and sycamores that line its bank. And there is the subtle smell of the fish that swarm and team beneath its waters.

Tom had asked me to come along on the electro-fishing trip to help him and his aide process fish. Tom's goal for the day was to collect Asian carp in order to further his understanding of the fish and to collect meat for fish fries at educational programs. Electro-fishing involves passing electrical current through water and collecting the fish that pop to the surface temporarily stunned from the current. Biological data is collected and the fish are typically returned to the water unharmed, except for Asian carp which are culled due to their invasive nature.

At the time, I was the property manager at Sugar Ridge Fish and Wildlife Area, working with Tom and several other fisheries biologists out of the Sugar Ridge office. My work focused on wildlife management.

Partly because I was eager to do a little fisheries work for a change of pace and partly because of my love of rivers, I accepted Tom's invitation.

Tom swings the boat downriver and lets the big Honda run fast until we are below the deep pool again. "All right take the helm," he says to his aide as he throttles back the outboard to idle speed. His aide grabs the wheel and Tom makes his way to a red cooler. I watch, but say nothing as he produces a can of Pabst Blue Ribbon from the bottom of the cooler.

Holy crap, I think to myself, *all those stories I've heard about old fish biologists are actually true.*

He opens the can and starts pouring beer into the river. In lowered and solemn tones he begins to speak, "O Mother Wabash, we offer you this PBR as a token of respect to your greatness. O Mother Wabash, we sacrifice this beer in the hopes that you give us success in our endeavors today." As the last drops of foamy beer exit the can and Tom's voice begins to trail off, a huge Asian carp rockets from the water and lands crashing and thrashing on the bottom of the boat.

From that point on, we were into the carp thick. Tom would take the boat up into the deep hole and his aide and I would struggle to net the flying fish as hundreds of them shot up all around the boat. After an hour of good fishing, Tom slowed the boat and we all three looked at the tubs full of fish. He lit another cigarette, "O Mother Wabash," he said with a smile and a shake of his head as he exhaled a long breath of smoke, which faded deep into the recesses of memory.

*Not long after this trip, Tom lost a short battle with ALS and passed away in the fall of 2013. According to his wishes, his ashes were spread in the Wabash River not far from Lafayette, Indiana.

*The following series of short stories starting with "Sora Hunt"
and ending with "One for the Memory Bank" first appeared in my
column called "Patoka Valley Outdoors" that ran monthly in the
Press Dispatch, a weekly newspaper published in Pike County, Indiana.*

Sora Hunt

Around me the marsh lays like a massive bowl of chopped spinach soaking in water. The sedges and lotus pads are in full bloom and look like they couldn't be happier. Along the edges of the marsh stand tall trees whose green leaves are just beginning to lose life. The late September, mid-evening sun blankets it all in a rich yellow light. The air is still but crisp and carries a subtle hint of winter. The heat from the sun's rays feels good against the skin of my face and arms. With each step I take through the shin-deep water, tiny frogs jump and swim at random intervals in crooked and sideways trajectories giving the marsh a living, squirming feeling.

My hunting party this afternoon consists of a friend and his two young sons. From a distance I watch the boys struggling through the water. Every so often they trip and fall, soaking their pant legs from the knees down. Their father has given them instructions on how to walk through the marsh but they splash away, determined to learn the marsh on their own terms. When no one is looking, the older boy "accidentally" hits his younger brother with his wading stick. The younger reacts by giving a sharp cry and complaining to his father. The boys' watery traverse is not unlike that of the tiny frogs.

I have my bird dog Frans along on the hunt and I can tell he is thoroughly confused as to why we are searching for birds in a massive marsh. His liver-colored coat is dark from the marsh waters and hugs tightly to his skin, which makes his leg muscles look like a young Arnold Schwarzenegger's biceps. I watch as he makes his normal zigzag search pattern through the marsh which requires considerably more effort than running through a grassy field. I know he will be whooped when we make it home and he curls up in the fresh straw inside his dog house.

I've read a few stories written by Russian authors from the 1800s on bird hunting in marshes. The writers paint scenes of Russian aristocrats clad in traditional hunting garb firing muzzle-loading shotguns at fast-flying game birds. They write of peasants with long beards and threadbare clothing who know the marshes like the backs of their hands and will provide a good day's guiding for a bottle of Vodka and a loaf of rye bread. They write of cool nights spent in the Russian countryside bedded down with their dogs in a hayloft full of fresh hay after a long day afield. I think of their writing and that over one hundred years later I am here, gun in hand, seeing and doing some of the same things they wrote about.

Frans splashes through the marsh grass and I notice his tail wag has picked up, a sure sign birds are near. And then as he passes a green clump of marsh grass, he points, with tail up and head turned sharply toward where the scent of a Sora is strongest.

Here I must pause to describe the marshland bird of which I write. The bird, which belongs to the Rallidae or Rail family, is about the size of a quail or perhaps slightly smaller. Its beak is short and stout like that of a coot and its feathers are drab brown in color. The bird favors marshy areas and feeds primarily on seeds and small animal life including insects and snails. Since Sora migrate annually, they are best found in the fall months as they congregate enroute to southern over-wintering sites.

I move forward and begin splashing around, trying to find the bird that Frans knows for sure is there; and after much effort, the bird finally flushes. In flight the Sora is a relatively slow flyer and its appearance is ungainly, sort of like a wet quail with long legs that happened upon a spilt can of beer and had too much to drink. The Sora flies low and rushing the shot, I shoot behind the bird which continues its low ungainly flight before dropping down into the marsh again.

We begin our search anew and experience several more points and flushes, but my shot never seems to be in the right place at the right time and the drunk, long-legged quail gets the best of me. Since this is my first Sora hunt, I am eager to harvest a bird and I let my anticipation turn into anxiety and shoot poorly the entire afternoon. Thankfully my hunting partner shoots much better and manages to down a couple of birds which Frans proudly retrieves. He receives many good pats on the head from the boys in recognition of his efforts.

We continue hunting until I notice the sun is beginning to set. I think of how I told my wife I would only be gone an hour and glance at my watch noting that we have been afield at least two. Another kind of anxiety creeps in and I think of how it's always better to overestimate your hunt time and come home early. But when the dog and gun are loaded in the truck and you're ready to go, it's hard not to mindlessly blurt as you walk out the door, "Oh, I should be back in an hour or so."

We begin walking out of the marsh as the sun slips below the tree line and I have to call for Frans who doesn't want to quit the hunt. The younger boy proudly carries the downed birds, pinning them with his hand against his wading stick, watching his step with one eye and with the other doggedly watching his brother's wading stick for sudden unwanted movements. I begin to think about those Russian hunters and how although we hunt over a hundred years later and we have no bearded peasants on hand to guide us, the feeling at the end of a hunt that grips hold of your heart must be the same.

Cold Water Retrieve

I t's a sunny and unusually warm day in February. Rena and I are making the best of it by taking the children on a long hike to one of our favorite strip-pit lakes called "Frog Pit." We hike on a tractor trail that runs through gray woods and yellow fields and across a couple of small creeks that trickle with thin veins of icy water. Our two bird dogs, Anne and Frans, are along on the trip. They range out in front searching amongst the briar patches and grass thickets for any living thing that might make for a good chase.

My 5-year-old daughter Eva walks along briskly, keeping pace with her mother and me. On her face she wears the little smile that means she's having fun. The strong southerly wind ruffles the ends of her blond hair that stick out from beneath her knit hat.

My 3-year-old son Eli does his best to keep up, but constantly lags behind as he negotiates the trail wearing his little rubber boots. He stops every so often to pick up a stick and with much effort, toss it off the trail. Rena and I do our best to keep him motivated but it seems like we spend more time waiting on him to catch up than we do actually hiking.

As for our youngest who is just now 1, she rides on my back in a kid carrier backpack. And but for the extra weight I wouldn't know she was there except for the occasional baby noise and the brush of her tiny hand against the back of my neck.

Before we set out on the hike, we ate pancakes and scrambled eggs on the big wooden table that sits in the kitchen in front of the double window. Here you can look out and watch the birds feeding on the sunflower seeds Rena puts out in the winter. The eggs were mixed with small pieces of pork sausage and potatoes and I ate them with black pepper and parmesan cheese sprinkled on top. The pancakes were covered in maple syrup and some of the raspberries Rena had picked and frozen the past summer. My fork cut their soft yellowness easily and soon my plate was clean. All that was left to do was to look out the window and finish my coffee. The coffee was black and still steaming hot since it'd been resting on the top of our woodstove which oozed cozy heat for us on this Saturday morning.

We finally arrive at Frog Pit and I pick a good spot on the edge of the high-wall where we can look down and see the green waters which are still iced up in places. I break out the fruit snacks I had stuffed in my pockets as we walked out the door this morning and the children carefully examine the different Curious George shapes and colors before happily popping them into their mouths.

Frans comes running by and since he loves to water retrieve, I find a stick and fling it out over the bank and down into the water. He watches the stick's trajectory before scrambling down the nearly vertical high-wall after it. But instead of floating on top, it sinks below the water's surface. Frans, not knowing the stick has sunk, starts swimming for the limb of a large snag that sticks up above the water. When he gets to it, he grabs it and begins pulling with dogged determination. The snag doesn't budge. Rena and the children now stand next to me and we laugh as we watch the futile struggle. We can see the rapid kicking of his legs beneath the clear water.

Several seconds pass and Frans is still pulling. "Frans," I call, "that's enough boy, leave it."

But the pulling continues. *"Frans!"* I shout as loudly as I can. I know he can hear me, and if he can hear me, he always comes. But he doesn't, he just keeps frantically kicking his legs, not leaving the snag.

And then the rapid leg kicking begins to slow down. No one is laughing now. "Crap, I think he's caught," I say as I begin scrambling down the high-wall, the briar thorns ripping through my shirt giving me sharp pinches of pain as I go. My descent down the high-wall is more of a controlled fall than a climb down. I see that he is really slowing down now and struggling to keep his head above the water. I quickly realize that there's a good chance the children looking down from above may be about to make a memory that I'd rather they didn't.

When I reach the edge of the water, I feel a surge of emotion and my first thought is to jump in and save him. But he's out towards the middle where it's deep and water temperatures can't be much above freezing. The thought of my children watching my dog drown is quickly trumped by the thought of my children watching their daddy drown. So I stand by helplessly as my dog that I've had since he was a pup and happens to turn eight years old this very day, fights for his life.

For humans, immersion in cold water is extremely dangerous. Cold water immersion inhibits your body's ability to function and even the best swimmers can quickly drown in cold water. The spring months often lead to cold water drowning because people are fooled by warm air temperatures and fail to recognize the danger posed by cold waters. Since drowning is the biggest threat posed by cold water, wearing a life jacket is the best way to prepare for an accidental immersion. But hypothermia can quickly set in as cold water rapidly cools your body's core temperature. So even with the added protection of a life jacket, cold water can still be deadly.

Standing on the edge of the water, the only thing I can do is yell. So I do, and as I call his name, Frans turns his head towards me. His brown eyes meet mine and the urge to jump in hits me again. But in an instant he breaks free. The head movement was all that was needed to free his collar from the snag. He begins swimming towards the bank. He crawls onto the shore and hunkers down next to me exhausted from the struggle, his brown hair clinging tightly to his shivering body. I have to help him up to the top of the high-wall, but in 15 minutes or so he is running around acting normal again.

As we hike back to the house, I feel a huge sense of relief that Frans made it and I don't have to answer countless questions from the children about why he isn't coming home with us. I also feel a huge sense of relief that I was able to overcome my emotions and make the right decision. As a parent, I know that I must put my own thoughts, desires and urges second. I'm part of something bigger now, a life experience full of sacrifice, frustration and heartaches, but one of the most rewarding I will ever know.

As we near the house, I turn and smile at Rena as Eva and Eli run down the hill that leads to the back yard laughing and shouting as they go. The little one still cooing in her backpack, lays her tiny hand on my shoulder. I reach up with my own and hold it, never wanting to let it go.

Hunting the Rut

It's the third day of November and I'm slowly working my climber up a tall pine tree that sits on a wooded hillside. First, I brace myself by gripping the seat portion of the stand tightly. Then I lift with my feet which are strapped into the footrest portion of the stand and bring it up the tree until my knees are bent. By putting downward pressure on the footrest, I make sure it is firmly seated into the tree before straightening my legs and lifting the seat as high as I can get it. I repeat this process until I'm high enough to avoid being easily spotted by a deer.

I settle into my stand and look at my watch. Its 7:30 a.m. Sunlight, turned gray from cloudy skies, has made the woods light enough to shoot in and then some. I realize I should have been in my stand about a half hour ago to limit the potential of spooking deer in the daylight. When I feel along the edges of my right pants pocket for my hunting knife, it's not there. If I did harvest a deer today, I'd have no way of field dressing it. *So much for the old Boy Scout motto "Be Prepared"* I think to myself.

The wind is from the south and it pushes through the leafless woods much harder than I'd like. But no matter, I'm here in a tree stand watching for deer. As a husband and father of three small children, that's enough to paste a smile on your face that can overpower the wind, the lateness and the missing knife.

I had planned on putting my daughter Eva on the bus for pre-school this morning, but since the forecast called for mild temps in the 50s Rena did it so she could take her morning walk before a strong cold front came in. The first time Eva got on the bus, she climbed up the steps in the morning darkness and took the first seat she came to without any hesitation. She never once looked back and I could see her little blond head through the window as the bus went on down the road and out of sight.

I'm not in my stand more than 15 minutes before I see my first deer. It's a small buck that walks through the woods like a dog following a trail of biscuits, pausing every so often to put his nose to the ground. The buck is out of range but I stand up and get my bow ready anyway. I watch as he stays about 50 yards away before moving into a thicket and out of sight. I'm pumped and shaking a little when I sit down. I spent most of the past two seasons staring at empty woods. Just seeing a deer gets my heart beating faster than the rhythm of a pileated woodpecker whacking the side of a rotten tree.

Thirty minutes pass and as the world's most impatient deer hunter I decide to climb down and slowly hunt from the ground in the direction the buck went. I make my way carefully down the tree by reversing the climbing process. Once on the ground I pause with my shoulder leaned against a stout maple tree, holding my bow in one hand, watching the woods. The wind has picked up a little making it difficult to hear movement.

Suddenly a doe appears and is almost on top of me before I can get my bow ready. Her ears are pinned back flat against the top of her head and she runs as if the woods are on fire. She moves in rapid bounds by thrusting her front legs forward and then hurdling the rest of her body along after them like a crazed deer slinky. Bounding along after her is the same buck I saw earlier, looking like a happy-go-lucky fool who has had too much to drink and is chasing a piece of paper down a windy sidewalk. They quickly move out of sight and my excitement about seeing deer is developing into a fevered pitch.

I stand still for several more minutes before slowly letting my bow down. But then another deer comes into view just as unexpectedly as the first buck and doe. Two spike antlers stand on the top of his head which tells me he is a young buck, probably in his second summer. He sniffs the ground cautiously as if unsure how close to get to the scene of the chase.

He is standing a little farther away than the distance I normally practice. But, I think, he is broadside and I have a clear shot so I get my bow up and get ready again. When the moment seems right, I release my arrow. I watch in helpless agony as it flies over the buck's back and on into the woods. He raises his head in alarm and trots back into thicker cover.

Male whitetail breeding behavior or rutting behavior is generally initiated by decreases in day-length. The rut consists of several phases including sparring, courtship, tending and breeding. Sparring initiates the rut and involves bucks facing off in dominance battles to establish breeding hierarchy. The courtship phase involves bucks chasing mature does. Does want no part of rutting bucks during this period, which means they are constantly on the move making this one of the best times to hunt the rut. But the mature buck keeps chasing because he knows eventually the doe will stop running. When she does, this period is called tending and breeding. Pairs isolate themselves and the buck tends the doe until breeding occurs. Tending lasts from 24 to 48 hours.

Rutting behavior typically initiates in September and terminates in January. During these months the woods are littered with signs left behind by rutting bucks. The most common signs are scrapes and rubs. The skin on a buck's forehead contains scent glands that become active during the rut. A buck "rubs" his forehead on saplings to communicate his scent signature to other deer. To make a scrape, a buck reaches up and pulls a small branch down with his mouth, letting it rub across the scent glands on his forehead. Branches are often broken during this process and hang down over the scrape site. He then paws the ground to remove leaf litter and urinates on the spot, letting the urine pass across another set of scent glands on his hind legs called "tarsal glands." Again the buck has communicated his scent signature to other deer.

I stand crestfallen. I really screwed up this time and I think of how awesome it would've been for the kids to see Daddy coming out of the woods dragging along a freshly harvested deer. "Way to go, Daddy!" they'd scream as I proudly displayed my catch. But not today. Today I will come home like all the other days, empty- handed.

"See anything?" my wife will ask. "Not really," will come the automatic reply from my dejected self.

And then I see him. I see his antlers first and know that he is big. He is walking straight towards me and I start to shake and freak out inside worse than a child on Christmas morning when he first sees the pile of presents under the tree. The buck keeps coming towards me and when he is about 10 yards away, he walks behind a large tree and I draw my bow back.

Two seasons spent staring at empty woods and countless hours shooting at 3D targets in the back yard and it's finally here, the moment of truth. My breath slows and I feel like the world around me is suspended in slow motion. A falling leaf would take hours to hit the forest floor under the current time constraints of my disabled mind. When he finally comes out from behind the tree, he looks my way and our eyes meet. The deep blackness of his eyes stirs a wild place in my heart like a hot ember from a wildfire that drifts back into the darkness of a cave. I let loose my arrow and hear a deep thunk as it hits hard into his side.

He flinches and trots off before slowing to a walk. I watch him walk out of the woods, into an adjoining field and out of sight.

I lean against the tree and try to calm myself. Since my arrow was loosed, time seems to move in a frenzied rush. All kinds of thoughts race through my head. *Was the shot good?...Will he go very far?...Was I too high or too low?* I stand by the tree fighting to keep control of myself before deciding to look for the blood trail. All the hunting articles I have ever read say to stay put after shooting a deer, but my impatient nature takes over once again.

I start scanning the ground and easily find splatters of blood every three yards or so that paint the leaves and twigs of the forest floor dark red. The trail is easy to follow and soon I'm in the open field. I scan the field carefully. For a moment all I see are the brown and yellow grasses that move gently in the breeze.

But then, towards the back of the field, I see the curved white bone of an antler sticking up above the grasses. A tide of joy rises inside of me. I approach the spot carefully. I find him there, lying on his side, quiet and still.

I pause to admire the beauty of the beast before me: the striking color and density of his brown and white coat, the thick, muscular neck that means he's a mature buck in rut, and the elegant curvature and branching of his antlers.

I call a co-worker and ask for help dragging the deer back to the house. "Oh, and by the way, can you bring a knife?" I ask.

When he arrives and we field dress the deer, I find my broad head in the chest cavity having sliced through both lungs. I rest assured in the fact that this is one of the most ethical ways to harvest a deer.

After a short but hard drag back to the house, the children are watching for me. When they see us, they run across the yard and crunch through the brown leaves that lay along the edge of the woods before pausing to admire Daddy's deer.

"What do you think, Eli?" I ask. Eli's blue eyes look up from the deer and he says "deer" before dropping them back to the animal. "Yes, it is a deer. Daddy harvested it from the woods. It will make for good eating this winter."

"Yeah," says Eva who is reaching down to touch its antlers.

This time Dad has something to show for his hours spent alone in the woods away from his family. I'm fulfilling a role that providers have occupied for thousands of years. And it feels good, it feels right.

Shades of Gray and Red (and Sometimes Black)

The woods are still and the heavy morning air hangs thick among the trees as if all night long the forest has held in a deep breath of green mustiness. I watch fuzzy gray shapes and blobs that my imagination has turned into a standing deer or some haunting shadow of a forest creature slowly morph into leafy branches and rotten stumps as the gray light of dawn begins penetrating the forest floor. This first light is much different than the golden yellow light that will follow making every green thing shine, and driving away the forest's morning breath.

Sound now reaches my ears as tiny songbirds flit from branch to branch chirping softly, occasionally letting loose a song so vibrant and clear that no human musician could even come close to replicating it. Out of the corner of my eye, I see movement and turn my head to focus on a gray squirrel that is bouncing from limb to limb in a tall hickory tree. I raise my rifle and begin tracking it in my scope and much to my delight, it begins a head-first descent down the tall tree. I give a scalding squirrel call with my mouth and it stops, raising its head to search for a rival squirrel. I focus my cross hairs on its shoulder and hold steady as a mosquito buzzes my ear, the noise sounding like the howl from a semitruck on a distant interstate coming closer and closer. I begin to squeeze the trigger making sure my eye is aligned with the cross hairs and is focused on the squirrel's shoulder.

Gray squirrels, as a rule, are early risers preferring to feed hard in the morning before kicking back and taking it easy in the midday hours. Fox squirrels, on the other hand, prefer the slow but steady approach, feeding on and off throughout the day. For both species, September and October are their most active months as they prepare for the lean winter months to come, making these months the best time to hunt them.

Gray squirrels tend to select upland hardwoods with a dense understory while fox squirrels prefer woodlands with a more open understory. The two species will inhabit the same areas and can sometimes be found feeding together in the same tree. Both species favor hickory nuts, beech nuts, acorns, black walnuts and corn.

The crack of my rifle breaks the hushed aura of the woods and the squirrel drops from the tree, making a soft thud as gray fur meets brown earth. I pick the squirrel up and examine its testicles and note they are black and hairless, which tells me this is an adult, since juvenile male testicles have soft fur.

Sometimes it's difficult being a wildlife biologist. I wish I could just pick up a harvested animal, check it out briefly and then throw it in my game bag. But that's next to impossible for me and nine times out of ten I find myself performing a full examination of the specimen, checking for ecto-parasites such as fleas or ticks, looking for tumors or growths, areas of missing hair caused by mites, and of course determining sex and age if possible. This is probably why I primarily hunt alone as most men would consider examining a squirrel's testicles taboo and would probably make a hasty exit from the woods telling their wives over supper, "First thing that dude did was flip the squirrel over and check out its testicles."

But knowing as much as possible about the animal I pursue is half the fun. Observations made while hunting help me expand my knowledge base. Want to really know about mink behavior? Ask a wildlife professor with a PhD, right? Wrong. Ask a mink trapper whose beard has long ago turned white and you'll find out everything you ever wanted to know about mink behavior. Of course, if you want scientific explanations as to why the mink behaves like it does, go back to the PhD wildlife professor. A good biologist possesses both field and book knowledge. What better way to get your field observations than in the woods, rifle in hand, on a cool autumn morning with the smell of fresh gunpowder hanging lightly in the air.

Wading for Smallies

I pull back and with a mighty heave, cast a crank-bait as far out as my small ultra-light pole will allow. The bait splashes down in a torrent of water so clear and clean that one can easily see the bottom in shallow areas. In the deeper pools, the water turns a deep turquoise green that makes me think of the green emeralds I've seen in the glossy pages of *National Geographic*.

I stand on a rock above where the river drops over what is left of a dam. The current is swift here and I have been watching two large smallmouth bass hunting along the edge of the pool. They move with explosive bursts of speed in pursuit of prey before disappearing out of sight again into deeper water. In general, a spot like this with deep water, swift current and preferably some submerged cover like a big rock or tree are good places to look for smallmouth, which prefer cool and clear streams and rivers.

I look at the other side of the creek and notice a small spit of sand that gleams white against the blue sky. I think of how it would be a perfect place for the kids to play if I had them with me today. But they are at home with their grandmother and mother playing with the toys that are kept in a small box under a bookshelf and watching cartoons. This warm summer day will be spent wade-fishing the Whitewater River with my father-in-law, Mark.

The rock I'm standing on used to be part of a larger dam that once stood here before an angry property owner used dynamite to blow it up because he felt it was causing the creek to flood his crops. There is still enough of the dam left to create a small waterfall that stretches the width of the river and dumps a small surge of white water into the pool below. After several failed attempts at hooking into the big fish that taunt me, I climb off the rock and drop into the cool water below the dam and begin wading downriver, casting and reeling as I go.

I look into the water and see the frays and threads of my wading shorts that move with the current like a water snake moves when it dives quick and deep. The shorts have been with me on countless wade trips and you'd know it right away if you saw me wearing them. You'd probably wonder what ditch I had just crawled out of and suspect that I had a drinking problem that kept me from buying new shorts. But I've worn them for years and they still provide me with pockets and a means for sheltering my middle section, although with the recent gaping holes that have appeared above both rear pockets the latter is questionable to some, in particular my wife who harbors a strong prejudice toward the shorts.

Mark and I stopped at Walmart before we hit the river and I felt a little self-conscious in the shorts as we walked through the parking lot towards the store. As we approached, the big sliding doors whooshed apart like some accelerated and commercialized parting of the Red Sea and out marched a woman wearing pink sweat-shorts that were at least three sizes too small for her. I felt my confidence build and headed straight to the sporting goods section, although I still pulled down on my shirt tail every once in a while to make sure it covered the majority of the holes.

I make another cast, aiming for a submerged log in a deep pool and reel my crank bait so close that I think it will snag the log any second. I am using a crayfish bait today because I like the diving action and I especially like the two sharp treble hooks that hang from the bait. I sometimes use a tube jig/twister-tail combo that I work in short bumps letting it fall to the bottom periodically. But the fact that it only has a single barbed hook and I'm not quite coordinated enough to react to a smallmouth bite leaves me with a lot of hits but few hookups, thus my preference for treble hooks.

As the lure passes the log, I feel the sharp bump of a hit and watch as my pole tip bends sharply and starts moving up and down like a dog's hind leg when he's scratched in that sweet spot just behind the ear. The fish runs hard and even makes a jump or two as I reel him in slow, relishing every second of the fight like the way you eat a tender venison steak that came straight off a smoky campfire.

Smallmouth seem to draw their fight from an ancient source: a well, lined with moss-covered river rock that is cool and dark when you stick your head down into it. You drop a rock into its emerald-green waters and watch as it falls deeper and finally out of sight. It contains the secrets of the universe and the source of a smallmouth's ability to fight. And it's that fight that keeps me wading cool waters on sunny days, trip after trip. The waters never say a word or raise a brow at the condition of my wading shorts but simply part as I make my way downstream casting and reeling and casting again.

River Trip

I take a deep breath and dive into the muddy water. I try to follow the line down to the anchor, which I know is caught underneath a log and wouldn't be that hard to free if I could just reach it. Our depth finder reads eight feet which is a doable dive if it weren't for the current that pushes against me forcing me to dive at an angle.

I reach up and with a wrinkled hand grab the sidewall of the jon boat. "Get out of the water, Son. That's enough," Bob says as he sits in his boat looking down at me below the rim of a camouflage bucket hat. It's the only hat I've ever seen him wear and I've seen him wearing it in Polaroid pictures from the 80s. He's been known to wear the hat as a solo ensemble while on the river as a way to display his freedom from secular norms and confines. Thankfully, today the hat shares his lanky frame with a pair of cut-off shorts.

I met Bob when we both worked out of the same Fish and Wildlife office. Bob was a highly experienced and highly respected biologist. He had the uncanny ability to learn something and then pull it from the recesses of his brain at will, sometimes years after he had learned it — a rare trait and one that gave Bob a distinct advantage over other biologists. He was independent by nature, paying little attention to what others thought of him or his views on biology, politics, etc. This trait gave him an eccentric quality which I admired.

By the tone of his voice and the steady look in his eyes beneath the rims of his large-framed military style glasses, I can tell his mind has run through the possible outcomes of my diving stunts and dwells on an ending he doesn't like. "We can cut the line. We'll cut the line, Son."

But I have to go down one more time because I know that Bob has recently purchased the anchor, which wasn't cheap. Since we are in his boat and this trip was my idea, I feel partly responsible. And once a feeling like that grips me, it can sometimes press me into places I shouldn't be before I can think about what I'm doing, a fault I hope never to see in my son.

I take a deep breath, tuck my head down and kick hard. I feel the cool river water against my skin. Its current is a steady push that can't be stopped and doesn't care what gets in its way or what body it may pin down to its muddy bottom for eternity like a giant boa constrictor that never tires. My world goes quiet and dark and I think of my family and what they would do without me.

How foolish it would seem for someone to read in the paper how on a warm summer day, while a soft breeze rustled the leaves of the tall silver maples that grow along the riverbank, and tree swallows skimmed carelessly over the water catching bugs, a man drowned while trying to save an anchor.

We had picked the spot to fish because it was a deep hole immediately below a riffle. Bob had been watching his depth finder while we cruised and immediately stopped the boat when he saw the drop-off. This scenario can produce fish as it combines two things that attract them: current and deep water.

Another good spot on a river to fish is the outside bank of a bend. The current is swift and the depth of a bend is deepest on the outside. Tight lining with a night crawler here can produce a wide variety of fish including drum, channel cat and white bass. Either scenario coupled with structure such as a submerged tree can be highly productive.

My head breaks the water surface and I pull a breath of air deep into my lungs and hold it there before releasing it along with the anguish I've felt over losing the anchor. I put both hands on the side wall of the boat and with a big pull, haul myself in. River water runs from my shorts and gathers in a small pool on the bottom of the boat.

I've given it up. I start to think again and quickly ask to borrow Bob's knife. "I'll get another anchor, Son," he says as he hands it to me. I cut the line and the boat starts drifting with the current. I rest against the side of the boat and look out over the river. The green leaves of the silver maple trees hang down gently toward the water and the tree swallows skim effortlessly over the muddy water as it moves endlessly forward in its unstoppable push towards the sea.

Going Deep for Redear

Before we had kids my wife and I spent many hours together fishing for panfish. We'd rise early, when the sun was just beginning to redden the eastern sky, and take a light breakfast of coffee, cereal and toast. I would hook our boat up to my red Jeep Cherokee and we'd head for the lake. Rena would be wearing her pink jersey shorts and a faded white t-shirt. The shorts made her tanned legs look even longer and the well-worn shirt would hang loosely across her slender shoulders showing the outlines of her prominent collar bones, a trait inherited from her mother. Her blond-brown hair would be pulled back into a pony tail with the white scrunchy that resided next to our bathroom sink when not in use. A loose strand or two would escape the grasp of the scrunchy and run down past her blue eyes and lay gently against the side of her face.

The lake we fished the most was Dogwood Lake located in southern Indiana. Here the water is clear and clean. In the summer, the big lotus pads ring the edges of the lake like a living necklace of green. The lake is full of stumps, trees that hang on stubbornly below the water surface long after the upper portions have snapped off and rotted. In the shallows amongst the stumps and lotus we'd troll looking for the spot where our bobbers would get sucked out of sight by slab bluegill. Our boat was small and gray, just big enough for two people. Since the trolling motor was mounted on the bow, the person in front could take the boat where they wanted.

141

We'd take turns sitting in front and inevitably, I mean like every single time we went out, an argument would break out. It went something like this:

> *Person in the back:* "Quit putting me in a bad spot back here!"

> *Person in front:* "I can't help it, the wind must be blowing us that way." (The lake is flat from the lack of wind.)

> *Person in back:* "Now I'm snagged up because I had to cast through all of these lotus pads and stumps."

> *Person in front* (as they are reeling in another fish): "All right, just hang on a minute. As soon as I get this fish in I'll get you un-snagged."

This would go on until the person in the front could no longer defend their blatantly selfish actions and we'd switch. But after the switch the only change was who was doing the criticizing and who was doing the reeling.

I had been married long enough to know that if a recreational activity repeatedly produces arguments, avoid that activity like the plague and move on to something else. But I couldn't leave fishing like I couldn't leave breathing. And so I was caught in a deep dilemma until the day I discovered it's possible to catch redear sunfish, a close relative of bluegill, in deep water away from any snags. Since you can anchor in one spot and still catch fish, there is no need to troll. Problem solved and marriage saved.

Redear sunfish can be distinguished from bluegill by the presence of a red or orange border on their ear flap. Redear also get bigger than bluegill, sometimes reaching lengths in excess of 12 inches. Most fishermen encounter redear in May when they go shallow to spawn. But after the spawn, when summer begins to settle in and one needs only a pair of shorts and a t-shirt to fish comfortably, the fish move into deeper water. They prefer feeding on aquatic snails found on the bottom and in some parts of the country they are referred to as "shell crackers" due to their ability to crack the shells of snails to get to the juicy insides.

All that is required is a decent fishing pole, some split shot and some hooks. For bait, red worms are preferable but they need to be fresh and lively because the movement on the bottom is what attracts fish. Finding your spots is the real trick but looking for deeper water, say between 10 and 12 feet, along the outside edge of a weed bed where the fish can easily see your bait is a good place to start.

As far as technique, let line out until your bait is on the bottom then lean your pole against the side of the boat, sit back, relax and wait until you get a bite. But always keep your pole within reach because when a fish is on, your pole will slam hard against the boat and double over towards the water. If it's a big fish, your pole will flop up and over the side and go down to a watery grave — a lesson I learned the hard way.

I sometimes think back on the warm summer days spent with my wife on Dogwood. The lake is calm, we are calm. "There you go!" I say as one of her poles doubles over and she cranks in another good one. Life was a little simpler then when it was just the two of us and our schedules were much less hectic. We would sit quietly on the big lake clad in shorts and t-shirts, our bare feet gripping the deck of the little gray boat as the green lotus pads along the shore waved back and forth in the soft breezes that drifted across the water.

Freezing for Turkeys

It's the last day of spring turkey season and I watch as sunbeams cut through the green leaves of oaks and hickories growing on the bluff where I sit. It's spring and the morning air is just warm enough to harbor a small swarm of mosquitoes that buzz around my face like feral dogs around a deer carcass. I pull out my bug spray and with camouflaged hands rapidly push the pump up and down until the swarm subsides. I can taste the chemical in my mouth and feel it turn my tongue numb. I watch the songbirds as they begin to chirp and flit about the tree branches looking for tiny bugs. Every so often I'll catch a glimpse of a chipmunk darting from one log to another, a brown blur of fur, searching for its breakfast like the birds.

And then I hear him, the cutting rattle of his gobble trumps all other bird sounds in both volume and intensity and gets my heart going every time. If I hear a gobble in the early morning hours while lounging on my front deck with a cup of coffee, I immediately start fidget thinking. I wonder where the bird might be and how I can get to him. Sometimes before I know what's happening, I'm halfway into the woods in a turkey-crazed trance sneaking towards the gobbler. I'm only awakened by the pain of a briar cutting through my sleep-pants the way a sleepwalker wakes after stumbling into a wall.

His gobble keeps coming like clockwork: a blast-rattle, then 30 seconds of nothing, then another blast-rattle. He picks up in intensity and I get ready. I make sure my gun is pointed where I think he will come and glance down at my camouflage pants to make sure my white socks are not showing above the tops of my combat boots.

The boots were issued to me at an Air Force training base in San Antonio, Texas, several years ago. Here my fellow trainees and I were made to march around in long-sleeve fatigues and long pants for several hours a day, all the while the hot Texas sun beating down on us. When the big sweat beads rolled down your face you couldn't wipe them away because your arms had to be swinging properly while you marched. You knew the drill sergeant was always watching and would go out of his way to humiliate a trainee for the slightest infraction, like wiping sweat away while marching. My foot sweat combined with the constant marching made the leather form snugly around my feet, giving the boots a firm fit that allows for a quiet tread in the woods.

I hold my hunched-over position looking down the barrel of the gun, my body hid behind some small leafy branches I cut and stuck in the ground in front of me to hide my outline better. I know from experience that if a gobbler catches the slightest movement from an object that looks out of place, even from a good distance away, he immediately runs or launches into flight in the opposite direction. This overgrown chicken with a brain smaller than a walnut has a serious case of OCD when it comes to sensing danger and fleeing. He has developed his keen sight by eons of searching for tiny insects in grassy fields and by being the first turkey to see danger and flee, thus passing on his genes in a survival of the fittest pattern that has created his unmatchable sight. By turning his head and looking at things from slightly different angles he can get a good estimate of relative distance and also gain a 360-degree field of vision. When he cranes his neck and focuses on you with those black eyes, don't blink, don't twitch your upper lip, don't swallow hard or he's gone, you can depend on it.

As quickly as the gobbling started, it has suddenly stopped. The bird has flown down from his roost and quit gobbling, leaving me with no clues to his whereabouts. As minutes of silence tick by I start to unfreeze myself, lifting my head up from the gun and leaning back against the tree I'm sitting under. I begin second-guessing which way he went and that maybe he walked off in the opposite direction and I'm sitting here for no reason. The mosquitoes begin to swarm again and my hopes start looking for the next bus out of town.

And then I see him. He is steadily walking right toward me. I can see his big searching eyes and the deep black feathers of his chest. I ever so slowly begin to put my cheek down on the stock of the gun so I can aim properly. I fall into a state of panic now as he comes closer and closer and I start to worry he'll see me before I'm ready to shoot. So, even though my cheek is not quite on the stock, I point in his direction and pull the trigger.

The woods erupt with sound as the gun kicks hard against my shoulder. Instead of seeing flopping wings and a turkey on its side, I see a turkey that sprints towards the edge of the bluff unharmed by my shot. He leaps into flight, weaving through the trees on the bluff headed toward the bottom where the creek runs.

For a split second I can't believe what just happened. When it finally sinks in, I recklessly dash down the bluff trying to run him down, unable to accept the fact that I missed a turkey from 10 yards away. Actually, I don't know what I was hoping to do except make an idiot of myself in front of all the watching songbirds and chipmunks. I wish I had just sat back down against the tree and took the miss like any rational thinking person would.

Next year, second day of season I sat hunched over my gun with my cheek on the stock and my eye down the barrel for a good 45 minutes straight. Never once did I unfreeze myself, even when the turkey I was hunting was silent for several agonizing minutes. When he finally did appear, I was ready. This time the report of my gun was followed by a flopping turkey on its side. I was soon headed for home, gobbler in hand. My black combat boots were tucked away under my work bench in the garage early that year, giving them plenty of time to rest up for next season.

Snowy Riverbank

The big diesel truck lumbers to a stop along the edge of a woodlot draped in white. The brown bark of the twisted trees brings out the brightness of the new snow. Inside the truck cab, the three of us are plunged into silence as my father-in-law, Mark, kills the clamoring engine. We have spent the morning cooped up in my in-laws' house eating ham and watching kids open Christmas presents. But once the ham was reduced to one lonely bone and the living room floor was so packed with wrapping paper you needed a snow shovel to escape, Mark, my brother-in-law Jacob, and I headed for the nearest woodlot.

Mark breaks the silence by explaining the plan. He methodically plots our route of travel and explains where we should sit with a slow, faint southern drawl. The plan accounts for all possible coyote approach paths, the most viable shooting lanes and most importantly wind direction. Silence again claims the truck cab. Seconds morph into minutes before my brother-in-law Jacob breaks the silence with his own tactical plan which varies slightly from that of Mark's. A debate ensues between father and son before Mark's plan emerges as champion. I nod my head in agreement, refusing to assert my own plan, all too aware of the reserved criticism that lies in wait for the guy who marries your daughter or your sister.

As we begin to exit the truck cab, I look at my watch and note that 15 minutes have passed since the truck first rolled to a stop. When I first began hunting with Mark and Jake, these frequent spans of inactivity frustrated me to no end (I have a hard time sitting still…). After many years I've come to anticipate the slow pace of our hunts, often bringing along a magazine or newspaper to keep myself occupied until the reckoning, discussing, and mulling over are done and we finally get to the action.

Outside the cab, the brightness of the snow stands in stark contrast with the gray cloud cover above us. I take note of a slight but cutting wind as I pull my brown hunting coat snuggly over my shoulders. Rifles are loaded and checked. Electronic coyote call, shooting sticks, snow camouflage, binoculars and ammunition are all readied and stowed for the walk in. I watch as Jake helps Mark sling his rifle and glance at my watch which reads 30 minutes longer than when the voice of the diesel engine was first silenced.

We begin to move, Mark taking lead while I bring up the rear, in somber display of my prominence in the hierarchy of my wife's family. Our path leads through dense woods to the edge of a shallow but swift-moving river. The icy waters are crystal clear and flow over large gray rocks. The banks are covered with snow and dotted with twisted roots and large chunks of driftwood. The trees on either bank hang their branches as far out as gravity will allow, overlapping in the middle like the arched ceiling of a gothic cathedral. I look upriver and notice a group of drake mallards resting on the water's surface. Their green necks and white rumps bring dramatic color to the otherwise brown and white river. They spot me and explode into flight with rapid wing beat and raspy quacking. To my right, a beaver has left behind a muddy slide and countless wood shavings scattered about like some mad woodcarver had whittled his magnum opus here. Mark, who has hunted along these banks many times before, pauses, clearing his throat to say, "I love hunting here."

Our route meanders along the river for what seems like a good mile and a half. Our pace is slow but steady. I observe my father-in-law's stride which is an efficient shuffle of feet where one lifts the foot just high enough to clear an obstacle but no higher. It brings to mind the energy-saving step of the mules I've seen on the Bright Angel trail in Grand Canyon National Park. Of course, the shuffle has its drawbacks, as occasionally the height of an obstacle is miscalculated resulting in a trip-up. On these occasions I look at Jake and smile as Mark lets a few choice words fly into the frosty air.

We veer away from the river and are soon standing along the edge of an expansive cornfield. I lean against a tree as Mark and Jake carefully place the electronic caller in the field and discuss where we all should sit. Jacob assigns me my position. As I settle into the snow next to a big tree, I look at my watch and note that it has taken us nearly two hours for our hunt to officially start. Shortly after Jake leaves my position, the sound of a rabbit in distress begins erupting from the caller. I scan the woods with my eyes only, shot gun at ready, in the hopes that a coyote will appear from the woods tempted by the prospect of an easy meal.

But nothing happens. I sit quietly for several long minutes before letting my gun down and leaning back heavily against the tree. The warmth from my jacket, the trickle of running water from the nearby river and the pale gray light of the day all work methodically against my consciousness. I fall victim to these natural sirens and pass into a light but peaceful sleep.

I am soon wakened by the sound of crunching snow as Jake approaches my position. I quickly realize our hunt, which consisted of several hours of preparation and about 15 minutes of actual hunt time is over. "See anything?" Jake asks.

"No," I reply as we both walk to the edge of the field where Mark is gathering and stowing his gear for the walk out.

On our walk back to the truck the three of us are quiet. On one hand, we have failed in our efforts to outsmart a coyote. On the other hand, we have succeeded by getting out of the house and making it to the woods for a hunt. We pause in the woods one last time before we reach the truck.

"I love hunting these woods," Mark says, his words carrying across the snowy banks of the river.

Whitney Pit

"It's green all around us," Jacob says as he looks up from his iPhone. Over his t-shirt-clad shoulder I glance at the yellow rays from the sun's last few minutes of light jetting up the side of a billowing cumulus cloud that towers over our small boat. The reflection of the cloud rests peacefully on the surface of the undisturbed water surface. I say nothing in response to Jake's statement and make a long cast toward the bank where I know a willing bluegill is waiting. As my lure strikes the surface and sinks, my eye focuses on the stripper bank with its green vegetation and dogwood trees in full bloom next to a crumbling rock high-wall that leers decrepitly above the water. The sound of distant thunder rolls through the air with a voice full of a contained energy. A turkey gobbles in response, as if trying to trump the noise with its own voice. The sound of the gobble is a throaty eruption of cutting notes descending deeper and deeper in tone and volume.

I cast again. I notice how the fading evening light brings a mysterious air to the place. It's that sort of eerie half dark, half light that one encounters just prior to sunset. It's a time when shadows creep and the eye an*d the brain attempt to reconcile over every slight movement but never seem to reach any sort of agreement except for a steady state of uneasiness. This Luna Moth lighting adds to the remarkable stillness of the pit and I am easily sucked into a drifting respite until distant lightning reminds me again of the looming storm. Ours is a landscape on pause. It's so beautiful that I put all my concentration into engraving the experience deep into my brain, like a smoker holding a breath of smoke in the lungs before slowly letting it back out again.

We fish on. One cast is followed by another until I feel the quick pull-pull of a bluegill hitting my lure. He pulls, turns, flips side to side, before making a long run away from the boat causing my fishing pole to sing as it lets line out. When I finally pull the fish into our boat, I admire its crimson yellow, ocean blue and rustic orange coloration.

Manmade noise now draws my attention as a rusty truck pops past on the dirt road near the pit. Old trucks with loud exhausts are a common site in this area. Often occupying the cabs are men with long beards who wear bib overalls and Charlie Daniels t-Shirts, honest and hard-working men, never bearing any false airs; what you see is what you get. Theirs is a land full of stripper hills, stripper pits, high-walls, stripper banks, and gob piles all covered with tangled woods and alive with wild things. Decades ago, the pit that Jake and I fish was an active coal mine. To get to the coal, workers "stripped" away the earth above it. What was once a quagmire of men operating noisy, exhaust-spewing earthmovers, booming with dynamite explosions, has now been reclaimed by the flora and fauna of southern Indiana. Men once came here to earn their pay, now they come here to earn their respite.

Another rolling throb of thunder is followed closely by a lightning flash. Jake and I glance at each other. A mind game of physiological endurance ensues. I want so bad to say "we better go in" but the words will not come. I will not be the first one to call it quits. Jake says nothing but steadily flings and retrieves a top water jig hoping for a bass strike. All the stories and warnings I've read about fishermen getting struck by lightning now start to nag at my conscience. I picture my wife quietly weeping as she reads the weekend headlines, *Two men killed by lightning while fishing Pike County strip pit.*

"Let's fish our way along the bank back to the boat ramp."

"Probably a good idea," Jake quickly responds.

I know I've lost, and I'm OK with it. For I should love another chance to live these moments again, if only to pull them from my memory bank and relive a moment of quiet beauty on the verge of a looming spring thunderstorm.

Running Beagle Dogs

It's a cold gray afternoon and since the winter wind licks down my back I reach around and pull my hood up a little higher and a little tighter. I move through the tall prairie grass that is a bright golden yellow color, which pushes back against the gray skies but can't seem to overcome the dreariness of the day. Snow begins to spit and rolls past me in rapid swirls blown by frequent wind gusts. Bo-Jay, my father-in-law's beagle, is a step or two ahead of me and looks back occasionally for reassurance. "He's in there, boy. Find the rabbit," I say as he delves a little deeper into the thick grass.

As a kid I was introduced to hunting with beagles by my dad's cousin, Brad. We hunted a woodlot in northern Indiana. When we got to a thick patch towards the back of the woods, Brad had me stand at the far end while he worked the beagle dogs towards me. As I stood in the northern Indiana cold holding my single-shot Ithaca with the hammer that was hard to pull back with frozen fingers, rabbits began to squirt from the patch like beans running out of a gunny sack. I waited until one ran out and stopped in front of me and I can still see the rabbit's black eye as it sat and I drew down and fired. I felt a little guilty about shooting a sitting rabbit but since it was my first shot at one, I wanted to make it count. And it did.

We ran several rabbits that day. When we got back to the truck, I can remember my dad's other cousin Neal sitting on the tailgate feeding the dogs donuts, saying things like "that's a good boy" in tender tones to the dogs as they jumped up and down on his leg and licked his hands, stained red from rabbit blood. Neal reminded me of a real-life version of Red Skelton's character "Freddy the Freeloader." I later learned that he actually led a life that would have made a decent backdrop for Skelton's character.

I walk a little further and see a gray streak go running through the grass, so I call Bo-Jay over by saying the word "here" fast and loud, a call you only make when you've seen a rabbit so there's no question in the dog's mind about what's going on. Bo-Jay comes running quick. After sucking with his nose at the ground so much you wonder how he keeps from filling it with dirt and chaff, he pulls his head up and lets loose a loud rolling bay.

The way he sucks at the ground reminds me of a hog gobbling up scraps, except Bo-Jay gobbles up scent. He follows the rabbit's trail until the scent hits him again and he lets loose another bay. The way he bays when he hits scent reminds me of the way your leg kicks out when the doctor tests your reflexes by hitting you in the kneecap with that little hammer. My father-in-law's other two dogs join in and a racket of bays, barks and yips fills the cold winter air.

Rabbit hunting with beagles is based on the premise that most rabbits, when pursued, will run in a circle, returning to the same general area where they were jumped. Rabbits feed heavily in the early morning and late evening hours and spend the rest of the day loafing in one location called a "form." The form is usually located in thick grasses or briars that provide the rabbit with good side and overhead cover but will be open in the front allowing for an easy escape route. Once the rabbit flees his daytime rest site and the beagles are in pursuit, the goal is to station yourself along the route you think the rabbit will run in order to get the best shot opportunity.

When beagles chase a rabbit back to where it was originally jumped, this is called running a full circle. Most serious beagle hunters will not shoot at the rabbit until the dogs bring him back around. If the rabbit is not harvested on the first circle, the process is repeated and some runs may last for two or even three circles. Some rabbits will run a tight circle while others will range out so far that the dogs can run out of earshot before bringing him back around. As with other types of hunting, the thrill is in the chase. Guessing what route the rabbit will run and where to stand is a big part of the fun too.

The beagles are coming back around now and as the barking comes close, I get ready. I watch in the weeds for the slightest movement, which is difficult because my eye constantly catches on the grasses as they blow in the wind. Watching like this makes me feel like the red-tailed hawks that sit along the highway for hours, scanning the grass for a mouse or vole.

I see him as he punches out of the grass and runs through a clear area. I shoulder my gun and pull the big hammer back, but by the time I'm on him he's made it to the next patch of cover. The day is quickly fading and the cold wind and snow keep on coming, so we decide to head back to the house. When we get back, I walk inside and open the woodstove door. The heat from the glowing coals wipes away the cold and the wind. As we put Bo-Jay up for the night, I reach down and pat his head telling him how good he was today. Even though I don't have any donuts, he jumps up and down on my leg all the same.

Crane Flight

It's an unusually warm winter day and I am sitting in a plastic lawn chair next to a hot fire. The sky still has plenty of blue left, but I know I better get these pork chops done because even though it's warm, the sun is still operating on its winter schedule and will set before suppertime. The chops pop and sizzle and I have to move them to the side when the grease drippings hit the hot coals and they erupt into meaty fireballs. The scent of sizzling pork fat mixed with hickory smoke smells so good I'm sure I could give the world's staunchest vegetarian a ravenous foam-at-the-mouth type of hunger for pork meat.

The children have used the warm winter day as an opportunity to turn the front yard into a mud pit that looks something like a Tonka truck mud derby. They are completely and entirely covered in mud. My oldest daughter who is five leads my three-year-old son in the rowdy pursuits of making mud pies and running as fast as possible through a large mud puddle. She takes off and Eli attempts to follow but only makes it about halfway before tripping and falling face first in the puddle. The water has soaked all through the front of his pants and has gone down over the tops of his little rubber boots. I hear him start to cry as he slowly pulls his muddy self up, but he soon starts running after his sister again and his sobbing turns to laughter.

As I sit, I begin to hear a faint broken call that comes from the blue skies above. I look up and see a group of big birds flapping their wings in steady rhythm. They are flying high in a loose "V" that keeps shifting and changing but always seems to stay together, heading in a unified direction. The birds are Sandhill Cranes. Since I haven't had much time to hunt or fish this month, I appreciate the fact that I at least get the chance see some wildlife.

Sandhill Cranes are a common sight in Indiana, especially in the fall and spring when they migrate through the state in large numbers. Sandhills will also overwinter in Indiana. So the birds you see in the middle of winter may not be coming or going from any far-off destination but rather making a daily movement from a roosting site to a feeding site.

Last year when we took a winter trip to Florida, there were Sandhill Cranes that frequented the subdivision we were staying in. As we drove through the rows of houses one morning on the way to the beach, I noticed a group of Sandhills walking along a sidewalk. The birds walked with their long legs and necks like they owned the place. I stopped the car and pointed them out to the children and the birds looked at us with their red-topped heads, which were almost eye level with the children.

I continue to watch the cranes as they fly out of sight into the blue sky. The day is fading quickly and I can feel cold air on my ears as I take the last pork chop off the fire and head inside. After supper I build a fire in the woodstove and think of how the cranes are probably at their roost site for the night. I look forward to the next time I hear their trumpeting calls and see their outstretched wings set high up against blue sky.

Roosted

I look out across the river and see through the treetops that the sunset tonight is a blood red orange color, the kind of color that your eyes don't want to let go. The past few days have been nothing but hectic as Rena and I struggled to get all of our earthly possessions moved into our new home. The move was complicated some, complicated a lot actually, by the fact that we have three young children and about as soon as we got a box packed our one-year-old would totter over and diligently take the contents out and strew them all over the floor like it was her job for the day. As I sit on the deck, I feel the wound-up tightness inside of me slowly unwinding and drifting away in the unusually warm March air and I lean a little further back into my plastic lawn chair.

The children are all in bed, quietly drifting to sleep, well fed from the T-bone steaks I cooked on the grill for supper. When I cooked the steaks, I let the flames from the grill crisp the fat so that when I took them off they were crispy in places but still red and juicy in the middle. Rena and I drank red wine with the steaks, which was chilled slightly and tasted crisp and sweet when paired with the seasoned steak.

Just as the sunset looks like it couldn't get any redder, I start to see fast-flying ducks in small groups of fives and sixes buzz past the back deck and on down the river. I watch them a little longer and by the way they fly, I figure they are wood ducks and I think of how they are probably heading for their nighttime roost.

Wood ducks are a common sight in Indiana, especially in the fall and spring when they migrate in large numbers across our state.

161

Wood ducks also nest here, preferring to raise young in tree cavities near water. Large sycamore trees growing along riverbanks offer good nesting sites because they are usually full of holes and crevices.

I begin to see the first stars in the evening sky before the little duck groups finally taper off. The day is done and the wood ducks are all at their roost. And I am glad too that the Whiteleather family is finally moved into our new roost. Hopefully the wound-up tightness of moving won't be experienced by this family again anytime soon.

Drum Fishing

It's Saturday afternoon and since the garage staining project is finally finished, I ask Eva if she wants to go fishing. "Yes," she says with a smile and runs to get her shoes. We walk down the 70 steps that lead from our cabin to the river and take the trail to the right that winds along the bank and goes to our fishing spot. Here we always find shade and a good breeze and the sweat from a weekend project is quickly forgotten. The exposed roots of two big trees have formed a platform which makes a good place to sit as it's close to the water.

I reach in my pockets and pull out some hooks, sinkers, a container of redworms and a small pair of pliers — all the tackle we'll need for the evening. I hook a red worm on my line and throw out, letting the sinker take the hook and worm to the bottom.

Now we wait. E has taken her shoes off and I notice how the brown river dirt sticks between the toes of her little feet. This is how kids' feet should look, I think, in the middle of summer, in the middle of Indiana.

Before long, E's attention turns from watching the fishing pole to watching everything else. "There goes an ant, Daddy," she says.

"Yep, looks like he's looking for something to eat," I respond. No sooner are the words out of my mouth than E follows with a question,

"What do ants eat, Daddy?"

I tell her how they eat other insects and dead stuff they find on the ground and she asks what kind of insects they eat. When I give her a few examples of other insects ants might eat, she asks how they find them and so on and so forth until the barrage of questioning that only a 5-year-old can conjure up is interrupted by the bending of my pole.

"Fish on," I say as E anxiously watches me fight the fish. By the strong steady pull and deliberate runs, I know the fish is a drum and I do my best to work it up to the bank.

Freshwater drum inhabit Indiana's rivers and streams in great numbers. The fish is named after the low drumming noise males make during spawning season. The noise is a low-pitched running croak that's heard best on warm summer evenings when the leaves on the silver maples hang motionless and the river is quiet. The drum is a bottom feeder, feeding primarily on aquatic insects and crayfish. It is readily caught on night crawlers fished on the bottom and when hooked puts up a good fight. The meat is white and mild flavored. I prefer it fried and between two pieces of bread, piled high with cheese and lettuce and slathered with mayonnaise.

After a good fight, I haul the fish up on the bank and E tells me how good the fish is and how we'll have to tell Mommy all about it when we get back. I remove the hook and we listen to the fish make its drumming noise before we release it back into the river.

I put a fresh worm on and cast back out again as E sets me up for a series of questions concerning what worms eat. The river rolls quietly on as we talk, flowing past our spot like it has long before E and I ever sat here, like it will long after we no longer do.

The Great Horned Owl

A s I step outside into the early winter night on my way to put the trash in the garage, I hear a soft but deep-toned call of an owl. The night is still but for the call, which is a series of subdued hoots that while not necessarily loud have a deep penetrating quality to them.

I pause for a moment and listen; this bird calling softly in the darkness pulls my thoughts away from my nightly routine and into the realm of wild things. I think of how the bird, a great horned owl, is possibly a male calling in order to attract a mate. And on this night, while many things consume my thoughts, his thoughts consist of only two things: finding a mate and finding something to eat.

If the owl is successful in finding a mate (a relationship that can last for life), owlets will be hatched in January. How odd it seems for a critter to be raising young in the coldest and snowiest time of the year. Some biologists speculate that owlets hatch early in the year so that they have ample time to develop survival skills before they face their first winter on their own as first-year adults.

My thoughts wander to my own owlets tucked away in their beds inside the cabin. Up the stairs that lead to the loft you'll find the two oldest, their blond heads sticking out from a layer of colorful quilts and Space Ranger blankets. The loft is the warmest room in the house. When you stand against the railing, you get a good view of the great room down below and the big stone fireplace that reaches all the way up to the rafters.

The youngest lies in the small bedroom just down the hall from the great room. This room was once used as a den by the previous owner. The walls were still covered with the old man's war pictures and Vietnam-era war paraphernalia when we first came to look at the place. Now instead of war medals and folded American flags, pictures from Dr. Seuss books and little white dresses with flowers embroidered on them adorn the walls.

My mate who I somehow attracted through a series of calls, like the owl, except I used a cell phone instead of a beak, resides on the couch next to the fireplace reading one of her non-fiction books. In the morning when her brood awakes hungry and sleepy-eyed, she'll feed them pancakes with raspberries on top, the raspberries she picked last summer and froze in quart bags. When the bacon gets to just the right crispiness, she'll lay it on a paper towel and use the hot bacon-flavored griddle to cook eggs on.

Later that night, as I lie down to sleep, the owl's call comes in clear through the thick cabin walls and I know he is still calling in the night. Rena hears it too and asks, "Why do you think he calls so often? Seems like I hear him every night."

"Not sure," I respond. "Great horns nest and mate for life; maybe he thinks getting it right is worth the effort."

Winter Hunting

When I first look out the window, the sun is showing pale red and orange through the brown trees that stand along the edge of the snow-covered field across the road from the house. I feel the heat from the big woodstove that sits in the living room and know that my father-in-law must have loaded it already. "Coffee's ready," he announces when he sees me standing by the window, a customary morning greeting between us. I pour a cup and go back to the window and look out across the field again as thin strands of steam wisp up from the coffee in a steady line of aromatic vapor.

In the next couple of minutes my mother-in-law arrives on the scene and the thick smell of frying bacon soon fills the air. The children start to file out of the back bedroom and after a quick trip to the bathroom shuffle down to the couch where a man in a yellow hat chases a monkey on the TV. From the back of the couch, all you can see are the tops of their heads. Their blond hair is tangled worse than the Christmas lights in our attic.

Soon breakfast is on the table and I sit down to biscuits and gravy, fried eggs and two thick slabs of bacon. I push my fork into the eggs and yolk runs out mixing with the white gravy before being soaked up like a sponge by the biscuits. I eat till I'm full, caring little that I'm getting my daily calorie intake all in one meal because I know I will be on my feet all day watching beagle dogs run rabbits through snow-covered fields and woods.

Outside the house the air is cold and a slight wind can be felt, but the dogs don't care. Once they figure out what's happening, they bark, bay and bounce off their kennel doors as if their back legs are tightly wound springs. Their little black eyes gleam with excitement as their hot breath pours out into the cold morning air.

When we get to the rabbit patch, there's enough snow for my boots to make prints but brown dirt can be seen in the spaces between the treads, good conditions for running rabbits. We tromp through thick patches of goldenrod, their stems bare except for the white fluffy seeds that cling to them like tiny clumps of pin feathers. In late summer, when the goldenrod bloom was in full swing, the flowers were golden yellow and alive with honey bees. The stems were covered in large green leaves. But now the stems are barren and stand over the snow-covered ground blowing steadily back and forth in the cold winter wind. Instead of standing out with their deep golden colors, they now blend in with the rest of the dormant colors of winter.

After stomping around for several minutes, a rabbit bursts from its hiding place. Soon the dogs are in pursuit, sending a chorus of bays, howls, squeals and barks out over the rabbit patch. The dogs are hot on the track and before long they have turned and are coming back towards me. I get ready, but when the rabbit darts past and I fire, my shot falls behind it. The next rabbit we find, the dogs don't do so well and my father-and-law and I come to the conclusion that scent conditions must have changed.

When hunting with dogs, scent conditions determine how well the dogs will do. The bodies of animals, and humans too, generate microscopic molecules commonly referred to as scent. Scent can hang in the air or cling to substrates such as dirt, grass and snow. If scent conditions are good, scent will stay in the area where it was deposited leaving a good scent trail. If scent conditions are poor, scent molecules will dissipate, leaving little for the dog's nose to pick up.

Wind, humidity, sunlight level and temperature all play a factor in how quickly scent is dispersed. Generally speaking, scent conditions are best when ground temperature and air temperature are close to the same and winds are at minimum.

When the hunt is over and the beagles are all put away and fed, I step into the house and stand next to the woodstove until I can feel the heat through my pant legs. My cheeks are slow to warm up and tingle a little, telling me they are wind burnt and red. The kids are all in bed and the house is quiet like the dark night around it. Before I go to bed, I look out the front window again and in the gleam of moonbeam reflecting off snow, I can see the trees along the field edge bending slowly back and forth in the cold winter wind.

On Any Summer Evening

If you come to our cabin on a summer evening, walk down the 70 steps that lead to the river, take the well-worn trail to your right that's always in the deep shade, walk over the two planks that straddle a small stream, duck once or twice to avoid the low-hanging branches that droop across the trail and look down to your left at the spot where the two big sycamore trees grow close together along the edge of the river — you'll find me.

I'll likely be eyeing my lines, watching for the small jerks and twitches that mean a fish is taking the bait. If it's later in the evening and the fish are starting to bite, I might be hooked into a fish and will be slowly reeling it in, savoring every second of fight.

River fish are the best of fighters having dealt all their lives with relentless currents in their daily struggle for survival. My fish will make long runs as line sheds from my drag like a gutter sheds water, before it turns and gives whole-body shakes and flops. When I finally get it to the bank just before I reach down to grab it, it'll start shaking and pulling again, getting water on my shirt as if to say, "I'll fight to the last, and then some."

Out will come the pliers. The circle hook that always ends up in the corner of the fish's mouth will be carefully removed, the long black whiskers of the fish lying wetly against the sides of my hands. Soon the fish will be back in the water, darting away into muddy darkness and I'll be reaching for another shrimp to re-bait with.

If you look out past me over the river, you'll see its deep green waters moving slowly within tree-lined banks. If there's enough light yet, you may see the sun's last rays glinting off a group of insects swarming over the water surface like some shapeless river phantom. If it's a red sunset, you'll see the oranges, reds and purples of a fiery sky reflected in the waters of the river. You may hear a belted kingfisher let go a raspy call as it flies downriver headed for its roost, its white-feathered breast reflecting the last glimpses of light.

I'll sit quietly as I fish so I can hear and see more wildlife, like the muskrats that come up on the rocks to clean themselves and the big beavers that cut strong "V"s in the water as they swim by. Occasionally, a deer will walk the trail and I will hear it before I see it, the same way I heard you before I saw you.

When you ask if I'm doing any good, I'll simply reply, "Oh caught a few," no matter how many I've caught, paying homage to the river-rat code of conduct which permits a fisherman to underestimate his catch in order to keep his best spots a secret. You may stand and watch for a while and we may talk, but all the while my eyes will be on the lines, watching for signs of underwater activity. When a rod begins to twitch before doubling over, the conversation will end until the fight is over and the fish is landed.

And then when the lightning bug darkness descends on the river and the songbirds in the woods have all quieted and gone to roost, I'll know I should go up to the cabin but I won't want to. You'll tire of waiting in the darkness and decide to head back up.

As you leave I'll call over my shoulder, "I'll be up in a minute or two, after I throw out just one more time."

Cicada Days

It's Saturday afternoon and I'm sitting on the back deck, my bare feet resting on its surface. The wood is dry and slightly abrasive, like 150 grit sandpaper, but since my feet are worn out from working all day, it feels good against my skin. A slight breeze stirs the leaves, but only momentarily and soon dies away. Here and there a bird flits from branch to branch in the tall trees that grow along the river bluff. Other than the birds, the woods are quiet and still. The sun, which has blazed hotly all day, is slowly slipping toward the horizon. It lights up the back sides of the leaves making them glow in tones of yellow and green.

And then they start. First it's a slow creaking, sputtering sound in the distance. But soon the sound gathers in intensity and volume and seems to be all around me. It rises in waves before reaching a throbbing pitch and fading away. It ceases momentarily before starting up again. It's like the sound of a distant train that roars past you and fades off in the distance. But then the train turns around and comes back.

The noise brings back memories from my childhood. On hot summer nights every window in the old 1800s-era farmhouse I grew up in would be open. I'd lie in bed huddled close to the window taking advantage of any breeze that might pass through. I could hear the noise loud and clear coming from the tall pine trees that grew close to the house. I would drift asleep to the sound, the same sound that had played through the house on hot summer nights for decades.

The noise heard across our state in late summer is produced by annual cicadas. Unlike periodical cicadas, which only occur every 7, 13 or 17 years, annual cicadas are found every year. Annuals have green bodies with brown and black markings whereas the bodies of periodicals are solid black.

Adult annual cicadas emerge in late May and June. The exoskeletons they shed as they emerge can be found clinging to the trees where they were left behind. Males call to attract a mate, and they do so by vibrating membranes on their undersides. In around a month's time adults will breed, females will lay eggs and both male and female will die. The eggs will hatch, overwinter in the soil by feeding on tree sap found in roots, before emerging next summer to start the process over again.

It's getting late now but the cicadas are still calling. The air is a little heavy tonight and a few sweat beads are starting to form on my brow. It's been a long summer and I'm looking forward to the time when all the cicadas are gone, the days are much cooler and the trees are dressed in their fall colors. But after fall will surely come winter. In the evenings I'll stand by the big glass doors and look out at the deck. The woodstove will be going and inside will be the big orange coals that come after a full day of burning wood. The deck will be covered in a blanket of white snow and icicles will hang from the gutters. A cold wind will rise up from the gray evening sky and swirl the snow. The songbirds at the bird feeder will be buffeted by it, their fine feathers ruffling like tiny banners in the wind. Deep underground, young cicadas will be tucked away from it all happily sucking tree sap. I'll stand and stare at the winter scene thinking of the cicadas and longing for the days of summer when their chorus will again fill the air.

Family Hiking

It's an overcast day in late August. A threatening chance of rain puts a damper on our spirits, but the unusually cool weather brought about by cloud cover brings them right back up again. I guide our Chevy Trailblazer to the parking lot next to the trailhead and as soon as I turn the key off, seat belts are thrown over shoulders and doors are thrown open with abandon.

First out is the tallest. Her shoulder-length blond hair trails in the wind as she runs to the back of the Trailblazer where I am opening the hatch. "Daddy, can you fix my shoe lace?" she asks.

"Sure," I say as I reach down to untie the knot in the pink laces of her blue tennis shoes. She fixes her large blue eyes on me as I work. Her mouth is held slightly open and her brow is knit with attention, a sure sign she is studying my methods so she can try to untie the knot on her own next time.

Next out is my son. His short legs stick out from his plaid shorts and run down until they are swallowed up again by his socks, which are pulled up level with his knees. The knee socks coupled with his hiking boots give him the look of a serious hiker. He mills about in the gravel of the parking lot, stopping to study the rocks before picking one out to kick into the grass.

Last out is the youngest. She walks over and wraps one arm around my leg. The thumb of her other arm is planted squarely in her mouth. She kicks at rocks a little with her feet while she watches me fiddling with her sister's shoe. I reach down and ruffle her fine red-brown hair until it looks like a little pile of hay on the top of her head.

After the day pack is loaded with all the necessities (fruit snacks, water, wet wipes, first-aid supplies, a spare pair of shorts for the little one, rain coats, cameras and more wet wipes), we head for the trail.

The woods are dark. Here and there large drips of rainwater drop from the green leaves of the pawpaw trees that dot the forest floor. The drops are big, cold and clear and if you stop and listen you can hear them falling in a steady rhythm in the still, dim-lit forest: drip...drip... drip...drip...drip. Large ferns grow on either side of the trail. In several places they come together in the middle, swallowing the trail in their leafy greenness.

Through a series of switchbacks, the trail descends into a steep ravine. The forest becomes darker and darker the further down we go. As we descend, I begin to spot several different species of fall mush-rooms growing on the forest floor. There's shelf and oyster fungus grow-ing from rotted stumps and logs. The shelf fungus is light brown with darker edges and is hard and brittle to the touch. The oysters are brilliant white and grow in clusters of 10 to 15. Unlike the shelf fungus, they are delicate to the touch. When I pick them and break them open their moist insides produce a clean and fresh smell.

There are also toadstools sticking up from the brown earth in tones of oranges, browns and yellows. These are difficult to pick without the wide, flat, circular caps breaking away from their thin stems. There is also a small shelf-like fungus that is the color of burnt orange and grows on rotted logs. The edges are waved and its body is rather thin. It's not much for texture or smell but its presence adds a dash of dramatic color to the forest floor.

The variety of fungus found here is unusual and I'm quickly absorbed in examining and photographing each one I come across. I soon find myself a good distance back from my family and hurry to catch up with them.

Up ahead the two older children are traversing the switchbacks with abandon, their feet thumping along the hard-packed trail as they go. The youngest struggles to keep up, her little legs working hard to keep her body under control.

But then the inevitable happens. Her downhill dash reaches a tipping point and she falls headlong onto the forest floor, her body making a soft thump against the dirt.

Rena and I wait for the wail that will surely follow. As she takes in a deep breath, the calm before the storm, I hear one last drip from a paw-paw leaf fall. And then the forest is filled with the sound and fury of a toddler expressing herself in the aftermath of a tumble. She pours all of her frustration, pain of a skinned knee, disappointment at not catching up with her siblings, into the wail that runs in one long wave of sound down through the ravine and up into the forest above. But as soon as the torrent begins it suddenly ends. She's up and going again, the dirt that clings to her little pink shorts the only reminder of the fall.

We finally reach the bottom of the gorge and find a little creek. Small trickles of clear water run and bubble over dark slabs of rock. I pick up small rocks and fossils and show them to the children. Their interest is short-lived and soon they are running full tilt along the trail again.

After another spill and a good cry from the little one, we begin to climb up and out of the ravine. When we reach the top, I spot a group of oyster mushrooms growing on the end of a moss-covered log. They grow in the forest opening that was left when the massive tree fell. A few rays of sunlight that manage to break through the clouds strike the fungus making it gleam white. I take out my camera and begin to snap shots and before long I'm alone again. I take one last shot before pausing a moment to listen. It's still and quiet, except for the dripping which continues in regular intervals. I stow my camera and run up the trail. Soon I'm back into the sights and sounds of a family hiking trip.

Fall Canoeing

U p ahead the river runs straight for a while before turning to the west in a long, sweeping bend. Here, when the water is low, a gravel bar lies in the center of the river. On one side of the bar it's shallow, a mere two or three inches of clear water running over thousands of tiny pebbles. On the other side, it drops off into deeper water. Also on this side are two gigantic logs. One sticks up out of the water, rising at an angle of 45 degrees before splitting into two big limbs that are about 10 feet above the water. The other teeters horizontally on the end of the first, like some fancy driftwood sculpture you would see in an art museum.

The shallow water and the large logs make it a good place to spend an afternoon with kids, which is why Rena and I are sitting in a canoe slowly paddling toward the spot with three towheaded kids along for the ride.

As I dip my paddle into the brown water and pull against it, pushing the boat forward, one of the kids asks, "When are we going to get to the sandbar, Daddy?"

I pretend not to hear the question and instead focus on a belted kingfisher that is flying low over the water in front of us. It makes a high-pitched chattering warning call as it flies. It's as if the bird is scolding us for disturbing its river realm.

"*DADDY*, when are we going to get to the *SANDBAR*?" This time, which is maybe the twentieth or thirtieth time I've heard the question asked, the questioner's voice is louder and carries a threatening tone.

"Look there goes a kingfisher," I announce. All three look for the bird.

The youngest asks, "Where, Daddy?" so I point to it and she watches the bird as it dips low over the water before rising up again to perch on a limb.

"Can you see its bill? It's thick and pointed which makes it good for catching fish. And look at the blue feathers on its head; see how they stand up in the back giving the bird a feisty look, like it's fixing for a fight?"

I end my descriptive narrative when I notice that the children have lost interest. They begin to pester each other by pulling on the straps of each other's life vests and by pushing ever so slightly against each other with their Croc-clad feet.

I study the kingfisher for one more moment, admiring the deep blue shades of its feathers which make the white on its neck stand out. It's all topped off with the spikes of its head feathers. Now there's a bird that knows how to dress.

I read about the kingfisher one time in a book by the famous nature writer Gene Stratton-Porter. According to Gene, kingfishers nest in holes made in the banks of rivers. They prefer high vertical banks like those found on outside bends. The fact intrigued me at the time and I have since kept a sharp eye out for a nest. I have yet to find one, but I'll keep looking.

"Daddy, Eli keeps kicking me." I ignore this too and look downriver to see how far we are from the gravel bar.

The afternoon sun lies golden on its waters and a slight breeze rustles the green leaves of the silver maples that grow along its banks. Here and there the wind catches the water and bunches it into small waves that cause the sunlight to sparkle and glint like a diamond ring held under a light. I can see the high bank on the outside sweep of the river where the gravel bar lies. We are getting close and the next stroke I take I push a little harder against the water to speed our arrival.

We near the gravel bar, but the children are so caught up in their continual, creative and pragmatic pestering of each other that they have failed to notice. I can see the big logs and the thousands of ripples from the shallow water passing over tiny pebbles. A few more pushes and we will be there. "Daddy, when are we going to be—"

"HERE!" I announce as the aluminum hull of the boat scrapes against rock and comes to rest on the gravel bar.

Deer Heart

Out in the dark, hanging from the limb of a tall hickory tree, is a deer. The limb is stout and could hold a bigger deer, but this one is big enough. Jake, my brother-in-law, is proud of him. The rest of us, my family and his, are proud too.

The darkness surrounding the deer is chased away by the silver beam of my flashlight. The white hair of its belly comes into view as Jake slowly swings him around to begin his work. Jake held off on field dressing the deer until he got it back to the house and hung by the neck. He figured he could do a cleaner and neater job that way. With a wheelbarrow underneath the deer to catch the internal organs and the deer hanging where dirt and leaves won't stick to exposed meat, I figured he was right.

Jake brings out his knife and checks its sharpness against his thumb. Then he slowly cuts his way up the middle of the deer, careful to keep the knife just below the skin. Along each side of the cut the skin stretches under the pressure of the internal organs pushing out. Here and there, smooth gray stomach skin bulges through. It looks as if a giant gray balloon has been stuffed into a coat and now the zipper is slowly being unzipped. The night is cold and outside of the flashlight beam, dark. Our breath steams in the cold air and hangs like a gray wisp of fog before disappearing.

As Jake gets higher and higher, the bulging and splitting at the cut increases. The dropping of the big gray balloon into the wheelbarrow looks imminent. I hold the light steady as he reaches the chest cavity. Most of the internal organs are exposed now, their smooth shiny skin gleaming in the flashlight beam. Sheets of blood run over the stomach like rain water running over a blacktop road. The blood runs down the deer and collects in the bottom of the wheelbarrow where it lays steaming like a pond on a cold morning.

When it happens, it catches us both off-guard. The massive stomach, liver and intestines of a mature buck fall in one steaming heap into the wheelbarrow, sending a shower of blood splattering through the air. Even though I jump back, I feel a few hot spots on my face where I've been hit. Jake is hit too. I shine my flashlight into the drink I've been holding and see at least one small droplet. It sits on a piece of ice like a red island in an arctic sea of bourbon. "There's blood in my drink," I say.

"They call that a Bloody Mary," Jake responds.

Next Jake reaches up into the chest cavity and brings out the heart. It's dark red with white and purple veins running on the outside like thick blood-filled spider webs. "Drop it in here," I say as I extend a large metal bowl towards Jake. The heart hits the bottom of the bowl with a splat and a small pool of blood oozes out around it onto the shiny metal.

When I step inside the house and put the bowl on the big granite-topped island, I can feel the heat from the woodstove on the skin of my face and hands. The big hickory pieces that were loaded before we left to get the deer are now large orange coals.

I put the heart on a cutting board and begin trimming all the valves and veins away, leaving only dark brown tender strips of meat. I've got a skillet on the stove heating and when the butter in it starts to pop and crackle, I drop the heart strips in one by one. Worcestershire sauce and seasoned salt are added in liberal amounts as the meat cooks.

When the pieces start to curl along the edges, I take them out, laying them to dry and cool on a piece of paper towel. Jake walks in and cleans the blood from his hands. "Try a piece of heart," I say.

He takes one and eats it. "Good," he says and grabs another.

The first one I try is still hot and steams a little in my mouth. There is hot blood and salty juices in the middle just the way I like. The warmth and fullness it brings to my pallet puts the dark and coldness of the winter night far from mind.

When the paper towel is empty, drink glasses are dry, and the stove has been banked, we all turn in for the night. I look outside one last time before going to bed. The buck is there hanging in the cold darkness of the night, its life now given over for another purpose as all things must do.

Spare Change

"That'll be $4.39," the convenience store clerk says courteously. I look down at the counter where I've dumped all the money I have on me. One crumpled up dollar bill, eight or ten quarters and a few sorry-looking pennies lay in a scattered mess.

"Crap," I say to her, "I don't have enough and I left my wallet at home."

She gives me a blank stare waiting for my next move. *Wow,* I imagine she's thinking to herself, *I've seen people run short of cash when trying to buy beer or cigarettes but never when trying to buy bait. This guy must be really hard up.*

She smiles politely before turning her back to me to grab a pack of Marlboro lights from the cigarette rack for the next customer in line. I scoop up the money on the counter, put the night crawlers back in the mini fridge and head for the door.

When I climb into the truck, my father-in-law Mark asks me where the night crawlers are. "The money we scrounged from the cab wasn't enough," I reply.

"I have a 20-dollar bill on me but I didn't want to break it," he says.

That's nice, I think to myself. *I just made myself look like a bum while my father-in-law sat out in the truck with a 20-dollar bill.* But I really can't say much since I'm the guy who left his wallet at home.

"They wanted too much for their bait anyway," I say. Mark quickly agrees, thereby putting the blame for the mishap onto the store. He pulls the diesel truck onto the highway and we head for the banks of the local river where we hope to spend the day catching smallmouth bass.

When we get to the river, Mark pulls the truck to a stop and shuts the clattering diesel engine off. I'm the first one out of the cab and quickly tie a tub jig to the end of my ultra-light fishing pole. Walking to the edge of the river, I wade knee-deep into its cool, clear waters and begin to cast.

Above me the sky is blue and spotted with white fluffy clouds. The woods that grow down to the edge of the river are lush and in places form a dense jungle of stinging nettle, sycamore saplings and touch-me-nots in full bloom with orange and yellow flowers. The spot I'm casting is a deep pool below a low-head dam. The noise from the water falling over the dam is a low roar that adds a feeling of underlying energy to the place.

I cast behind a large boulder that looks promising. As my bait drops, a bronze blur darts out from the boulder to intercept it. After a good hook set, I'm soon doing battle with one of Indiana's top fighting fish, the smallmouth bass. After a series of several runs and one jump, the fish is played out and I lip it to work my hook free. When I release it back into its cool water home, it darts for cover and is quickly lost amongst the moss-covered boulders.

I continue fishing upriver from the dam and catch and release several more nice smallmouth. Each time I set the hook and feel the strong shoulder of a fish behind it, my heart rate quickens and rises into my throat. All of the random thoughts and worries that continually float around my mind drop away until it's only me and the fish. When it's all over and I've sent the fish on its way, I start casting again, hoping anxiously for the next bite.

The bright sun that has warmed the back of my neck all morning is now starting to work its way towards the horizon. I meet up with Mark back at the dam. I raise my voice to project over the sound of rushing water and ask how he did. "What?" he calls back. "Did you catch anything?" I say almost shouting. "Yeah, caught several," he replies. We continue fishing for a little longer before deciding it's time to head for home. We climb into the truck and are soon on the state highway winding our way through fields of corn. When we drive past the convenience store, I think of how we didn't need live bait anyway and hope that I won't have to go back there anytime soon.

Fall Camping

"All right, who wants some orange Hi-C?" I ask the three tow-headed children that are standing around the back of the car where our red cooler sits in the dirt.

"I do!" they respond in unison. I dig around in the food bag past a crushed box of fruit snacks and a half-empty bag of pretzels to find three cups of equal size but differing colors.

I hand a yellow cup to my son Eli. He sees the color and knits his brow. "Take it," I say.

"I don't want the yellow one, I want the green one." I give the yellow cup to my youngest daughter instead. She takes it and patiently waits for her Hi-C ration.

Next, I give a blue cup to my oldest daughter Eva. "I want the green cup," she says.

"You both can't have the green cup, there's only one. What difference does it make anyway? They're all the same size," I respond. Eva takes the cup but puts on her scowly face, which at 8 years old she hasn't yet managed to outgrow.

Eli grabs the green cup relishing the fact that he has won the cup war. I open the cooler and grab the one-gallon value jug of Hi-C and pour a little in each of the cups. I fill the cups to the half mark, mitigating the risk of wasting a full cup when someone spills it in the dirt. The kids start gulping it down and soon each one sports a faint orange mustache over their upper lips.

For our fall vacation, we've traveled to central Illinois to spend a few days tent camping at a state park and visiting the zoos, historical sites and museums of St. Louis, Missouri. Most attractions are free, which makes it a great trip for budget minded families. The weather forecast looks favorable for tent camping except for night-time lows in the 40s making me worry about the kids getting cold at night. Luckily for them, Dad has spent some time tent camping in cold weather so we're prepared.

When tent camping in colder weather, I prefer to sleep directly on the ground, avoiding air mattresses or cots which tend to allow cold air to creep in beneath you. To prepare for our first night, I've laid several thick blankets on our tent floor which will give us comfort while still keeping us close to the ground. Instead of sleeping in individual sleeping bags I've unzipped our bags which will go over the top of us allowing our body heat to be shared. I would only apply this technique with my family; this could get a little awkward with a group of friends. I've also made sure that all of us have stocking caps and wool socks that we can wear at night to keep our feet and heads warm. It is important to put on a fresh pair of clean and dry socks right before going to bed. Wearing the socks you've sweated in all day will result in cold feet.

After our Hi-C ordeal is over, I put the kids to work helping me set up the tent. Now that they are old enough to help out, I've found that not only do we get the job done quicker as a family but the kids enjoy the interaction and the feeling of doing something useful. Once the tent is up, we load back into our car and head to a nearby small town for pizza.

Later in the evening when we get back to camp, night has fallen. The kids bail out of the car and are soon running under the big oaks that dot our campsite sporting the glow sticks we bought them in town. I busy myself with the campfire and soon bright orange flames are casting yellow light up into the spreading branches of the oaks. I work on the fire until large coals throw heat on my hands and face, insulating me from the chilly night air.

"Let's go for a night hike," I call to the kids. They form a pack around me and we leave the glowing fire to walk out onto a nearby peninsula that juts out into a large lake. A gentle breeze blows across the lake causing small waves to lap against its shore in the darkness. Above us stretches a vast expanse of black sky set with thousands of sparkling stars. We lay on our backs and I point out the Little Dipper and Orion's belt to the kids.

Eva and Eli seem interested but soon the little one is overwhelmed by the darkness and pleads to be led back to the relative safety of the campfire. I relent and we are soon back at camp. Rena, who has returned from taking a shower at the shower house, lets the kids know it's time for bed. After a long day of driving in the car and a night full of running around in dark woods, no one complains and soon all three are quietly sleeping in the tent.

I sit by the fire, letting the ancient pull of glowing coals and flickering flames hold me just a little longer. I think of the day and the fun we've had together as a family. And although at times having the kids around on a camping trip can drive a person to insanity quicker than it takes a dog to eat a piece of bacon, I wouldn't have it any other way.

Splitting Wood
and the Cost of Living with Kids

"What happened?" Rena asks as I walk into the house holding my bloody finger.

"I cut myself splitting wood."

She shakes her head and I know she's thinking, *How is that even possible?*

In the bathroom I clean the wound which is deep and about a half-inch long.

"You should probably go to urgent care," Rena says.

I look at the wound and see that it is a clean cut and seems to be staying closed on its own. "No, I think it'll be OK," I respond.

It had been a normal afternoon splitting wood. I was using a metal wedge to split some bigger pieces. After taking a big swing, the wedge shot into the air. I watched it in slow motion come back toward my body. Before I could move, its razor edge sliced through my index finger.

Part of my reasoning for not going to the emergency room was because we had already spent a fortune on healthcare costs this year. After jumping from a tree, Eli had broken an arm. Esther, jumping from a slide, had to have a tooth fixed that was busted from the fall. Eli had also developed a bad cough that required many doctor visits and treatments.

It seems like a parent never knows what might be around the corner. Just last week a simple trip to the grocery store resulted in injury. The four of us had gone to town to get some supplies for a birthday party. After pulling into a parking spot, I carried Esther in my arms as we walked towards the store. Eva walked next to me and Eli brought up the rear. As we neared the store front, Eli cut in front of me. He did it so fast that I had little time to react. I tripped on his feet and since I had Esther in my arms, I couldn't do anything but fall straight forward. And so down Esther and I went, with Eli beneath us.

I managed to roll Esther off to the side before we landed, but Eli went face down into the hard pavement. Eva, the only family member left standing, stared in bewilderment as the rest of us lay on the ground, sprawled out in a pile. I quickly got back to my feet, pulled the two crying kids off the ground and walked into the store like nothing happened. Luckily the fall didn't result in an urgent care visit, but Eli had to go to school the next day with a skinned-up forehead and a black eye.

One minute you're walking into a store with your three kids, the next minute you're face down in the parking lot. What goes on in a kid's brain? When is it ever a good idea to run in front of Daddy and cut him off when he's carrying one of your siblings? I know as a kid I did the same type of stuff, and now I can appreciate my parents' frustration.

As I lie on the couch, I try not to let my mind focus on my wounded finger. Even a small injury can shake a person up and make him slow down a bit. I think of what I did wrong with the wedge and how next time I'll be more careful. I think of how if the wedge had flown closer to my body I'd likely be at the ER. I tell Rena that if it had hit me in the groin area, I probably wouldn't need to go in for that family planning surgery she's been after me to get done. I'm certainly grateful that although this injury was a minor incident, it served as a good wake-up call for how important it is to be safe. With my home doctoring skills saving a trip to urgent care, I'll have a little bit more in the health savings account, which odds are, will be put to good use when the next unexpected kid adventure goes awry.

Winter Hiking

"Mom, my bibs aren't staying up," says a rosy cheeked six-year-old clad in snow bibs, a heavy jacket and a blue monster stocking cap complete with horns. Rena bends over and fixes his bibs.

"Here, put your scarf on," she calls to the oldest who has wandered away from the car.

Eva beckons the call and runs back. "I don't need a scarf," she protests.

"Yes you do," Rena says and on goes the scarf. Last the littlest one climbs out of the car and plunges into the snow.

"Mom," she says, "I need a Kleenex."

If I had a nickel for every time I've heard "I need a Kleenex" this winter I would be rich beyond measure. Runny noses, sore throats and incessant coughing (both day and night) have ravaged the kids' immune systems for what seems like four weeks straight. When the cold bugs make a coordinated strike and all three kids are sick at the same time, we can easily go through a box of Kleenex a day.

"Come on, let's go," I call to the kids. We start moving away from the car and towards the trail. The afternoon sun shines bright off the fresh three inches of snow we received the day before. It doesn't take long for the kids to get out ahead of Rena and me.

They are a constant blur of motion, knocking into each other before falling into the snow over and over again. "Let's make snow angels," Eva shouts and soon all three are on their backs, arms and legs squirming in the snow. We make slow progress down the trail, three snow angels made for every ten yards of trail gained.

As we walk, I look at the river that runs near the trail. Along its muddy banks grow sycamore and silver maple trees. It's wide and flowing swiftly from recent rain and snow. On the opposite side I see a few ducks moving away from the commotion of our group. My eye catches movement on the trunk of a nearby tree. A small bird moves upwards, pausing every so often to work the bark with its beak. Higher and higher the bird climbs until I lose sight of it in the tree's upper branches.

The bird is a brown creeper. Brown creepers are small, a little smaller than a chickadee. Their plumage is drab, very similar in color to brown tree bark. They forage for insects found beneath bark by climbing the trunks of large trees in a series of small hops. When they get to the top, they fly to the base of another tree and start again. On your winter hikes, look for them by pausing often to scan the trunks of large trees for movement.

"Mom, my ears are cold." Even with scarves, hoods and monster-hats, someone's ears are always cold. I look at the little one and wonder if she is really cold or just bored and ready to go back. "My ears are *COLD,*" she says again. This time I grab her hat and pull it down, then pull her hood up and over. This seems to satisfy her and we walk on.

We leave the trail and walk to the river's edge near a big bend. I hear a volley of shots and not long after a duck comes zipping upriver, splashing down in the water just past us.

"Looks like a merganser of some sort," I say to Rena, "and those guys need to brush up on their wing-shooting." We stand along the banks until the brisk wind that rolls over the open fields across the river turns the kids' cheeks a little too rosy.

"We better head back," I say. "Yep," Rena responds and we walk back to the trail.

On the way back, we hear a boat coming downriver. All five of us walk to the bank and watch as a camouflaged duck-hunting boat roars past. One man runs the motor while another sits with his back to the wind in the bow. The kids all wave and the hunters wave back. A third man appears from the bottom of the boat, huddled against the cold wind. He lifts his head above the sidewall and waves too. We watch until they are out of sight and the sound of the noisy motor fades into the distance.

About halfway back to the car, littlest calls out, "My legs are tired."

"I know, Girl, just a little bit further," I reply. She puts her head down and plods on. When we finally make it to the car, the kids pile in and we head for home.

Back at the cabin I stoke the woodstove and put some deer meat on for tacos, one of the kids' favorite meals. We eat our tacos in the warmth and comfort of the cabin as another cold winter night sets in. The kids watch a movie before going to bed and to my amazement, not one time do I hear "I need a Kleenex."

As I lie in bed I think of the fun we've had taking the kids on a winter hike. I also think of the duck hunters and how I haven't done any duck hunting at all this year. But I know when the kids are grown and out of the house and I have plenty of time for duck hunting, I'll look back on these days of snow angel hikes and wish I could live them all over again.

Christmas Cooking, the Wild Way

L ooking out from the cabin, the river looks like a ribbon of crystal green running through a sea of white. The snow that fell the night before sparkles from the rising sun. "The sky will be blue this morning," I say to myself.

Inside, the cabin is aglow with Christmas lights. The lights run across the wooden mantle, over the stone fireplace and up and around the beams of the open ceiling. Over in the woodstove, blue flames flicker over glowing red coals.

Long wisps of steam hit my face as I take a sip of coffee, welcomed refreshment after an early rise from a warm bed. Under the tree, presents are piled in a heap, spilling out onto the floor. From the stereo Nat King Cole softly sings Christmas songs. I remember the soft tone of his voice from the days when my dad was the coffee drinker, waiting for wee ones to wake on Christmas morning.

The shuffling of feet reaches my ears as Eva and Esther slowly make their way down the stairs from the loft. Although still half asleep and still in their Christmas pajamas, their eyes light up when they see the tree. "Good morning, girls. Merry Christmas," I say.

They make no reply but look at each other and smile.

Next up is Eli, who shuffles down the hall to join his sisters. Now they all three sit on the couch, eyes fixed on the tree.

Last up is Rena. She has her Christmas pajamas on too. "Merry Christmas," I tell her. "You ready for the kids to open the presents?"

"Yes, let me get my camera first though," she replies sleepily.

Soon we give the kids the green light and wrapping paper begins to fly. The moment they have been impatiently waiting for, losing sleep over and pestering Rena and me about for weeks is finally here.

When the presents are all unwrapped and the kids are busy playing with new toys, I turn my attention to Christmas dinner, and of course in our house that means a main dish of wild game.

Incorporating wild game into your Christmas dinner is a rewarding experience and adds an element of outdoor tradition to the holidays. Not only is wild game delicious, but because it's low in fat and rich in protein it's also healthy. One of my favorite Christmas dishes is rabbit with noodles.

To start, I stew the rabbit for several hours until the meat falls from the bone. Then I pour off the broth, add a couple of chicken bouillon cubes and set the pot on the stove to boil. Once the broth boils, I add noodles (scratch noodles are best but dried store-bought will work too) and cook until the noodles are done. Next, I add the meat back to the mix and put it on the stove to simmer. Rabbit and noodles are best paired with mashed potatoes. Rena is the mashed potatoes expert at our house, as my cooking skills start and end with meat. For a bread choice I prefer German rye bread. I like to warm the bread on the woodstove until it's warm enough for a slab of butter to melt and drizzle down the sides. The icing on the cake (for me anyway, Rena and the kids turn their noses up) is sauerkraut. For beverage pairing, I like a dry red wine or a stout glass of ale.

Rabbit and noodles shared with three bright-eyed kids and a beautiful wife on Christmas day; it's about as good as it gets.

Splitting Wood Rings a Bell

When we're finished eating, I take all of the dirty plates and stack them at the end of the table. The plates are scattered with the remains of taco salads, shrimp tacos and tiny pieces of rice. The kids are starting to get restless and are out of their chairs circling around the table like a pack of fidgety sharks.

On the sidewalk that runs past our table, people walk to the local festival that is taking place a couple blocks away. There are groups of teenage boys, with droopy pants and braided hair carrying on lively conversation sprinkled with expletives and spiked with hints of aggression. There are also parents with their children herding them down the sidewalk like cattle drivers. And there are couples too, clad in t-shirts and shorts, strolling hand in hand, conversing in low subtle tones.

The waiter comes back to the table and while the bill is being paid, I take the children and head for the sidewalk. We goof around for a minute until Rena, Uncle Tommy and Aunt Lisa, Rena's sister and her husband, join us.

We walk down a block and then turn the corner towards the festival as day slowly fades to night. A large Ferris wheel comes into view with neon lights running along its spokes. The lights illuminate the night sky with wild shades of pink, purple and blue. The children look up at the glowing light wheel and stare with open mouths.

The Florida air is pleasant tonight. It feels comfortable in short sleeves and the breeze from the Gulf stirs the leaves of the palm trees that dot the festival site. We pass a large barbeque smoker that pours blue smoke from small stacks sticking from the top of its rusty black body. Men tend the smoky fires as women handle corn on the cob, getting it ready for hungry customers.

We draw near a stage where a large crowd watches a rock band performing. Drum beats and the sounds of guitars are deafening near the stage, but as we continue walking they fade into the background.

In the carnival area workers stand beside games and rides. Everything exists in a constant swarm of motion, light and noise. We come across a high striker game manned by two carnies who heckle men as they pass, challenging them to put their manliness on display by striking a small pad with a big hammer and making the bell at the top ring.

I've always wanted to try this game and on the spur of the moment I decide tonight is the night. I hand one of the men my money and take the hammer. A small crowd, mostly made of our group, gathers. I walk up to the line and get ready.

I have been preparing for this moment for a very long time. Ever since I was old enough to swing a splitting maul, I have spent many a cold Indiana winter day splitting firewood. I started with a wood handled maul that my dad used. He put a piece of radiator hose on the handle to keep a mis-swung blow from breaking it. Over several years of practice, I learned that a good swing is an act of precision more than power.

It's best to pick a point on the log, like a small discoloration, and then hold your eye on the spot all the way through your swing. To do this you must maintain control of your swing to ensure you connect with the spot at the end. You should start with your hands apart on the handle, bringing the maul up high into the air directly over your head and then bring your hands together just before the blow.

With these things in mind I take my first try. I connect with the striking pad and send the ball up top where it makes a healthy connection with the bell. When I take my next swing, I hit the pad harder making the bell ring a little louder. On the third blow, the pressure of not messing up gets to me but I swing through and the bell tolls for a third time. I take a step back and look at the carney as if to say "now what?"

He dully replies, "You can pick any prize." The tone and volume of his voice has lost all of its former enthusiasm now that he has my money in his pouch.

I look to where our group stands and see that my youngest daughter Esther is the only one of the kids that is still interested in Daddy's display of manliness and power. "Come on, Girl, pick out a prize," I call to her.

She approaches the inflatable toys and looks carefully at the oversized baseball bats, gigantic hands and mallets. A pink "super bat" catches her eye and she grabs it with a quick glance at me for reassurance. "All right, good one," I say as she tucks the bat firmly under her arm like the way a man tucks a newspaper under his arm after buying it from a metal pay box. It's hers and you'll have to be pretty big (bigger than her two siblings…) and pretty scary (they aren't scary only irritating….) to take it from her.

As we walk through the carnival and along the busy streets of the town, she clings to the pink bat without fail. Her uncle sneaks up from behind and gives it a pull. She knits her brow and gives him the "scowly" face before he lets go and laughs at the determination of a three-year-old protecting her prize.

I study the children. They look at the rides and the lights and the crowds and observe them in their own way. I wonder which of the things they see tonight will stick the longest in their minds. When they are all grown up, which memory of this trip to Florida will they recall? Which will be their favorite?

For me it's easy. It's the sight of my little one walking in the warm night under the neon lights of a Ferris wheel, her light golden hair rustled softly by the breeze. She's wearing a pair of blue shorts and a pink mermaid shirt as her little legs move her rapidly forward through the crowd. And all the while the pink inflatable bat that Daddy won is clutched tightly under one arm.

Death Beetles

"**D**addy, come here! I have something to show you!" my eight-year-old daughter Eva says. She watches me closely with her blue eyes to see how I respond to her request. I've just arrived home from work and I'm on a mission to cut the grass. I really want to tell her "not right now E" without even slowing down on my beeline path to the garage. But that little voice inside my head which makes me a better parent.... if I listen to it that is....says: *STOP what you're doing! Your daughter obviously has something important to show you. The universe won't implode if the grass cutting has to wait 15 minutes.*

"OK," I say, "what is it?"

Eva's eyes brighten and a smile creeps across her face as she steps off the porch into the front yard. I follow her through the uncut grass, past the garden boxes that need weed-eating until she stops and points at the ground. "There," she says.

I look closely at the ground but notice nothing. "Where?" I ask.

She scans the grass carefully before pointing, "Right there, you see that?"

I look where she points and see a small pile of intestines and pieces of other internal organs, dried and blackened from the sun.

"Oh yeah," I say.

"What do you think they're from?" she asks.

"Maybe a rabbit," I reply. As I lean close to examine the guts for signs of rabbit fur, something else draws my attention. The guts are alive with bugs. There are the expected black flies that buzz the pile continually.

There are also large green blow flies with their shiny almost iridescent bodies that slowly crawl over every inch of the mess.

"Look at those beetles," I tell Eva.

"Yeah, they're really big," she says.

I watch as several large beetles crawl around the pile. They are all black except for a small splotch of yellow on their heads. Their bodies are blocky, almost rectangular and are about 1/2 to 1 inch long. The beetles are carrion beetles, and if there is a gut pile in your neighborhood, they're sure to be at the party.

The carrion beetle life cycle begins when adults lay eggs near rotting meat. The eggs hatch and larvae feed until they are adults, which typically takes 10-12 weeks. The new adults overwinter and emerge in early summer to breed and lay eggs. Thus, there is only one generation of carrion beetles per year. Thanks to scavenger bugs like carrion beetles, the road kill opossum that nobody in your neighborhood wants to pick up, will eventually go away.

"Thanks for showing me this, Eva," I say after we watch the beetles for a while.

She nods her head and smiles before running off into the yard to find her brother and sister. I walk over to the garage where I find my lawn mower patiently waiting.

See that wasn't so bad, the little voice says.

Yes, you're right, you're always right, I think as I start the mower and settle into my afternoon's work.

Spined Micrathena

"Go in front of me," Rena says stopping and turning around. I look down the well-worn trail winding its way through towering trees that darken the path.

"Why?" I ask.

"Just go," she says, her blue eyes steady and determined.

I walk around her and start down the path again. A few minutes later I feel something sticky hit my face. I bring my hand to wipe it away, and in the process cover my arm in the sticky mess. The creator of the mess somehow swings away and drops onto the forest floor. I turn and look at Rena. "Watch out for the spider webs," she says smiling.

"Thanks for the warning. I appreciate it." Now my eyes are steady and determined. I rummage through the leaves on the forest floor and find a stick. Walking with the stick out in front of me as a shield we press on.

If you're heading for the woods in late summer, you'll likely encounter spined micrathena spiders and their sticky webs. They are a common spider found in Indiana woodlands. If one takes the time to examine a spined micrathena, you'll be pleasantly surprised by its unique appearance. As indicated by its name, the spider's abdomen (the main part of a spider's body) is covered in seven or eight sharp spikes that protrude outward. Coloration can vary but most are dark black with decorative splotches of white. Micrathenas are small, easily fitting on the face of a penny. Males don't make webs, so you're most likely to encounter a female while walking in the woods. If you look closely at her web you will see that it's circular and you should find a single strand going away from the web. This is her escape strand. By the time you plaster her web all over your face, she's likely scurrying up her escape strand for safety. Females build webs across narrow forest openings, such as those made by hiking trails, to catch insects that use the openings as flyways. Females spin a new web daily, so not only are they pretty to look at but they're also hard workers, which brings me back to Rena.

"Where are the kids?" Rena asks.

"They're on up ahead. I wish they were tall enough to break some of these webs," I reply still brandishing the stick.

After hiking for a good hour, we finish the loop trail, pile into the car and head for home.

Back along the trail the woods go quiet again. In the green darkness tucked away beneath a hickory leaf, a micrathena slowly crawls back to the edge of the trail. Web begins flowing from her abdomen as she makes her first string across the trail. She keeps weaving until she has a circular web in place. Finally, she makes her escape strand. Crickets provide the background music as she works. Then quietly positioning herself in the middle, she watches and waits. All along the trail, other micrathenas weave their webs and the traps for a wandering fly, or perhaps a hiker, are set.

Spring Nights

"**D**addy, where are we going?" my youngest daughter asks.

"Just follow me and try to stay in the beam of the flashlight," I respond.

As we walk, a high-pitched chorus of "peeping" noises grows louder and louder. We pause at the edge of a shallow wetland. Large trees crowd around the edges like dark pillars holding up the night sky. "Keep your voices low and try not to move much," I say.

"What are we doing—"

"Shh!" I quickly respond to the question from my son Eli. Both kids crouch down beside me as I troll my flashlight slowly across the water surface. Our breaths steam lightly in the night air.

"There, you see that? That's one." We watch as a small creature about as round as a quarter floats to the surface. With rapid kicks of its tiny legs it swims towards us.

"Take the flashlight and shine the beam right into its eyes," I tell Eli. Eli makes its eyes shine green and I get poised for my grab. I position my body and extend my hand. Ever so slowly I reach toward the critter. I call this my "blue heron" pose as it reminds me of the way a blue heron moves its neck down towards the water just before striking for a fish.

Esther stares on with wide eyes.

And then I strike. I plunge my hand into the water with a splash, eyes focused on my target.

"Did you get it, Daddy?" Esther asks.

Eli shines the light into my closed hand as I slowly open my wet fingers. In the white light of the flashlight a small frog lies still, its legs tucked tightly against its body.

"You see that 'X' on its back?" I ask the kids. "That means this is a spring peeper, and he is the one that has been making all that loud peeping noise."

Spring peepers are found commonly in southern Indiana. Males begin calling to attract mates on warm nights in February and March. They produce a single "peep" note that is repeated roughly every second. Their peep is a sharp and loud note, and the noise from a group of peepers calling is almost ear deafening.

We look at the spring peeper some more before I place him back in the water and Eli follows him with the flashlight as he swims away. As we walk away the peepers start calling again.

Above us the sky is aglow with thousands of stars. "Look at those stars in a line," I say to the kids as I point out Orion's belt.

Back at the house, Rena and I put the kids to bed. When all is quiet, I notice a window that has been left open. The cool spring air drifts through it, rustling a faded curtain and bringing the sound of peeping into the darkness.

Blessed

"What is it, Eva?" I call out to my daughter who has stopped dead in her tracks.

She points to the ground, her mouth held tightly closed and her face tense. I walk back along the stream towards her. "There, Dad, look!" she says.

From a distance I hear a rustling sound and see a dark object lying coiled on the ground in front of her. "Just hold still, Eva," I say. As I walk, panicked thoughts flicker through my mind. *I walked right past where she is without even noticing anything. How could I be so careless? This is timber rattler territory. I should have been more alert for snakes!*

When I finally reach Eva, the snake lets loose a loud hiss and flattens its wide head, which makes it look like a cobra's hood. The snake puffs its body up and hisses loudly again. Eva remains frozen in her tracks.

Earlier in the day, Rena and I had decided to take the kids hiking in a creek in southern Indiana. The creek was full of geodes and fossils and even though the sun was bright and hot above us, we were kept in comfort by the deep shade of the woods. The sunlight that did make it through was dappled and fell softly on the wet rocks of the creek bed. The kids were having a great time splashing in the creek and Rena and I shared some quiet moments as we followed along after them.

I study the snake closer, relaxing a little as my fears start to fade away.

"What is it, Daddy?" Eva asks.

"It won't hurt you, Girl. That's a hognose snake."

Seeing a hognose snake in southern Indiana is a rare treat. The hognose burrows or roots with its shovel-like nose, hence the name. Their preferred diet is toads. What makes seeing a hognose a real treat is their defensive behavior. Their first line of defense is to puff their bodies up to make them look bigger than they are and to release loud hisses to make them sound meaner than they really are. They also flatten their heads for added effect. They will on occasion strike, but they are not an aggressive snake and prefer to bluff their way out of a confrontation, as evidenced by their final defense which is to play dead. Yep, they take a page out of the opossum's book on this one. If threatened enough they flop over on their backs, thrash around a little bit and then roll into a neat coil before lying still.

Rena and the kids all gather around the snake as it continues to hiss. I wait for it to flip over on its back, but this snake's game is all hiss and no possum.

"Come on guys, let's leave it alone," I say and we make our way on down the creek. Seeing a creature that is so unique only adds to the day.

The kids are happy and free splashing in the creek, on a scale of one to ten the weather is a definite ten. My wife is here with me enjoying the moment, and yes I could probably find something wrong with the day if I tried hard enough, but I know in my heart that I am truly blessed.

On the River at Last

"Eli, get away from the boat!" I yell at my 7-year-old son. He stands on the riverbank staring down at me, his blue eyes steady and firm under the brim of his camo hat. I look back towards the canoe. A cloud of large bumble bees swarms around one end. They look angry. One buzzes at me and I feel a tingle of pain in my leg. Another attacks my hands, which by this time are flailing wildly around my head (when attacked by bumble bees, never flail around like one of those inflatable air dancers businesses use to grab attention; it just makes the bees madder!). They've got me zeroed, it's man versus bees.

Thinking quickly I shove the boat into the river. It hits the green water with a splash along with my paddle, which had somehow slid down the bank in the midst of the battle. Catching in the current, the boat and paddle drift rapidly away under the shade of the silver maple trees that grow along the riverbank. The pair look peaceful floating side by side, except for the swarm of angry bees that still hovers over one end of the canoe.

I look back at Eli. He is standing in the same place, staring down at me with that calm look in his eyes. He hasn't said a word, but I know what he's thinking: *Oh, no, here we go again...*

As I stand on the bank watching the boat drift away, I feel relieved to be rid of the bees and their painful stinging. But now a new problem enters my brain, *If I let the canoe drift away, how will we ever go canoeing again?* I leap off the bank and into the river. My head goes under the cool water and things go quiet and dark for a moment. The water relieves some of the pain from my stung legs. I resurface with a gasp and swim rapidly towards the canoe.

This has been a tough summer for the Whiteleather family when it comes to canoeing trips. The White River has been high from constant heavy rains. Just when it started to come down, another storm would come along and turn it into a brown swirling beast again. Not to mention the fact that my oldest daughter Eva was at the Riley Children's Hospital for six days from a burst appendix. Rena and I took turns living at the hospital so one of us could be with her at all times. Rena was there when she underwent emergency surgery while I stayed at home with our other two kids. Every time I pictured my little blond-haired girl that I've loved from the moment I looked into her blue eyes lying on the surgeon's bed, it crushed my heart. I prayed and worshiped my Creator. I never asked Him for anything. He knew what I wanted.

But she recovered like a champ and soon the halls of Riley were graced by two less parents with worried looks in their eyes. I was moved by the stories I heard when talking to other parents and the support my family felt from so many volunteers and donated resources during Eva's stay there.

And now the first opportunity we've had to hit the water is in peril from a pack of angry bees.

Swimming low in the water I sneak towards the end of the canoe opposite the bees. With one swift motion I reach up and flip the canoe over sending the bees to a watery grave. Victory!

Flipping the canoe back over I pull it up to the bank. "Eli, you up there?" I call out. Slowly he peers from the foliage of the riverbank and looks down towards me. Those blue eyes are just as calm and steady as when the whole ordeal started. "The bees are gone, Son. I think we can get the boat upright and still go canoeing."

He nods but looks at the canoe half full of water with dead bees floating around and I know he has his doubts. But soon we've got all of the water out of the boat and are both seated, ready to start. With one push of my paddle, I send the boat forward and we are on our way, on the river at last.

One for the Memory Bank

"**B**ring the camera up here, Babe" I yell downriver to Rena who is wading ankle-deep in the riffle below me. I move towards the snag that the fish pulled my line under. The water around my legs swirls like a thousand hot-tub jets turned on high. My feet feel weightless against the river bottom but I go deeper. If I can keep good pressure on the fish and get up to the snag, I might be able to land it.

The water creeps up towards my chest. I'm on the verge of being swept away and I know it. In my brain a battle between the urge to land the fish and the urge to not drown is being waged. Just when I think I can't go any further the bottom starts to shallow and I'm quickly within arm's reach of the snag.

I reach down and grab the line with my hand and feel tension. He's still on! I back away from the snag, the line cutting into my hand from the pressure of the fish. Carefully I ease the fish out of the snag and into open water where I can use my pole to control him. It pulls in short bursts, causing my drag to pulse out line.

Now another battle brews in my mind. *You got this, just take your time* wrestles with *You're going to lose this fish no matter what you do!*

As I reel the fish in, I see him for the first time. His wide bronze body looks dark in the clear waters of the river. It's the biggest smallmouth bass I have ever caught and likely will ever catch, if I can land him that is.

Fishing rivers and streams for smallmouth in the fall can be very productive. Waters are typically clear and low, which means you can see underwater structure, and the fish are more concentrated in deeper holes. I like to fish deep water with good current and plenty of places for bigger fish to hide.

Over the years, the smallmouth that I've watched feeding seem to focus their attention on the bottom. That's why I prefer tub jigs or other jigs that sink rapidly and can be worked in short hops. I also like a weighted jig because it allows me to get my bait close to structure such as logs and rocks. Smallmouth tend to hold very tight to structure especially in stronger current.

"Eva, come here!" I yell to my daughter who is looking at mussel shells on a gravel bar.

By now Rena and the kids know something is up and everyone starts splashing their way toward me. I've got the fish closer and I need Eva to hold my pole so I can get a good grip on it. When she comes over, I grab the fish and push its body against my leg so I can lip it.

My thumb firmly in its mouth I hoist the big fish up out of the water. I smile at Rena and she smiles back, the afternoon sun sparkling in her blue eyes. It takes two hands to hold the fish properly.

There aren't any battles being waged inside my brain now, just a feeling of elation that I actually landed a fish like this.

The kids all gather around me and Rena snaps a few pictures. A blue heron flies over us, its wings black against the blue sky. The sun glints yellow off the river's crimpled water and makes the trees on the bank look golden green. "I guess we should go back now," I tell Rena and the kids. I look at the fish one last time before placing it gently back in the water. It pauses a minute before disappearing into the river's depths. The fish is gone forever but the feeling of elation stays with me, although I know it will fade with time. But the memory will remain, and maybe on a dreary winter day when I've had a tough day at work and I'm worn out with life, I'll remember the warm late summer day when our paths crossed.

Fall Travels

"**D**addy...I'm starving!" a voice from the back seat calls out.

"You should've eaten more when we stopped for lunch," I call back, my voice carrying a hint of the irritation I've been working hard to suppress all day.

In the rearview mirror I can see my five-year-old daughter Esther strapped into her pink car seat. Her big green eyes are downcast and her golden brown hair droops loosely on either side of her rosy cheeks. Her lips are pressed into a frown and I can tell a storm of discontent is brewing under the surface, just waiting to burst out like a shook-up 2 liter opened too quickly.

I look at the road stretching out in front of our SUV. It's a gray interstate that snakes over the rolling wine country of northern New York. We are within an hour of our final destination. If I can somehow keep a lid on the stewing 5-year-old in the back seat, we all can make it to Niagara Falls with at least a portion of our sanity intact.

The car goes quiet again, the only noise the clipping of the road joints beneath us as we press on towards Niagara. All is good in the world: Rena is lost in a book in her seat beside me and the kids are busy drawing colorful illustrations on notebook paper.

"Daddy...how much further!" Esther asks with a pleading "if I don't get out of this car soon the world will end" kind of tone in her voice. I keep driving, choosing to ignore the most ominous question ever posed to Dad-kind. Esther pauses to regroup and plot her next move.

And then she pulls out the big guns, "Daddy, I have to go potty!"

I take the bait and decide to engage. "No you don't, we just stopped a half hour ago!"

She pauses for a moment before letting out a long, slow, groaning whine that I'm pretty sure could be recorded and played repeatedly in a jail cell to get a confession out of the most hardened criminal. I know the whining groan is leading up to something big, something earth shattering, something the likes of which Dad-kind has never heard. And then she lets it drop. "Daddy…*MY PINKY HURTS!*"

"Your what hurts?" I ask in disbelief.

"MY PINKY!" I look over at Rena who is smiling and shaking her head. I smile back at her and drive on.

After a few more hours of driving and a night in a hotel, we finally make it to the falls. The five of us stand against a metal railing looking down at a plunging torrent of water. Mist rises up and settles all around us, soaking our hair and clothes. The roar of the falls is so loud you can feel it in your bones. The kids don't say much but simply stare at the falls. I know it's been a long trip in the car for them, but surely this is something they will never forget.

I grab Esther and raise her head above the railing so she can look down. We stand quietly as thousands of gallons of water rocket past our feet. For once on the trip her and I are in the same place. Neither one of us is thinking of hurting pinkies or strange car noises, but are both lost in the wonders of creation.

Where Your Heart Is

"What was that?" my daughter Eva asks, looking up from her art project.

"I don't know, but it didn't sound good," I reply as I grab my jacket and gloves. A loud ground-shaking thud had just come from outside. Looking out through the cabin window I see trees swaying back and forth like the drunken pendulum of a grandfather clock. Every time a wind gust hits, the pendulums swing faster and further. A whooshing sound can be heard as the wind seeps through every tiny crack and crevice of our doors and windows.

Ever since the emerald ash borer reared its ugly head in our neighborhood, I've been dropping dead ash trees all around our cabin. The tiny bug has had a dramatic impact on our woods and in woods all across the state for that matter. We've lost upwards of 30 trees in our yard all within the past two or three years. In the place of the tall ash trees will soon be a new plant community as the plants on the forest floor make the best of their new-found share of spring and summer sunlight. With the new plants will come new bugs and critters. Leave it to Mother Nature to make the best of a bad situation…and she'll do it every time.

I've cut most of the trees down that are close to the house, except for one or two…

I open the front door and head out. It doesn't take long to discover where the sound of the thud came from. A large ash has busted in half and swiped the side of the house on its way down. My heart sinks when I see the damage. Our cabin that I work so hard to maintain and put so much of my paycheck into has been wrecked. A large piece of trim has been ripped off the gable and the front guttering is hanging twisted in the wind. A row of shingles and trim looks to be damaged too.

As a man I feel obligated to make sure my family is protected from the elements in a comfortable and safe structure. When something bad happens to that structure, I feel like I have failed them. This feeling that works up through my body almost brings me to tears as I survey the damage. It feels like my world has been shattered.

But I soon come to my senses and start thinking about how I will fix the damage. *It's not that bad,* I tell myself. *Some new guttering, trim and shingle repair and it'll be as good as new.* But I'm still mad. Mad at the emerald ash borer, mad at this changing climate that brings spring wind storms in the middle of winter and mad at myself for not cutting the tree down. I walk back into the house and take my coat off.

"What was it?" Rena asks.

"A tree came down and swiped the house. I'll have to call the insurance company."

She nods and I can tell she is not nearly as concerned as I am. But maybe I shouldn't be. Maybe if I didn't put so much of my heart into the treasures of this earth I wouldn't be so shaken. Treasures...things I can see, touch and feel. Things that are shiny and bright and make me feel good inside. The problem is the feeling doesn't last that long and soon after one treasure is obtained or one project is completed, my heart is off to the races to find the next shiny thing to long for. And all of it for something that will soon enough be taken. Either by worm, wind, rain, or by the eventual departure of my spirit from this physical earth, they will be taken from me.

These bad things that happen to a person, the loss of a loved one, the loss or damage of a house and the loss of health can sometimes be a test of the heart. Where is my treasure stored? Is it in these possessions of mine? Or is it in my relationship with Jesus? The first will be taken. Putting my heart in them is like building my house on a foundation of sand. The latter can never be taken, ever. Not in life or in death.

Backpacking with Kids

Author's Note: This article originally ran in Backwoodsman *magazine*

When I open my eyes I see stars peeping through the leaves of the tall trees above me. The night is quiet, the air thick, but cool. The call of a barred owl breaks the silence. The rich tones of "who cooks for you" pierce the woods like an arrow slicing through soft ice. Barred owls are common in Midwestern hardwoods and use their distinct calls to establish and defend territories. Around me in the darkness, the complex drama of territorial defense is being played out.

I prop myself up on one elbow and watch my fire. Its short flames push weakly against the darkness, creating yellow shadows that dance across the forest floor. By the tents where my wife Rena and the kids sleep, I notice small points of light on the ground. "What could that be?" I think to myself. I grab for one of the lights and find a bug resembling a pill bug in the palm of my hand. On its underside is a small area that looks like the underside of a firefly. The "glow bugs" add another element of mystery to the dark woods. Things are happening around me in the darkness that I don't fully understand. I can only hear or catch a glimpse of them in my small circle of light in an otherwise vast sea of darkness.

There is something that makes a person feel uneasy sleeping in the backwoods miles from civilization. There are no light switches here. If something goes bump in the night you might as well be at peace with not knowing what it might be. You can build your fire up or shine your flashlight but sometimes that only makes the darkness seem bigger. The things beyond the light are outside of your control and maybe understanding. If you choose to accept and embrace the feeling, it's a great way to realize your small significance on earth when stripped of modern human contrivances. And if you can become one with the wilderness night, you'll find a peace of mind unlike any other.

I put the glow bug (actually a larval firefly) back and rise to answer the call of nature. Walking towards the edge of our camp I hear a noise coming from a nearby tree. I shine my flashlight towards the tree and see a pair of black marble-like eyes staring into the light. My pulse rises. The creature clings to the side of the tree mesmerized by my light. We lock eyes for what seems like minutes. "Holy crap!" I think, "it's a southern flying squirrel."

The squirrel finally makes its break and scurries up the tree. Its fur is tawny brown and a small tail protrudes from its wide body. I chase the squirrel with my flashlight beam before it plunges from the upper branches of the tree and "flies" through the night air, landing on the forest floor several yards away before scurrying into the darkness.

"That was awesome," I think as I lie back down by the fire. I look into the glowing embers and think about the day's events. I think of how good the kids did on the hike to our camping spot. They plodded along the trail carrying their sleeping bags on their backs without too much complaint. The barred owls sleeping in their roosts probably heard a "Daddy, how much further?" a few times along the way, but for the most part it was smooth sailing. I think of the smile Rena gave me once our camp was set up and the kids were playing happily in a nearby creek. And although I dreaded our first backpacking trip with a 4, 6, and 8-year-old along, I am glad we made the commitment to expose our kids to backwoods living at an early age.

Backpacking with small kids can be an intimidating thought, but below are several tips that will help ensure your trip is successful:
- Pick the right time of the year: Planning a trip around the weather forecast can be tricky and frustrating. In general, the best months

222

of the year in the Midwest are September and October. These months are typically your best shot at getting ideal weather conditions: no rain, highs in the 70s with lows in the 50s.

- Don't get too aggressive with your itinerary: One to two nights is about right for my family. The easiest trip is a 2-3 mile hike into a backcountry area with a 2-3 mile hike out the next day. While not as exciting as hiking a longer loop trail, planning for shorter hikes will keep from wearing the kids out.

- Involve the kids in trip planning, sharing the load and camp duties. Why do everything yourself when you have helpers with abundant energy? Yes, it can be frustrating trying to keep a child on task, but if you take the time to teach and let them participate, it's rewarding and beneficial for child development. Have the kids carry light items in backpacks (kids' school backpacks will work) such as their own sleeping bags, snacks and pillows. Get buy-in from the kids on where to camp and assign them camp duties such as unrolling the tent or gathering firewood.

- Always know and abide by backcountry rules and regulations: Explain to the kids why you are "leaving no trace" and what responsible backcountry camping is. By setting an example, you'll encourage your kids to develop into responsible stewards of our natural resources.

- Don't think you have to live in Montana or Colorado to go backpacking. Even in my home state of Indiana, a person can find places to backpack if they are willing to do some research.

The next time I open my eyes, the stars are gone and the woods are draped in pale light. The calls of songbirds reverberate through the forest like small bells ringing on and off in an empty church. I rise to my feet, my back tweaked from sleeping on the hard earth. With a little work, my fire is soon spitting long flames. I hang a pot of water over it and wait for the lid to dance and spout steam. As the woods come to life, I look at the tree where my flying squirrel was. "Not there this morning," I think to myself. "Probably curled up in a tree sleeping the morning away."

Before long my water is boiling and I dump it through a strainer full of coffee grounds into my coffee cup. The coffee steams lightly from the cup and raises my spirits, overcoming the soreness in my back. Soon the kids are up and, coffee cup in hand, I walk with my oldest daughter Eva to the creek. We sit on an old log, our bare feet dangling lightly in the clear waters of the creek. "Nice morning isn't it E?" I say to her. The woods are quiet except for the calling of a few nearby birds.

"Yeah, it is," she replies.

"Are you glad we hiked out here?" I ask. She sits for a moment looking into the woods.

"Yes," she says smiling at me.

We sit quietly as the woods awake around us. Deep in my heart, I'm glad I left the comfort of my soft bed and the security of light switches and closed doors to live in the backwoods with my family, albeit just for a couple of days. I encourage you to do the same and I promise you'll not be disappointed.

Retracing the Whetzel Trace

Authors note: This story first ran in Muzzle Blasts *magazine, the official magazine of the National Muzzle Loader Association.*

As I walk out the cabin door, the gray clouds that have hung low in the sky all morning begin to release heavy drops of rain. The drops pelt the bill of my hat before rolling down past my face. The big mulberry tree by our drive drips from its green leaves in a steady rhythm. I strap the kids into their car seats while the rain works on soaking through the back of my shirt. By the time we pull onto the road, the windshield wipers swipe back and forth with abandon at the sheets of water that stream down the windshield. "Daddy ... where are we going?" one of the kids asks.

"On a historical road trip," I reply with enthusiasm.

They don't seem to share my excitement and one of them asks, "Will it take long to get there?"

I ignore the question as I'm sure it's not the first time I'll get asked it today and point our SUV east, headed for the starting point of the famous Whetzel Trace.

Since the day we moved into our cabin on the bluffs of the West Fork of the White River near Waverly, Indiana, I've heard of the man named Jacob Whetzel who first settled the area in the early 1800s. I've driven past the shady cemetery where his bones rest on a high grassy hill. Here you can look to the west on a summer evening and watch the sun set over the White River bottoms. I've read the historical marker located at the cemetery that tells of the trail he blazed in 1818 through the wilderness of central Indiana, beginning at Laurel and ending 60 miles to the east at Waverly. I've read accounts of his famous brother Lewis and his legendary Indian fighting skills which helped subdue the edges of the frontier in the late 1700s. And I've looked upon Jacobs's big musket with its dark and well-worn stock that resides in the Indiana State Museum in Indianapolis.

But I've always wanted to know more about the man and his role in settling central Indiana. How did he end up in Waverly? What was the lay of the land over which he cut his trace? What obstacles did he face in completing his task? And so one Saturday morning, I set out with my wife and three small children to find out more.

When we pull into Laurel the rain has finally stopped, but the clouds persist, leaving the air heavy with humidity. The small town sits in a long valley of scattered farm fields bordered by the West Fork of the Whitewater River and surrounded by heavily wooded hills. Laurel contains many historic buildings and homes. Many stand proudly with freshly painted windows and doors, while others show their age more blatantly with cracked paint and crumbled brick.

I turn off the state highway and roll down Main Street to get a better feel for the place. We pass the Long Branch Tavern situated in a low white building. Outside, two men clad in jeans and faded t-shirts stand near the open door talking and keeping a watchful eye on Main Street. Next to them a man with a white beard sits on a bench keeping an eye on nothing in particular.

The town is a combination of well-maintained historic homes and not-so-well-maintained modern dwellings. It's an all too typical Midwestern small town. In its heyday it would have been a thriving economic center where country folks could come to buy and sell things and find entertainment. But somewhere along the way, time passed the town up. The people who live here have changed but the buildings, homes and overall feel of the place belongs to another time.

Jacob Whetzel lived near here with his wife and children on a small farm prior to the establishment of his trace in 1818. Laurel, which wasn't officially a town until 1837, probably wasn't much more than a loose settlement when Jacob lived in the area. Life must have been easy enough in the Laurel Valley for the Whetzel family. The days of frequent Indian raiding parties were over, leaving settlers free to tend their crops and livestock. But for Whetzel, the promise of a better life in unsettled lands to the west was a tempting proposition. And while other settlers hesitated at the thought of hacking out a living in new territories far from roads, grist mills and general stores, Whetzel was willing and ready to blaze a path of his own.

Whetzel was born September 16, 1765 in Virginia and spent most of his life on the very fringes of the frontier, living in areas ever westward as the sun slowly set on the days of Indian influence and power. As a boy, Jacob and his famous Indian-fighting brother Lewis were captured by Indians. After a short time in captivity both were able to escape to safety. Jacob's father, John, was killed by Indians during a period of frontier upheaval in 1786. Jacob had even served in the war of 1812, helping pave the way for American settlement of Indiana.

In 1818 Jacob decided the time was right to head west. He soon set about making plans to relocate his family to a site on the Eel River, due west from Laurel near present-day Worthington, Indiana. His only problem was getting there. In those days the best way to move women and children, household belongings and livestock was by loading them onto a flat boat and utilizing rivers. But utilizing rivers to reach central Indiana wasn't practical due to the fact that most rivers near Laurel flowed south before flowing west. And so Whetzel, being the stout-hearted frontiersman that he was, decided to go the route less traveled and hack his own path through the wilderness.

In July of 1818, Whetzel set out with his eighteen-year-old son Cyrus and four other able-bodied men from the Laurel Valley. Their goal was to make it to the Worthington area by cutting a path due west that could later be widened allowing for wagon travel. Jacob and another man traveled in the lead of the party marking the best route while the others brought up the rear, hauling gear and provisions. Their initial trek would take them around a month to complete while the eventual widening and completion of the trace would take much longer.

Putting Laurel to our backs we head west. Rising out of the Laurel Valley we wind through narrow country roads hemmed on one side by densely wooded hills and on the other side by small creeks whose clear waters trickle over brown rock. It must have been difficult picking a route through this type of terrain for Whetzel and his crew. He'd need to determine the best way to scale a ravine keeping in mind that wagons would eventually be used on the route. The rugged hills around Laurel, however, are short-lived and as we continue west the terrain levels out. Soon we ride through expansive farm fields that stretch to the horizon, broken only by distant tree lines. This type of level terrain, although heavily wooded in 1818, would have made for much easier going.

We travel state highways through this sea of agriculture before turning off onto backroads headed for the general area where the trace crossed the Flatrock River south of Rushville.

"Daddy, how much further?" the littlest one strapped in the middle seat asks. I ignore the question and push the pedal down on the Trailblazer as the farm fields and white clapboard farmhouses blur by.

When we reach the Flatrock, we find a white covered bridge spanning the river. I pull over and everyone piles out to walk across the bridge. The bridge is old but in good condition, its bright white paint gleaming in the mid-afternoon sun. Inside it's dark and smells of old wood. A group of three young boys shirtless and barefooted mill about the far side of the bridge looking down at the water as if deciding whether or not to jump from the limestone bridge abutment. Below the bridge the waters are running swift and brown from the recent rains we've had. As I look at the river, I consider what would make a good river crossing in the 1800s. Gently sloping banks on either side, a hard, rocky bottom and shallow waters would have been essential to allowing wagon passage during normal river conditions. Even at the best crossing though, the temperament of the river would be the determining factor as horse and wagon would be no match for swift waters.

From the thick woods growing along the riverbank comes the call of an Eastern Towhee which rings through the woods like an anvil being struck in a dark cavern. The bird and others like it would have provided the background music for Jacob and his men as they traveled. I listen to the bird calling as we strap the kids into their seats and put the white bridge, the Flatrock River and the three Indiana boys loafing on a summer day to our backs and head west again.

Our next stop is the Big Blue River near a small town called Marion. In the middle of the tiny town, sitting in a well-groomed grassy area, is a large rock that gives the town's date of establishment as 1820. The date of establishment, only two years after Whetzel began work on his trace, leads me to believe that the settling of the small burg was a direct result of Whetzel's work.

After crossing the Big Blue, we head west once again, passing through more flat farm ground. Due to recent heavy rains, water stands in small pools here and there throughout the fields. In Whetzel's day, before drainage tiles and ditches, water persisted much longer on the Indiana landscape. Seasonal wetlands would have dotted his route. Although likely shallow and easy enough for a frontiersman to traverse, Whetzel probably routed his trace around some of these wetlands to allow for easier wagon passage. How many of these wetlands he encountered can only be guessed at, but I imagine they had a significant impact on the final trajectory of the trace.

Our last stop before reaching Waverly is on Sugar Creek just north of Boggsville. The terrain here is much the same as our last stop, flat with heavy forest growing on either side of the creek. Of the many creeks and rivers we've crossed today, all ran through flat terrain and one could easily fling a stone across most of them. Water crossings under normal conditions would not have been a threat to wagon passage along the trace.

Evening is settling in over the countryside as we draw near Waverly. We've been in the car several hours and the kids in the back seat are well past the car riding limits of their impatient, live-in-the-moment minds.

Since their constant barrage of "how much longer" hasn't had much effect on their history-enthused dad, they change their tune to "Daddy... I'm hungry" in the hopes that the announcement of their dire state of starvation will produce better results.

When we finally reach the small town of Waverly, I pull into the parking lot of Whiskey River Barbeque. We're soon walking across well-worn hardwood floors, following our waitress towards a large wooden table that sits in the back of the low-lit establishment. The tables and floor around us are wiped clean and the other patrons in the restaurant converse amongst themselves quietly. Over in the bar area a large jukebox decked with neon lights plays old Hank Williams songs. As we wait for our food, I look out the large window next to our table into the woods that crowd the edge of the restaurant. Dusk is gathering. This is the time of day Whetzel and his crew would be locating a suitable campsite for the night. A fire would be made and soon beans and venison would be simmering over hot coals and flame. The men would sit by the fire as night drew near, smoking and talking about the day's events and what might lie ahead in the morning. With their bellies full, they would wrap up in their blankets and drift off to sleep as wood smoke drifted through the leafy canopy above them and dissipated in a star-studded wilderness sky.

When Whetzel and his crew finally reached the banks of the West Fork of the White River, he decided they had gone far enough. The location, known today as Waverly, was many miles short of the Worthington area. But the Waverly area was appealing in many ways. The White River offered transportation and natural resources and the ground to the east was flat and suitable for farming. The high bluffs along the river provided protection from flooding events. For Whetzel, his days of moving ever westward had finally come to an end. After work was completed to allow for wagon passage on the trace, Whetzel and his family relocated to Waverly. He would live out his last days here before passing away July 2, 1827.

His trace served as an important wagon road for settlers heading west for several years. Many families and small towns owe their establishment to Whetzel and his trace. Eventually, once more substantial roads were established, the trace was abandoned.

Our waitress comes to our table and lays a plate full of walleye fillets, fries and fried okra in front of me. I pick up a piece of the fried fish and break it in half as steam escapes from the white flesh in little wisps. The flavor is rich and salty, the way good fish should taste. The large green hunks of fried okra pair nicely with the fish. For a man with a simple pallet such as mine, it doesn't get much better.

We leave Whiskey River with full bellies and drive along the White River bluffs before dropping down in the bottoms where the old town of Waverly used to lie. The town established by Whetzel's descendents has seen its heyday come and go, much like the town of Laurel. Residents of Waverly used to live, work and do business in their little town. Now, while many folks call Waverly their home, they only live here, working and shopping in other towns and cities. But thanks to the establishment of a new County historical park in the old town, the legacy of Jacob Whetzel and the town he helped establish has taken on a new life. The park contains many interpretive displays telling Whetzel's story and is host to annual history-oriented festivals.

I've decided to end our trip with a visit to Whetzel's grave. We arrive at the small cemetery and walk up the hill to search the rows of headstones. We find Whetzel's and stand in front of the simple sandstone slab with words and letters that are worn thin and hard to read. We pause at the grave and I tell the kids about the man who is buried there. They are quiet for the first time in the day, taken aback at the thought of someone's bones lying beneath their feet. They stare up at me for a few seconds and then start asking a series of questions centered on why people die, when will Daddy die, when will Mommy die, etc. I attempt to answer their questions the best I can before breaking off the mortality question-and-answer session by telling them to get back in the car. The sun which is now barely above the horizon sheds its last rays of orange light over the river bottoms as we pull away.

When we reach the cabin, the kids are quickly put to bed and soon the house is quiet. I look out the big glass doors and see that darkness has fallen over the thick woods and the brown river running silently down below. As I drift off to sleep, I think of the many frontiersmen who helped make the settling of this area possible. I'm glad for the opportunity to live in a place like this, thanks in part to the efforts of men like Jacob Whetzel who sacrificed and suffered for the greater good.

White Sail on Blue Sky

Author's Note (a version of this story originally ran in Cruising Outpost, *a boating magazine)*

It's just my uncle and I on the boat and even though I've been out plenty of times I still can't remember how to raise the sail. I feel a little guilty as my elder clambers onto the deck, fixes the lines and cranks the sail up the tall mast. But I can steer the boat and know enough to hold directly into the wind as the white sail meets blue sky. The sail bucks wildly until I roll us down wind. It gives a couple of hard slaps then holds tight and flat and Uncle Dave eases down from the upper deck into the cockpit. I feel the warm lake breeze hit my bare legs as the boat gently rocks up and down, tilting on a mild heel from the push of the steady wind. The bottoms of my bare feet grip the floor of the cockpit holding firmly on the tiny traction bumps as I lean back to pull on the tiller to keep the boat straight. Many times I've watched Uncle Dave steer the boat by moving the tiller with the slightest pulls and pushes. I try to emulate the controlled movements but still find myself occasionally pulling like a 5-year-old child walking a stubborn dog.

When I arrived at the slip this morning, I noticed small pieces of brown crumbled dirt on the deck and that a piece of trim was missing from along the outside edge of the walkway. Normally the boat's gel coat gleams white and broken hardware or trim is quickly shored up as Uncle Dave can fix about anything. This summer was anything but normal however as this was the summer my grandfather passed away.

I know that if it weren't for all the time spent with Grandpa in his last weeks and managing affairs after his passing, the boat would look just as good as ever.

The very last time Grandpa was on the boat I had to walk him down the dock holding both of his arms while he shuffled along in front of me. I stood on the top of the dock ladder and Uncle Dave stood on the boat and we lowered all 130 pounds of him down to the cockpit. We motored through the harbor and out past the breaker walls but the waves were big which unsettled Grandpa some, so we came back in.

* * *

Grandpa was an avid sailor and as a kid I'd listen to him recount with pride stories of racing Snipe sailboats on Birch Lake in Michigan. He'd tell me about which one of his kids liked to sail the most and crewed the boat the best. The trophies he won were proudly displayed in a wooden bookshelf in his home on Hermits Lake in Crown Point, Indiana.

Down along the shoreline he kept a couple of small sailboats in which I first tried my hand at the tiller. The best days were when the wind blew hard and you could go fast enough to capsize. You then spent half an hour splashing around in the water trying to get the boat back up.

The lake was a manmade impoundment that consisted of three lakes with narrow passages connecting them. When the wind was light it could be tough to sail through the narrow portions. On one occasion my cousin and I got stalled out within sight of the dock. I kept trying to sail the boat into the wind but would lose momentum and drift further back every time. Standing on the dock my grandfather was watching and yelled directions to us. He was too far away for us to tell what he was saying but close enough to know he was irritated. We finally were able to break through and when we got back to the dock, we both stood and listened as he told us what we were doing wrong with a smile and shake of his head.

Grandpa also kept a sailboat in Florida on Lake Tarpon. When my family would come down for spring break, he'd take us out on the big lake where the osprey dove for fish and the alligators lurked in the shallows along the cattail-covered shoreline. Dad, being the loyal son-in-law that he was, always attempted to help crew the boat. I can see Grandpa at the tiller wearing a flat cap, windbreaker and a pair of tan slacks telling my Dad to loosen the boom vang, Dad on the deck in blue jeans and a tucked-in t-shirt, moving from one line to another as Grandpa yelled, "The boom vang! No, the boom vang!...*THE BOOM VANG!*" Grandpa was a nervous sailor and sometimes an irritable one, but he loved to sail nonetheless.

I was given one of the small boats that was kept on Hermits Lake. The boat is about 11 feet long and on the red and yellow sail is the outline of a little fish next to a bigger fish illustrating the boat's model name of Minifish. One year I took the boat to the Outer Banks in North Carolina by strapping it and the mast on top of our Chevy Trailblazer. I drove the 14-hour trip looking like a Beverly Hillbilly with a water-sport addiction.

I spent a sunny day sailing the small boat on the Atlantic Ocean, taking short trips back and forth along the beach on Hatteras Island, the boat sailing nicely in the steady breeze and light seas. My daughter, Eva, who was three at the time wanted to come out with me so we sailed off together toward the far end of the beach. We talked about the sandy beach and the white and black lighthouse that stood tall in the blue sky on a point a ways down from us. She asked me several times if there were sharks here.

Before we went on the trip, my wife and I let her sit with us as we watched a movie about a young girl who lost her arm to a shark while surfing. When I saw the look on Eva's face when the shark came up and got the girl's arm, I knew we had made a mistake and that the scene would be burned into her brain for good.

As we sailed, we talked about sharks and I reassured her several times as she stared into the blue depths that there probably weren't any under the boat. It was quiet and warm as the wind nudged us along and there was nothing but blue sky, blue water and the two of us in my little boat.

* * *

Before we started out, I asked Uncle Dave what the wave and wind forecast was for the day. He said he didn't know but we would find out what the lake was like once we got out there. Every time I come up for a sail, my Aunt Judy tells me about the last time she had to call Uncle Dave and tell him to get off the water because there was a huge storm on the radar. He would come in like she wanted him to, but I've never known him to get excited about the weather — except perhaps for the time he went out on Mother's Day with my cousin Darin and his wife and almost didn't make it back. He recounts how the waves were so big that the boat was pitching back and forth violently and when the bow would drop down to descend a big wave he wasn't sure it would come back up again. On a couple of different occasions, he and Darin had to go down below because the motor quit. The boat was pitching hard and they had to work in a confined space around diesel fuel. They took turns going down because they couldn't hold their stomachs, the vomit mixing in with the diesel and the pitching boat to create a mariner's worst nightmare. They eventually made it back to the harbor. My cousin's wife vowed never to go on the boat again. I think she thought they were all going to die and I know it must have been pretty bad for Uncle Dave to mark the conditions as noteworthy.

* * *

There's really only one way to learn when not to go sailing and finding out the hard way must run in the family. On the inland side of Hatteras Island there is an area of water called the Canadian hole. Windsurfers and kite boarders flock there in droves for the unusually strong winds. The last day of our trip I wanted to try to sail in the hole. When we got there, I parked the Trailblazer along the road which runs down the spit of sand that separates the Atlantic from the sound and pulled the boat down to the water. My wife, Rena, and the kids found a good spot in the sand and I set up the beach umbrellas to keep the sun off the children's skin. I quickly ate a sandwich while rigging the boat. The wind was strong and I watched a kite surfer zoom around the shallow water, every so often pulling on the line and sailing high into the air before splashing back down again.

When I got the boat into the water, I had a hard time holding the sail because it was pulling too hard in the brisk wind. I was able to hold the sail line down by lashing it to a small cleat. I started to go pretty good and made several short passes out and back, keeping within shouting distance of Rena and the kids. Although the wind was starting to pick up, I felt pretty good about my ability to control the boat and decided to make a run with the wind at my back. The boat moved faster than I thought it could. I got that tingling feeling in my spine, so I let the boat go and we rocketed along. I wished I had a video camera to capture the speed on film and a GPS to clock how fast I was moving. If I had filmed the speeding boat, though, I'd have had to edit out a long series of "woo hoos" that came bursting out of me like spouts of hot steam from Old Faithful. It was all I could do to hold onto the boat as we cut wildly through the water. I felt like I was free-falling from 20,000 feet and the reckless plummeting sensation overpowered any thoughts of what would happen when I reached the ground. The feeling burnt hot inside of me so I held the course and zoomed on like a kid sledding down the face of a giant dam right past the no-sledding signs and heading towards a watery spillway far below. I finally made it down to the far end of the beach where a swarm of agile windsurfers darted to and fro across the water with dazzling speed and precision. I cut through the center of the swarm and felt proud to be out where the real action was.

I looked back down the beach for Rena and the kids but couldn't see them anymore. I begrudgingly decided that I should make a go at getting back, especially since the wind was strong as hell and getting stronger yet. When I turned the boat into the wind, instead of going forward I was pushed sideways further down the beach. I refused to give up and kept trying to tack but now the front of the boat was diving under the water. I was soon sitting in a swamped cockpit, feeling rather foolish. The wind surfers who kept racing by gave me dirty looks and I knew they wished this rummy who thought he could sail in 25-mile-per-hour winds would get the hell off the water.

It was at this point I realized it was too windy to be out sailing. I let the sail flail completely out of control, the boom pointing straight off the bow, and sat with bowed head as I was slowly blown off the water. I beached the boat on shore. Carrying the mast and sail I walked along the highway back to where Rena and the kids were. It took me nearly 45 minutes to make the walk. Along the way I managed to find a small wake board that had probably blown out of the back of a Jeep Wrangler stuffed to the gills with coolers and beach chairs. When I made it back, I presented it to Eva who smiled and ran to the water to try it out. The wake board resides in our garage now and she still uses it when we go to the lake on weekends.

Rena, who was sitting in the sun because the wind was too strong for the beach umbrellas, looked up from her magazine and said, "Oh, there you are. I was starting to wonder what was going on when I looked up and couldn't see your sail anymore."

When we got back to our rental house it was cool and dark. Rena and I lay on the bed on top of the comforter while the children slept. We watched a documentary about the Jim Jones cult and how most of the people willingly drank the kool-aid. One lady escaped by lying among the bodies pretending to be dead. I drank two Leinencugels in cold brown bottles while we watched, which helped calm my nerves some.

* * *

We put our stern to the harbor now and sail towards open water before tacking and sailing parallel with the sandy shoreline. I see the big mansions that the rich people from Chicago call lake houses and I feel a little sick inside about how some of them probably rarely get used. I wonder how many of these folks who own the big boats in the harbor actually feel the same way I do about being on the water. Or maybe getting a big boat is just something you do when you have money so everyone knows it. They probably look down on people like my uncle who actually feel right when they're on the water and don't give a damn about what someone might think when they see the boat they own.

The boat leaves a trail of streaming and swirling water and I know that we are moving along with good speed. Uncle Dave goes down the steps into the cabin and hands up a can of Coors Light, its chilled silver skin snugged tight in a black koozie. The beer is cold and I think about how the fridge is working properly and that Uncle Dave has it turned down low enough for an American lager to taste like it should. We drink the beers then have another and I notice the big white rocks on the breaker wall getting smaller and smaller.

Uncle Dave looks out away from shore and says, "That looks like Harry's boat." We prepare to come about and I point the boat into the wind causing the big main to buck again as we start working the winches to change the jib. I crank my winch tight then cleat the line as the main sail goes flat again and we start pushing towards Harry's boat. As we approach, Harry looks up from his 30-foot center console, a fishing pole in his hand. We make a pass coming in close but not too close to keep from messing up his lines. Uncle Dave asks how the fishing is and Harry shouts that it's so-so and asks Uncle Dave how the sailing is. By this time we are too far away, so we tack around again coming a little closer and Uncle Dave finishes the conversation as the two big boats part ways. Uncle Dave tells me how Harry was practically born on a boat. When he's at the helm he makes a straight wake because when he was a kid on his father's boat, his father would watch the wake and coach him until he laid it out straight. Harry was fishing for yellow perch that afternoon and I take a moment to admire a guy who fishes for 12-inch pan fish out of a 30-foot center console.

The evening is beginning to wear on now but the wind keeps blowing good and I know Uncle Dave would stay out all night. I'd like to keep sailing too, but Rena and the kids are awaiting our return so I mention how I want to be back in time to walk the children down to the end of the breaker wall and watch the sun set over the lake. We tack around and head for the harbor. I see the whiteness of the sail and the boat set against the deep blue waters of Lake Michigan. I see Uncle Dave reclining with his back against the cockpit side, his eyes gazing out over the open water. I see the bow of the boat cutting and pushing a never-ending expanse of water powered by a never-ending supply of energy. I pull all these things into my brain and hold them there until they're stuck so I can retrieve them on a winter day when the air is cold and the skies are gray and I'm miles and months away from white sails on blue skies.

Hobo Gatherings

As evening approaches, I stand on the edge of our campsite with my daughter Eva, watching a strange personage approach on the gravel road that runs through the campground and down to the shelter house. The figure is stooped as with age and walks with a slow jerky gate. A flat cap and a brown cardigan sweater adorn the stranger and held over one shoulder is a stick with a handkerchief bundle on the end. Eva watches with a blank stare, her mouth held slightly open. As the stranger passes, they turn their head and smile at us. Eva stares on as my Aunt Mary continues on her way to the shelter house. "You never know what you'll see at a Milne family reunion," I say to Eva as we head toward the shelter house for "hobo night," the gravel under our feet making a chorus of crunchy sound as we go.

This is Eva's first experience around my mom's side of the family, the Milne side, which I think she will be old enough to remember. I have many childhood memories of Mom's side, mainly of Christmas and summer days spent at Grandpa Milne's house on Hermits Lake in Crown Point, Indiana. I remember packed living rooms with aunts and uncles sitting on couches and folding chairs all in a circle around a swarming pack of kids opening Christmas gifts, wrapping paper and boxes strewn across the floor so thick it was impossible to leave the room without walking on them.

I remember sunny Fourth of Julys with my grandpa on the back deck flipping hamburgers and hotdogs and spraying the grill when it flamed too much with a little green squirt gun. The squirt gun was always a conundrum for me. Here was a kid's toy that was used as a grill tool. I always wanted to grab it off the deck railing and squirt something just to see if it had any toy left in it.

I remember sitting in the back seat of my parents' baby blue Crown Victoria as we pulled in the drive at Hermits Lake. I'd wait for the car to stop before I flung the heavy door open and run down toward the lake, fishing pole and tackle box in hand. "Come in and see your grandma and grandpa before you go down to the lake, Sammy," I could faintly hear mom call as I ran down the hill. But I was far enough away that she couldn't be certain whether I heard her or not, so I kept up my dash for the lake, dashing a little faster to be on the safe side.

* * *

I hope she remembers the pitch and tone of her great aunts' voices or how Daddy's cousins chased her and her brother around the deck of the lodge building, hiding then jumping out before hiding again. I hope she remembers taking rides on her grandpa's mule in the big horse arena before sitting on the bench and watching the other children as they rode. I hope she remembers making crafts with her great aunts who so carefully and thoughtfully prepared them for her and the other children.

An entire campground and lodge facility were rented for our exclusive use for this year's reunion, partly because the Milne clan has become so big and I suspect partly because things like "hobo night" are best enjoyed in a private setting without the presence of strangers who would surely gawk excessively at such festivities. The origins of "hobo night" are a mystery to me but I have seen pictures of a Milne hobo gathering from the late '70s; it's a tradition with deep roots. The custom, uniquely Milne I'm guessing, involves family members dressing up like drifters and then preparing hobo-style food such as hobo dinners (meat and vegetables wrapped in foil and cooked on hot coals). When I was a teenager, activities like "hobo nights" would most certainly embarrass me, but in my heart I would relish them for their uniqueness and creativeness.

Along with unique customs, there are also unique physical characteristics that define my mom's side. A high percentage of red hair, unusually long toes and prevalence for light-colored skin with lots of moles are a few that come to mind. A distinguishing trait for men in the Milne clan is the prevalence of male pattern baldness which reeks havoc on our hair follicles worse than a pack of piranhas on a fresh-killed chicken carcass.

My Grandfather, who went bald early, passed all of his daughters' sons the trait. Most of my cousins and I lost our hair shortly after high school. We lived in a messed-up world where our dads had more hair than we did.

I used to get self-conscious and highly agitated about my hair loss, especially when I was in college. Over the years I've come to terms with it, although I still feel a little self-conscious in certain social situations, except of course when I'm at a Milne Reunion.

As we walk towards the shelter house, I hear the sound of many voices both young and old mixing together into one mush of noise. The lively hum stands in stark contrast to the stillness of the darkening woods. We have endured a few rain showers during the day and the remnants of the last shower drip slowly off the green leaves like the sweat that drips from my brow from the exertion of the slow walk. The midsummer air is heavy and the leaves on the trees hang perfectly still. As the woods darken, they remind me of the woods in the background of a Bugs Bunny cartoon I used to watch when I was a kid. In between the trees was a blackness that made the woods seem mysterious and almost threatening. I always thought this is how the woods in an African jungle would look, probably because I had once heard the phrase the "dark heart of Africa."

When I was a kid my parents took me to the Chicago museum of natural history. Towards the back of the museum there was a room that was lined ceiling to floor with African masks. African tribal music with heart-pounding drum beats blared from hidden speakers. Somehow I ended up alone in the room momentarily with the masks and the music. My dad, a deep lover of history, had probably moved on to the next exhibit not noticing I was still in the room. That night I had nightmares about the room. The room was dark except for a red light shining on the masks. The music blared loudly as the masks started coming to life. The music got louder and louder and the masks kept coming closer before I finally awoke. Apparently, the distance between the mask wearer's culture and that of a 6-year-old from Indiana made a deep impression on me.

The only sound that occasionally breaks the silence of the deep woods is the song of a wood thrush which rings out like a hammer striking an anvil in the middle of an empty gothic cathedral. It's a bubbly melodic song that stirs the recesses of my heart. The wood thrush primarily inhabits the deep woods which today are few and far between but 200 years ago covered most of Indiana. I think of the peoples that inhabited these woods during those times and wonder what feelings the wood thrush evoked in them on a still midsummer night.

When we reach the shelter house, everyone is gathered. I see faces and hear voices I have known from my earliest memories and which are embedded within me like the red marrow in my bones. Many of my aunts and uncles have become grandmas and grandpas and I am no longer a grandkid to anyone in the shelter house, but my daughter is.

And so it goes. It's as if we're all crewing a boat that steadily moves forward and can never stop. While the crew members change over time, the duties they perform never do. As one crew member fades into memory another rises up to take their place in one gigantic never-ending cycle.

And the crew gets their traits from the crew members who went before them. While they each have a unique personality, it is only a unique combination of traits that have already graced the decks of the boat. And I can honestly say that while I'm glad we have rented a private campground where we can be free to celebrate family in our own unique way, for those parts of me that are distinctly Milne, I am proud.

Nothing I Can Do to Stop Them

It's warm but overcast and even though it's not raining I see gray clouds out across the Gulf which worry me some. E comes running down the beach. The sand bogs her down a bit and the breeze off the water blows her light blond hair easily off to one side. Her hue is pale and the suntan lotion Mom has lathered on thick makes her appear even more so. "Come on, Daddy. I have something to show you."

I follow as she runs along the edge of the water, zigzagging to the side just out of reach of the bigger waves, her upper body tilted hard toward shore while her legs spin fast to outrun the surf.

We stop at a hermit crab. I see the crab is pulled firmly in its shell from being rolled about and prodded by a rowdy 4-year-old. E prods the crab some more and I explain that maybe if we stay still enough he will come out and make his way back to the sea. She nods and grins then sits beside me in the sand and we wait. I'm shirtless now and clad only in my blue billabong swim trunks. I bought them back in college when I was preparing for some spring break trip or another. They have faded some but are still capable of going along for a good trip to the beach, although the trips are much, much quieter now. E wears her one-piece Ariel swimsuit, the one with little pink ruffles around the arm and leg holes and a large graphic of the red-headed princess plastered across the front.

I first introduced her to the famous mermaid when she was dealing with a bout of bronchitis. I administered vapor treatments every night in the basement of our home before she went to bed. The basement wasn't finished but I had painted the walls and furnished it with a TV and a couple of dilapidated yet comfortable couches. The ensemble sat on a carpet remnant I picked up from a small-town carpet shop for 15 bucks. I would hook the mask up and place the little vapor cartridge in its place before turning on the machine. While the machine ran we would watch the little mermaid together. E never once tried to take the mask off. She'd look at me from time to time for reassurance. I would ask her if it was OK and she'd nod her head and take the medicine like I wanted her to. The little mermaid and the sea witch battled it out on screen as I sat with a mild heartache and wondered how I could ever manage myself if this was something more serious.

We watch as the crab starts to come to life. First its eyes come straight up like two periscopes. Next the rest of its body pulls out of the shell and it's soon sprinting for the surf. E's eyes get big as silver dollars as she watches. When she can't hold still any longer, she lets out a long scream of glee and runs after the crab. She comes close then backs away before coming close again. The scream draws the attention of little Eli who has been rummaging around in the sand with his plastic shovel trying to create some sort of castle that only he and E would recognize as something other than a loose pile of sand. He comes close to the crab and stops, looking up at me with a grin. His grin beams under the brim of a wide floppy hat which dwarfs his head. In turn, his head dwarfs his body and coupled with his little pair of swim trunks that run down well past his knees, he looks like a scrunched-up scarecrow. I look up past his left eye and see the scar. I note that it is looking better, but it's still a scar and I know it always will be.

The first time Dad came to the house we live in now, he noticed the brick platform that the woodstove sits on and how it had a rather sharp edge, "Boy, I don't like the looks of that with the little ones around, Son."

Fast forward to the next time my parents came down for a visit. Eli is running full tilt through the living room. Just as he starts to round the corner to go into the kitchen he trips and falls, his forehead hitting hard on the brick ledge. The wound was deep enough to warrant a trip to the emergency room where the decision to glue instead of stitch, although much easier on the boy at the time, probably won't do any favors to the noticeability of the scar. The next time my parents visited, a protective guard covered the ledge.

The crab finally makes it to the water and disappears in the white foam of a wave. Eli loses interest first and wanders back to his pile in the sand operation. E smiles and looks out over the endless water and up at the gray clouds that continue rolling in from the sea and onto the beach, like riders on an escalator who step off and walk on their way to some place or another all in one motion. Her gaze passes back to the beach and she pauses on a Willet. The shore bird, with its stilted legs that bend backwards, probes its long bill in the sand just on the edge of the surf. He probes then walks a bit before probing some more. E stands still and watches the bird like a lioness watching a gazelle and then gives chase. The bird dashes away with rapid leg beat before pausing. E pauses too then breaks for him again. This segment of action repeats itself until I notice she is too far down the beach and I rise to call her.

When I was a kid my grandfather would bring my family to this same beach. I can see him walking along in the sand, his tall slim body clad in a light windbreaker and gray slacks, a flat cap on his head and his glasses tinted dark from the sun. Grandpa and Grandma had a place in a trailer park on Lake Tarpon. Almost every year, Dad would drive us down for a visit during spring break. My parents would save their spare change all year in a big jar they kept under the sink to help fund the trip. When it was time for the trip, Mom would take the jar to the bank and I would watch as the bank clerk ran the coins through the machine before counting out the cash.

The trailer park was strewn with live oaks that dripped Spanish moss. At night you could walk down to the lake and listen to the alligators bellow. In the back of the park was a row of old airstream travel trailers. They were overgrown with saw palmetto and wild vines which kept the row enshrouded in permanent shade. I never saw anyone around them except for one time when I saw an old lady as tangled looking as the trailers peering from one of the windows. That must be where retired gypsies live, I remember thinking. The park is gone now and almost every last one of the live oaks has been removed to make way for fancy houses with fancy sterilized lawns leaving no room whatsoever for retired gypsies.

Out from the beach is a little sand island that Dad let me wade to, even though many years later he would recount the wade with a hint of worry in his voice because the water came up to my chest towards the end. The island has tidal pools full of horseshoe crabs and starfish. I would go from pool to pool spurred on by the addiction of a kid from Indiana who never knows what he might find in the next pool. While I explored, I proudly wore the captain's hat Dad bought me at the sponge docks from a Greek shopkeeper who nodded and took his money before looking back to the crowded street for the next customer. Every trip we would go to the sponge docks and look through the touristy stores with their piles of dried sunfish and endless racks of t-shirts. In front of the shops were benches where you could sit and watch the boats going down the Anclote River and out to the Gulf.

Eva comes back toward me now and piles down beside Eli and they continue the next phase of construction on their sand pile castle. I retreat to our spot in the shade next to a small row of short branchy trees that grow in a slender line down to the water. Behind them are small sand dunes covered in thick clumps of sea grass. Rena is quietly reading a book and the littlest one, Esther, is laying on her back on a beach towel half asleep. Since all is quiet, I take a respite from daddy duty and flip through my bird book. I read that the Willet is a common resident of Florida and is usually solitary, its gray plumage and lonesome nature making it easy to overlook, but still a fun bird to watch as it is constantly probing for food along the edge of the surf.

Rena has packed a can of ginger ale and I feel the cold wetness of the can as I take a drink. I reach into the cooler again and pull out a turkey and mayonnaise sandwich. I know my wife made the sandwich because the mayonnaise is extra thick just the way she likes it.

I finish the sandwich and pick up my binoculars again. I spot a group of pelicans diving a couple of hundred yards out in the Gulf. The big birds slow their flight before taking a suicide plunge beak-first for their prey. They seem to favor one area in particular and I think of how if I were in a boat that is the first spot I would fish.

Our spot is a good ways from the parking lot but a few beach combers trickle by; the older women dressed in Capri pants and sun hats stop to smile at the children and the younger women smile too but don't take the time to stop. The children come over and I feed them tiny bites of my sandwich. I watch the mayonnaise build up in the corners of their mouths before Mom spots it and wipes it away.

The gray clouds that have been hanging around all afternoon have begun to produce a thick fog that rolls in off the Gulf so I decide it's time to go. I gather all of our sandy things, placing them in the sandy backpack that I dutifully carry. We start off on the long walk back to the car. Rena carries the youngest and the other two run out in front along the water's edge. I notice that each small footprint left in the sand is wiped clean by the waves that keep coming one after the other and I know there is nothing I can do to stop them.

Made in the USA
Monee, IL
13 May 2021